SECRETS OF THE GLEN

A Novel

By Dorothy Ann Searing

East Lake Publishing
Printed In the United States

SECRETS OF THE GLEN

All Rights Reserved
Copyright - February 2013
Written by Dorothy Ann Searing

Secrets Of The Glen is copyrighted and all rights are reserved including the right to reproduce any portions thereof in any form whatsoever.

ISBN - 13 978-1492250128
ISBN – 13 149-2250120

Secrets Of The Glen is a work of fiction and all characters, places and events are the product of the author's imagination and are all purely fictitious. Any similarities to actual persons living or dead, or to actual events, or actual places, are purely coincidental.

East Lake Publishing
Printed In the United States

DEDICATION

My Irish immigrant grandparents told humorous, fanciful stories, often justifying their questionable facts with a simple caution, "Never let the truth stand in the way of a good story." It is from them that I inherited my wild imagination along with a compulsion to embellish on every narrative. I dedicate this book to them for their utter bravery in escaping starvation by crossing the Atlantic in order to begin a new life in a strange land. They never looked back, nor did they ever speak about who or what they left behind. I regret not knowing about their lives in Ireland. But I do know that in America they worked hard, raised a family, laughed heartily and often - and loved us all.

I also dedicate this book to my husband, Richard, who has provided me with a lifetime of love and support. I owe everything that is good in my life, including my beautiful daughters, my grandchildren, and the completion of this book to him.

ACKNOWLEDGEMENTS

To Deanna Bennett, founder and director of The East Lake Writers Workshop - thank you for giving me inspiration and confidence.

I will be eternally grateful to both Deanna and Ruth Duncan for helping me make the corrections to this novel in between my rounds of chemotherapy. Deanna has wonderful instincts regarding the written word and Ruth is blessed with a vision that extends far beyond mere human eye sight.

I also extend a heartfelt "thank you" to all the members of the East Lake Writers Workshop, past and present, especially Marge, Lore, Tricia, Maureen, Bob, John and Arlene - great writers all - their wise critiques have been very helpful to me.

And many, many, huge, grateful hugs to my husband, Richard, and my feline muse, Sox, both of whom are always there beside me as I toil at the computer.

CHARACTERS IN SECRETS OF THE GLEN
Aboard The Persian Princess
Desmond Lynch - The Dublin Workhouse
Frank O'Connor- Ardmore, Ireland

In The Glen
Sean O'Brien – Proprietor of O'Brien's Pub
Mrs. O'Brien – Sean's wife
Monsignor Murdock – Pastor, St. Joseph's Church
Boss Garrigan – Mayor of The Glen
Mr. Flannagan – Carpentry shop owner
Gregor Schmidt – Butcher shop owner
Greta Schmidt – Gregor's daughter, Frank's wife
Catherine O'Connor – Frank's daughter
Michael Brandon –Marries Catherine O'Connor
Keith Brandon – Catherine's son
Sarah Brandon – Catherine's daughter
Hannah O'Toole – Wife of Desmond Lynch
Mrs. O'Toole – Hannah's mother
Angela "Annie" Lynch - Desmond's daughter
Isaac Weinberg – Neighbour of Desmond Lynch
Esther Weinberg – Isaac's cousin from Europe
Doctor Smith – Doctor at Saint Joseph's Hospital
Elaina Smith – Dr. Smith's wife
Reggie Smith – Dr. Smith's son
Bernadette Smith – Dr. Smith's daughter
Hilda – Greta's cousin
Margaret Kelly – Catherine's high school friend
Henrietta – Madame at brothel in the Bronx
Peggy – Young prostitute
Joe Kline – Detective, works for Reggie Smith
Pat Madden – policeman
Liam Fogerty – Medical student
Fiona Fogerty – Liam's Mother
Dennis Shay – Desmond's driver
Dr.Warner - Obstetrician

St. Gerard's Convent Home For Unwed Mothers
Sister Rita – Mother Superior
Sister Muriel – Nurse
Sister Rafael – Midwife
Andrew – Annie's son
Dr. Harrison – Physician assigned to the convent
Joseph – The handyman
Father Henley – Priest assigned to the convent

In Houston at Taylor University
Karen – Annie's neighbour and friend
Fred – Karen's husband, classmate of Liam
Eric – Fred and Karen's son
Mrs. Evans – Dean of Nursing Program
Dr. DeBann – Director of Student Affairs

In Bamberg, West Germany
Helmut Rodiger – Friend of Esther Weinberg
Captain Lawrence – Keith's commanding officer
Colonel Nolan – Army psychiatrist
Maria Vanderhorne – Proprietor, Riveredge Inn
Captain Collins – Army Nurse

In New York City
Rosa Santos – Esther Weinberg's maid
Cassie Flack - Reggie Smith's secretary
Olga Krupchik - refugee from Czechoslovakia
Milos Krupchik - Olga's husband imprisoned with Keith
Stefan Krupchik - Olga's father-in-law

PROLOGUE

Only five years of age on that dark night at the Dublin Workhouse, Desmond Lynch waged a fierce battle against the two black-draped nuns who dragged him away from his mother. With her coarse red hair wound tight around his little fist, he begged to be left alone, to sleep beside her as he had always done.

"Yar Mam's dead, boy," The older nun said.

His tiny, frail body went limp as he cried for his mother.

The Sisters of St. Clare prayed aloud for his mother's soul as they dragged the helpless child down the long, dark corridor to a huge, wooden door.

A toothless man with a whip tucked into his belt flung the door open, growling, "You'll be livin' here in the ward for orphan boys now."

There were other boys there, bigger and older than he, wearing only rags, their faces dirty, their heads shaved. The tallest of them sneered, strings of green snot dripping from his filthy, stained nose. They called him a "wee baby." And when they tired of taunting him, they beat him. His broken nose and twisted arm healed but the pain in his heart never did. Still, his will to survive was so strong that he learned to live without so much as a smile or a kind word.

The nuns tried to teach him to read but he could barely focus on the letters, let alone tell them apart or make sense of them. So he took on the hardest and the dirtiest of work, putting in more hours than any grown man until one day the headmaster pulled him aside. "Boy, you've earned a ticket to America. I'm takin' ya to the dock, meself."

They reached Dublin's Kingstown Harbor just before dawn, walking the length of the dock, passing the big ships with their gangplanks outstretched like open arms - all the way to the end of the sea wall and out onto a wooden pier that extended beyond the jagged, rocky shoreline.

The headmaster shook Desmond's hand. "Good luck to ya, me boy. Keep workin' hard in America and you'll be very rich one day."

He stood alone now, unsheltered, shivering in the cold sea wind.

Others came, men and women, young and old.

They were taken by row boat, five at a time, to a freighter anchored in the harbor.

It was April 4, 1913 – his birthday.

Desmond Lynch turned fourteen years of age on the day that he left Ireland - and he never looked back.

PART I

THE VOYAGE

Chapter 1

The rattle of death echoed through the shadowy bowels of the old freighter as the frightened passengers stared at a young lad, face-down on the filthy floor, retching, and drowning in a curdled yellow puddle of his own vomit.

"Hey, you, get up." Grabbing the boy's shoulders, young Desmond Lynch yanked the young boy to his feet. "You're givin' these useless louts a fine show and they'll be laughin' their fackin' heads off when you die right here in front a them."

"Who are ya?"

"Just another starvin' Irisher like yourself. Me name's Desmond Lynch from the Dublin Workhouse."

"Frank O'Connor from Ardmore," The boy said as his wretched body went into uncontrollable, dry heaves again.

"You'd not be so sick up on deck with the fresh air but the likes of us aren't allowed there unless we're fackin' dead and bein' slipped into the sea. Are ye an orphan?"

"No, no, there's me Da but he's terrible sick. That's why he's sendin' me off to America."

"Well, stay on yer feet if ye want to live to see it."

The ship rolled and Frank began to shake.

Desmond pushed him up against the wall. "Ya got nothing left to throw up so don't go to the floor. Just stay on your feet and it'll pass."

Desmond and Frank were the youngest passengers aboard the old freighter, inaptly named The Persian Princess and both were traveling alone.

Only an hour out of Dublin's new Kingstown Harbor, they hit the first violent squall. Massive waves pummelled the ship broadside. The crew scrambled to tie everything down, and below, in the belly of the ship, the terrified passengers prayed.

There was nothing even remotely royal about The Persian Princess. She carried a cargo of whiskey, leaded glass and twenty Irish emigrants whose accommodations were only a step above the old time "coffin ships." They slept on triple-high bunks. Each was issued a metal plate, a cup and two utensils and they ate sitting on planks alongside a huge wooden table. Their only contact with the crew was when the ship's cook brought them a pot of oatmeal in the morning and some rancid stew in the late afternoon, barely enough to vomit back up when the sea sickness came.

The spring of 1913 was bitter cold in the North Atlantic. Winter's savage winds refused to yield to the warm spring breezes and their battles spawned fierce squalls. The beleaguered Persian Princess, heavy in the water, forged ahead, her portholes sealed tight, making the inside air foul.

When a desperate male passenger smashed a porthole to allow the fresh air in, the passengers cheered, except for one old woman who shouted, "Ya damn idjut! The rain'll be comin' in and we'll slip on the wet floor."

"That wicked stench will kill us long before we've had a chance to fall," the young man replied.

One lavatory on the starboard side of the ship, just aft of where the passengers slept, served both male and female passengers. They emptied their slop pails into a drain on the floor when the ship listed to port and washed themselves in the frigid salty, sea water that dripped from two sinks on the wall.

Young Desmond, the only passenger not suffering the sea sickness, paced the floor while the others writhed and retched. He knew every inch of the passenger quarters and came upon a Jacob's ladder rolled up and stashed beneath the bunks. Unravelling it, he called out to Frank, "Hey, I've an idea! How good are ye at climbin'?"

"I'm a terrible sailor but a good climber. I often fixed me Da's roof."

"Good! Can you get this rope ladder up on that beam? I'll give ya a boost on me shoulders."

Frank, older and taller, weighed less than Desmond. Climbing onto Desmond's shoulders, he wobbled as he threw the rope up over the high beam. Then he tied both ends together, losing some length, but forming a strong trapeze. Grabbing at the trapeze with both hands, Frank swung himself from Desmond's shoulders up onto the high ledge. Then he reached over and yanked the Jacob's ladder off the beam, tying it to the ledge and allowing it to hang to its full length.

"Come on up." Frank beckoned Desmond with a broad smile on his sickly-pale face.

Desmond climbed up to join Frank. Together, they crept along the ledge until they came to a hatch. Desmond pushed it open. It was a tight squeeze through the hatch that led out onto the lower deck. The fresh air hit their faces and they sucked it deep into their lungs.

Suddenly, the Persian Princess rolled to one side, catching Frank off guard. He slipped through the opening of the outer rail. Flailing about wildly, he barely managed to grab the rail with one hand as he struggled to pull himself back from the edge.

Desmond mumbled, "that was a close one."

"A bit too close. Let's get over to those stairs." Frank pointed ahead.

They ran along the walkway, up the stairway to the main deck and then inched along on their hands and knees to a shadowed area beneath one of the hanging lifeboats.

"This here's a good hiding spot," Frank whispered.

"Aye 'tis, indeed," Desmond agreed.

The two boys sat back, enjoying the simple, primal act of breathing. It was so cold they could see the white smoke of their own breath seeping from their mouths and nostrils. After only a half hour, they could barely feel their fingers and toes, so they headed back below.

But the very exhilaration of the adventure proved to be a healing experience for Frank.

Desmond said, "It won't so bad down below now that we know we can escape the stinkin' bowels of this fackin' old ship."

"Aye," Frank answered, smiling for the first time.

The two boys crept up on deck every night. And when, five days later, the weather turned a bit warmer, they slept all night beneath one of the hanging lifeboats.

It was almost dawn when Frank heard an ominous shuffling sound. "Desmond, wake up. We'd better get back below."

But before they could move, a huge hand grabbed the back of Desmond's shirt, and dragged him out onto the open deck. The enormous toothless brute then grabbed hold of Desmond's crotch with his other hand and lifted him up above his head. "You little scum. I should throw you to the sharks."

"Please, sir, I'm only a boy," Desmond pleaded.

Frank crawled out from under the lifeboat, reached up and grabbed the giant's testicles with both hands. He squeezed and crushed the bulk that dangled between the huge man's legs until the sailor shrieked in pain and dropped Desmond flat on his back.

Frank and Desmond ran.

"I kill you both." The giant yelled, limping after them.

The boys scrambled down the stairs two at a time and disappeared through the hatch. Frank pulled it closed behind them and locked it. They wriggled down the Ladder and jumped the last few feet onto the iron floor.

Four women sat at the dining table, mending clothes beside a candle lantern. The oldest said, "Quick lads, get down under." The women lifted their skirts and the boys slid beneath the plank bench, disappearing from sight under the ladies' ample skirts.

Terrified, Frank and Desmond hid silently, barely breathing.

Time passed and no one came below looking for them. Frank crawled out into the open. "Come on out Des. That beast doesn't want his cronies to know that he was bested by two young boys."

Desmond rolled out onto the floor next to Frank, grinning. "Aye, Frank, that's true. Thanks to you, laddie, ya saved me from a flogging or maybe even worse."

"Des, you were almost chum for the fish. You'd best keep your cap on and hide that red hair of yours for the rest of the trip."

"That I'll do." Desmond winked. "Tonight we'll hide right beside the crew's quarters. They won't expect us there." Desmond laughed, enjoying the prospect of danger as if it were a grand game.

Frank suddenly looked sad. "Why do they take our money and treat us so bad?"

"Ach 'tis just the way of the world and 'twill never be any different."

"I knew different and far better with me Da. I wish I'd never boarded this filthy ship."

"You'll see, 'twill be better in America," Desmond said, trying to comfort Frank, but wondering himself just what America would really be like.

Chapter 2

On April 16th, 1913 with over half her cargo damaged and only sixteen passengers left on board, The Persian Princess limped to a berth at the Hoboken Pier aided by a harbor tugboat. Four passengers had succumbed to fever and were left behind to rest in the dark waters of the Atlantic for all eternity.

Longshoremen swarmed the damaged freighter unloading anything salvageable as the weary immigrants boarded a harbor ferry to Ellis Island. There, they waited on long lines along with passengers from other ships. After perfunctory interviews and medical examinations, all but two passengers were cleared to enter their new country.

"Quick, we don't want to be hangin' here on this damn Ellis Island. Is that the right ferry?" Desmond asked, tightening his grip on Frank's arm.

Frank squinted, looking up at the sign. "Aye, this is it. It says Ferry to Manhattan Battery Pier. I don't relish another ride on the water."

"It's either take the ferry or swim," Desmond teased, pushing his way through the crowd to secure a spot along the rail.

Frank looked up to the sun and yelled into the wind, "We survived a hellish trip."

"That we did!" Desmond shouted, "and will ya look at those buildin's. They're gettin' even bigger as we get closer. We're Americans now and we're gonna be filthy rich." He jumped around doing a silly jig, spinning in circles, until he fell and slammed his head against the metal railing. "Good thing 'twas only me head and not me ankle or I'd be in big trouble."

When the ferry docked at Battery Pier, all the passengers on board hauled their meager belongings ashore and stared with envy at the one young man who was lucky enough to have someone there to greet him.

Desmond remembered overhearing a conversation about O'Brien's Pub in a place called "The Glen" where Irish immigrants were welcome to sleep on the floor for ten cents a night. Spotting the man who spoke of The Glen, Desmond asked, "Sir, would ya be kind enough to tell me how to get to this place called The Glen?"

"I will, indeed. Ya walk north to the Grand Central Station and take the train through the Bronx up to Yonkers. Get off there and walk west toward the Hudson River. You'll know you're in The Glen Center when you reach the very bottom of the valley. But, if you get lost, just ask a policeman. They're all Irish, ya know. Say, have you lads enough money for the train?"

"We've got the fare and more," Desmond bragged, his hands on his hips.

"Well don't you be telling people that. There's some who'd steal from ya. Here's a bit a luck to ya lads." He pressed two silver quarters into Desmond's hand and quickly disappeared into the crowd.

"Frank, we're only in America a few minutes and already we're makin' money. What say we go to The Glen together? Eh?"

"Sure, I'll go to O'Brien's Pub with you."

"Frank, I'm glad that I met up with ya."

As the boys hiked north toward the new Grand Central Station, they were distracted by the sights and sounds of New York City with its tall buildings that seemed to grow into the clouds and huge crowds of people walking about on the streets.

"Seems that America 'tis a country made of stone and concrete," Desmond said.

"Aye, and there's a powerful energy here," Frank declared.

Twice they asked policemen for directions and each time they were amazed that these men dressed in such fine uniforms were once immigrants like themselves.

At last, Frank spotted a new building with "Grand Central Station" etched in stone over an entrance of more than ten glass doors. He removed his cap as he walked into the grand edifice and nudged Desmond with his elbow. "Look 'tis a fine castle for sure. And will you look at the marble floors and all that shiny brass."

They walked up to one of the many windows and peered through the glass at a handsome young man who looked Irish but spoke with the harsh American accent. He sold them two tickets to Yonkers but never smiled or uttered a word of welcome.

"Americans aren't very friendly, are they?" Desmond commented.

"I fear that's true. I miss Ardmore and me own people."

"Aye 'tis easier for me, Frank. Bein' nothin' but a stray dog at the workhouse, I've no one and nothing to miss."

"Ach, 'tis a wonder you even survived being alone at such a young age."

"I don't need your pity." Desmond shrugged.

"I don't pity you, Desmond. I envy your courage."

By mid-afternoon they left the well-lit, grandiose station, entering a dark tunnel where they boarded the train for Yonkers. All the seats were taken so they stood, holding tight to a brass pole.

The train rolled as it started but then lurched forward and picked up speed, spinning around curves in the darkness. It burst out of the tunnel into the daylight and climbed higher and higher on narrow tracks. There was nothing on either side of the train and it was a long way down to the ground below.

Desmond's lips pursed as he gripped the pole tight with both hands.

Suddenly, the door of the rail car opened, allowing the deafening sound of wheels clacking and smashing against the iron rails to enter the quiet car. A black-skinned man wearing a brown uniform yelled out, "HARLEM HERE! YONKERS, NEXT STOP," smiled, checked the passenger's tickets and moved on to the next car.

When the train lurched to a stop at Yonkers, Desmond and Frank got off.

Desmond looked around. "Well I did not expect this."

"It's sort of country but not like Ireland's country," Frank said. Black-top roads meandered up and down hills, past wooden houses and fields where cows grazed. The boys walked west, their hands raised to shield their eyes from the sun.

"You know that black man on the train," Frank said, "Well he has a fine job."

"Aye!" Desmond answered, "I heard at the Workhouse that America has all kinds of people, whites and tans and blacks and some small yellow people and even red people who dress in feathers."

"Ya don't say? That's amazin'," Frank replied. "Once an Englishman came to Ardmore with a black servant but this black man here is a free man and earning his own keep. It's a good thing to be a free man."

"Aye and 'tis even better to be a free man with a full stomach," Desmond said, acknowledging the roaring and rumbling blaring from his near empty stomach.

They reached the top of a hill and looked down into a deep valley where two sprawling buildings sat on either side. Each had wide chimneys spewing out dark smoke. Roads ran up and down and all around the hills like snakes encircling a mound. There were rows of attached wooden houses interspersed with stretches of empty lots. The far side of the valley was bordered by another huge hill with a plateau on top holding fine big homes. Mid-way up that far hill, stood a stone church, and what appeared to be a hospital and a school.

The boys walked down to the very bottom of the valley, shadowed so completely by the hill to the west that it blocked the sun, making the streets dark and dreary. And in the shadows of the late afternoon, people rushed about, darting in and out of the small shops.

"This must be The Glen," Desmond said.

Frank spotted a sign hanging perpendicular to a building in the center of the main street. "There it is! O'Brien's Pub!"

Desmond moaned. "This street looks like a slum in Dublin."

"Aye 'tis far different from its name but we've nowhere else to go and it'll be dark soon."

Frank took money from the secret pocket his father had sewn inside of his shirt.

"Me Da' was real sick when he gave me this money and told me to find a better life in America. But I'm not so sure that he knew at all what this America was like."

Desmond reached into his pants pocket to count out the five dollars given to him by the headmaster at the Workhouse. That and his passage on the Persian Princess was all he had to show for all those years of bloody hard work.

They walked into O'Brien's Pub, right up to the mahogany bar, breathing in the sweet whiskey scent, the same as all the pubs back in Ireland.

An old man on a stool at the bar pointed his gnarled finger at them. "Look here now, will ya? Things must be gettin' even worse in the old country. Why, they're sendin' them greenies over younger and younger."

Frank ignored the old man, asking the bartender for two bowls of hot broth.

"And a wee bit a bread, if you don't mind," Desmond added, standing with his hands on his hips, legs apart, looking every bit like he was ready for a fight.

"You two lads can have all the soup you want for a quarter," the barkeep answered.

"And we'd like to sleep here tonight," Frank said, placing his foot on the rail the way his Da used to do at the Ardmore Pub.

"That'll be two dimes more. It's up those stairs when you're ready and the plumbin' is out in the back yard."

"Here's your money. 'Tis my treat, Des."

The walls were done in wood with lanterns every few feet. Families sat at the tables while men in work clothes occupied the stools or stood, leaning on the bar – all sipping frothy beer from thick glass mugs.

Desmond and Frank wolfed down the beef broth and wiped their bowls clean with the thick brown bread.

Bone tired, they climbed the narrow stairs to the second floor and spent their first night in America sleeping on the floor along with six other loud-snoring Irishmen.

PART II

IN THE GLEN

Chapter 3

The next morning Mrs. O'Brien asked if the boys wanted a hot bath for fifty cents.

"Indeed we would," Frank replied.

"Do you have any other clothes because that price also includes the washin' of your clothes in the bath water after you're done and the use of the clothes line out back to let them dry."

"We've just the clothes on our backs," Desmond responded.

"Run up the hill to St. Joseph's Church and ask for some clothes from the thrift shop in the basement. Tell them Mrs. O'Brien sent ya and that you'll pay for them when you find work."

When they got back to the Pub, Mrs. O'Brien said, "Go on into the kitchen through that door behind the bar."

A huge tub filled to the brim with hot steam rising from it, stood in the middle of the big commercial kitchen. Boxes filled with canned goods were stacked to the ceiling along the walls. Desmond bathed first, washing quickly so he could leave some hot water for Frank. But when Frank's turn came, Mrs. O'Brien marched into the kitchen and began to pour kettle after kettle of boiling water into the tub.

Frank's face turned beet red whenever Mrs. O'Brien came near.

"Aye, stop it, boy. I've had two husbands and five sons so you can't possibly have somethin' that I've not already seen more than enough of."

Desmond, dressed in the clothes from the Church, said, "Aye, it feels good to be free of that salt stickin' to me skin."

"And to be rid of that fish smell," Frank added, turning pale as he thought back on the sea voyage. They washed their clothes in the used bath water, hung them over the line in the back yard to dry and carried the tub outside, dumping the water onto Mrs. O'Brien's seedlings.

"Let's be gettin' a better look at The Glen." Desmond grinned, anticipating adventure.

They walked the length of main street and then up and down the side streets.

Frank smiled at people the way he did back in Ireland but they looked right past him, too busy to take notice.

"Will ya look at that dark haired girl with the big blue eyes." Desmond nudged Frank.

Hearing him, the girl said, "What are ya staring at, you carrot-haired greenhorn?"

"Who does she think she is, laughin' at me like that?"

"Ignore the foolish lassie. You'd not want to be friends with a cruel one like that," Frank warned, pale and much too thin from losing weight aboard ship. But his high cheek bones, brown hair and soft brown eyes held the promise that he'd be a handsome man one day. And the manners that he learned from the nuns at the Ardmore Primary School gave him the air of a gentleman. "Forget the girls for now, Des. We have to find work. Our money won't last very long."

That very afternoon Mrs. O'Brien offered to pay them to unload heavy whiskey crates from the delivery trucks and carry them down to the Pub's cellar. Every day for weeks, they found odd jobs of some sort. They slept and ate at O'Brien's Pub and everyone took them for brothers or, at least, cousins.

Frank read the discarded newspapers in the Pub and offered them to Desmond, who always declined, "No thanks."

Finally, Desmond sheepishly confessed, "Truth is, Frank, them nuns at the Workhouse would beat me silly but I could never make sense out a them squiggly little marks on paper."

"You're joking! Des, I thought sure you could read."

"I fake it good. And I'd appreciate you not tellin' anyone."

"Why would I tell? But you listen to me, Des. Don't you be puttin' your mark on a paper unless I read it first."

"That's decent of you, Frank. But I don't take no charity. So in return I'll just be watching yar back. Me head may be slow but me fists are fast."

The two lads grew to be close friends. They worked hard and studied the way of things in The Glen. And soon they began to think and act like Americans.

Desmond retained whatever he heard, able to repeat it all verbatim. At night, lying on the floor above O'Brien's Pub, he'd tell Frank everything that he'd overheard during the day.

"You know, Frank, 'twas the early Irish immigrants who gave The Glen its name. Back then, the valley had lots of green grass, like where you're from in Ireland."

An old man across the room shouted, "Shut up, you mutts, or I'll take me belt to you."

"Shut up yourself, you old fart," Desmond yelled back. He already had a reputation for fighting. Some even named him, "The Carrot Kid" because he'd take on any size bully rather than suffer the slightest disrespect.

"Well, The Glen is more concrete than grass now." Frank answered. "We'd better be quiet and get some sleep."

But Desmond kept talking, "That Garrigan guy is the boss of the whole Glen. They say he's got his hand in everyone's pocket. I know his kind real well. There were a lot like him back in Dublin."

"He probably owns the land this pub sits on," Frank said, yawning.

"Yes, and I know he owns the land under the elevator and carpet factories."

"You know, you've an excellent memory, Desmond."

"Aye, but there's some things I wish I could forget. Boss Garrigan is buildin' a lot a them row houses. I'm gonna work for him. I want to make big money and he can show me how."

"I'm takin' that job at Flannagan's Carpentry Shop. You can come with me and I'll split my wages with you."

"Nah, Frank, thanks but I can earn me own keep."

Desmond hired on with Garrigan's crew and soon everyone was talking about the young hooligan from Dublin's Workhouse who was good with his fists and willing to do anything for a buck. Even Garrigan himself took notice.

Frank and Desmond decided to move into a room at Leary's Boarding House just a few blocks from O'Brien's Pub. Maureen Leary, a buxom widow in her forties, rented four sparkling clean bedrooms and served a fine supper every night.

Desmond's stomach no longer roared. "I'm likin' me life in America, Frank. I've enough to eat and money in me pocket. And I say, to hell with the troubles in Ireland."

But Frank missed his Da and longed for his home in Ardmore. He saved every penny he could, planning to return to Ireland - until that evening when he came home to the boarding house to find a letter on his dresser that was not written by his Da's hand.

Dear Frank,

I'm sorry to tell you that your dear father passed away. His last words were of how proud he is that you're living a better life in America.

Things are still bad here. They arrested John Foley and word is that he'll hang for blowing up the mayor's house with him and his cronies still in it. Be glad that you're away from all the troubles.

Your Da was grateful for the money you sent and asked me to use it for his last expenses. If you could manage to send a bit more, I'll put a stone on your Mam and Da's grave with their names on it.

There's new renters in your Da's house and they kept all his things. Sad to say, I couldn't even get his rosary to send you. God Bless you, Frank. Everyone here in Ardmore is proud that they know a fine American gentleman, like yourself.
From your neighbour and friend,

Frank arranged for a special Mass to be said at St. Joseph's Church in memory of his father and he sent the money to Sean Reardon for the grave stone.

"I'm alone in the world now - like you, Desmond. I don't know how you did it, being so young and all. And I'm thinking that maybe the best way to honor me Da is to make a nice life for myself here in America. That's what he wanted."

"That's good news, Frank. It's time ya stopped lookin' back at them Micks and all their troubles. We're Americans now," Desmond said, placing his hand on Frank's shoulder.

But Frank found the world to be a very lonely place, knowing his Da was gone. He worked six days a week at the carpentry shop, discovering that he possessed a rare talent for designing and making fine furniture pieces.

On Sundays Frank taught Catechism at St. Joseph's Church after Mass, sometimes even managing to drag Desmond along.

Desmond Lynch and Frank O'Connor blended into The Glen just like the German, Jewish, Polish and Italian immigrants. The Glen even had a Chinese family that ran a laundry in the last shop at the far end of Broadway.

But it was the Irish who spoke the language and they got the jobs in the police and fire departments. And so it was that the Irish culture dominated, with Boss Garrigan, the grandson of an Irish immigrant, ruling The Glen as if it were his own little kingdom.

The different ethnic groups lived and worked together but they did not mix socially. With no public school in The Glen, all the immigrant children went to Saint Joseph's. O'Brien's Pub was the unofficial center of life in The Glen, a place where everyone was welcome as long as they had the price of a pint. But even there, at the long mahogany bar, the different ethnic groups drank with their own kind, speaking to each other in their own language.

Chapter 4

In 1917 Frank, tall and quite handsome, turned nineteen. But Desmond, only eighteen, gave the impression of being older. Wide-shouldered and strong, Desmond never hesitated to use physical force to gain advantage. The freckles that used to dominate his face had faded and the space between his front teeth was now less pronounced. But that bright red hair remained his trademark.

The boys continued sharing a room at Leary's Boarding House but their work schedules were so different that they only got a chance to talk once in while at dinner.

Desmond's work day for Boss Garrigan began in the evening and lasted late into the night so he usually slept well past noon. While Frank's work day at Flannagan's Carpentry Shop began in the early morning and ended just before the dinner hour.

The conversations at Leary's dining table were all about the political situation in Europe. And there was constant speculation about whether the United States would, or should, send troops.

When the United States finally did enter World War I, Boss Garrigan encouraged Desmond to enlist. Desmond, in turn, encouraged Frank to join up. "I'm always in a fight anyway. And I'll enjoy the adventure of it," he said to a skeptical Frank.

"Des, I'd love to see France but it's not my fight. Besides, I dread another sea voyage."

"But Frank, it'd be different this time. There'd be no slop pails and no bein' locked below. We'd be American soldiers, travelin' on a solid navy ship. And we'd be savin' the world."

"Des, me friend, I could of stayed in Ireland and done plenty of fightin' for my own kind."

"What are you gonna do, Frank? Sometimes you have to fight. You can't hide in books all your life."

"Des, I can teach you to read."

"Nah, I don't need to read. But I love a good fight and I'm goin' in the Army with or without you."

Frank couldn't let Desmond go alone. So the two young men enlisted on the very first day that the recruiting office opened in an empty storefront on Broadway. Within a week, they were on their way to Fort Dix in New Jersey for basic training.

Six weeks later, just as they were about to be shipped overseas, influenza broke out among the new recruits - ten cases in their barracks alone. With their entire company under quarantine, confined to quarters, the two boys felt cut off from the rest of the base as well as the rest of the world. They watched other young men get sick and die.

Somehow Desmond knew that he would not get sick.

But Frank worried that his life might end right there in a wooden barracks on the flat, mosquito-ridden fields of New Jersey. "All this waste of life is a terrible thing." Frank shook his head and prayed for every soldier who coughed and ranted with the madness of fever.

"Frank, you've grown stronger in America with enough to eat every day. Why, you'd a died back in Ireland for sure."

"Yeah, maybe so, Des. But I feel so sorry for these poor young souls."

"Aye, Frank, 'tis a shame. But it's the first time that you and me are on the lucky side a things so let's just be enjoyin' our good fortune for a change."

They spent four long, boring months in quarantine. And all that time Desmond feared that he might miss out on the fighting.

At last, they sailed from New York Harbor aboard the retrofitted USS Powhatan, an old German liner once known as the SS Hamburg. The old ship had gotten stranded in New York Harbor when the high seas became too dangerous for civilian travel and the United States seized it, converting it to a troop carrier. Protected by two destroyers, the Powhatan set sail for the port of Brest, France to deliver a fresh batch of raw, young recruits.

After stepping onto French soil, Desmond and Frank's unit joined a contingency of British soldiers marching toward the front lines.

"I can't believe that I'll be fightin' alongside the damned Brits," Frank moaned.

"To hell with it, Frank! Who cares? The Irish, Brits, the Krauts. I'm just takin' care a meself and fightin' for the fun of it."

Frank despised the fighting. Still, he did his job. "This is not the lovely countryside of France that I read about. Look at the charred skeletons of trees. Even the mud seems to be stained with blood."

Desmond laughed at Frank's assessment. "I can't wait to get into the real fightin'. Those guys up ahead sure dug us some fine trenches."

In their first skirmish with the enemy, Desmond rushed out of the bunker, firing, and even doing hand-to-hand combat. He killed three German soldiers, advancing the entire platoon to the next set of trenches. It appeared that nothing bothered Desmond - not the mud, not the screams of pain in the dark, not the miles of barbed wire, not even the stench of the dead rotting farm animals and cavalry horses.

But Frank hated everything about the war, "Desmond, me Da was right. This fighting is a waste. And for what?"

The next morning, with the trenches shrouded in fog, Desmond began setting up a ladder against the walls of the trench.

Suddenly, Frank spotted a German soldier right there in the trench running toward Desmond, bayonet unsheathed and aimed directly at Des' belly. Firing two shots, Frank hit the German in the face at close range. Bloody pieces of flesh splattered onto Frank's face and he recoiled in disgust.

Desmond gasped, "I never even seen him coming. Frank, this is the second time you've saved me sorry arse." Smiling at Frank, Desmond felt something in his heart for Frank that he had never felt for another human being.

Frank had acted out of reflex, shocking even himself. He stared blankly at Desmond and the dead German. And then he fell to his knees, vomiting.

And so it was on that foggy morning in that dreadful, muddy trench in France, that the lives of Frank O'Connor and Desmond Lynch, and the lives of their progeny, became forever and irrevocably entwined.

Chapter 5

Desmond Lynch and Frank O'Connor returned from the First World War as citizens and heroes. No longer greenhorns, they now called The Glen, "home" and everyone greeted them by name when they walked down Broadway.

Desmond relished the recognition and respect.

But Frank just wanted to go back to his old job at Flannagan's Carpentry Shop. He confided to old-man Flannagan, "It seems that I'm only able to forget the savagery when I'm carving something beautiful out of wood."

"I think a man like you is compelled to create beauty. You really have a gift, Frank."

"Well, 'twas you who gave me the chance to discover that gift."

"Aye, I'm glad you're back, boy."

Frank's hand-carved furniture became more and more popular with the wealthy housewives on Park Place and, in just a few short months, there was a waiting list of back orders for his work. "Frank, me boy, we've sold all the display pieces," Flannagan said in a panic, as two men hauled the last piece of furniture out of the store, leaving even the front display window empty.

"I'll work every night, and Sunday. Don't you worry! We'll have a fine display window again in no time."

"But first, Frank, you'd better finish Mrs. Garrigan's order. Ya got to please that old witch before anyone else. She's a spoiled one, looking down her nose at all of us living in The Glen."

"Aye, she's always got a complaint about something. I feel like telling her not to buy my furniture."

"Oh, no Frank, you can't cross her and she knows it. Just placate her with that handsome smile a yours."

Frank nodded, aware that his good looks often gave him an advantage with the female customers. But, in his heart, Frank only had eyes for Greta Schmidt, the beautiful daughter of the German butcher whose shop was right next door.

Frank purchased a meat sandwich for lunch every day at noon, waiting patiently in line just so he could smile at Greta. And Greta, blushing, always smiled back.

After several weeks of lunches and furtive looks, Frank asked the stern old butcher for permission to call on Greta.

But Gregor Schmidt refused.

Frank kept on asking.

Finally, after weeks of refusal, Gregor relented and invited Frank to spend Sunday afternoon at the Schmidt's row house.

Wearing a brand new suit and carrying a small Waterford vase filled with wild flowers, Frank rang the doorbell of the corner row house.

Greta opened the door, smiled and invited Frank to come in and sit on the living room sofa. She served tea and homemade cookies while Gregor Schmidt sat in the overstuffed chair across the room watching every move that Frank made.

After two more Sunday afternoon visits, Frank asked Gregor for Greta's hand in marriage. "I swear to you, Mr. Schmidt, that I will spend my life making Greta happy. No one will ever love Greta the way I do."

Gregor glared at Frank. "You are nut gud enough vor my Greta."

"You're right, Sir, I'm not. No one is good enough for Greta. But I will work day and night to make her happy."

"If you ver to marry my Greta, und I'm not saying dat you vill, den you vould live in dis house, my house, vith me und Greta."

"Yes, sir, of course."

"And you vill vork vith me in de butcher shop und take it over von day."

Frank shook his head, "No, sir, I can't do that. But I'll work hard making furniture. I swear on me Da's grave that I will give Greta a fine life."

"Der vill be no marriage," Gregor roared.

Weeks passed. Frank and Greta could only look longingly at one another when they passed on the street. But every day, Greta begged her father to change his mind. She tearfully professed her deep, unending love for the handsome Irish carpenter.

Finally, after weeks of Greta's pleading, Gregor stormed into the Carpentry shop on a dismal, rainy afternoon. "Eez done. I give you permission to marry my daughter. Greta, she cries vor you every day. But, by God, you vill be gud to her or I vill kill you."

"I will take good care of Greta. You have my word, Sir. Thank you, thank you. I adore your daughter."

Frank made a magnificent "hope chest" for Greta. It was carved from the finest cherry wood, with such elegance of design and so perfectly crafted, that even Gregor praised Frank's superior talent.

The wedding date was set and news of the engagement between the German butcher's daughter and the Irish carpenter spread through The Glen. It wasn't long before a dismayed Desmond Lynch rushed into Flannagan's Carpentry Shop. "What are ye thinkin' Frank? Greta's a Kraut. You, of all people, know what they're like."

"Greta's lived in The Glen since she was ten years old. She's hardly an enemy soldier."

"Ah Frank, couldn't you find an Irish girl? The Glen is crawlin' with em."

"Come on now, Des, don't be like that. I'll be needing you as my best man."

"Aye, you know that I'd do anything for you, Frank. Hell, I owe you me life. But with all this bad feelin' against the Germans, well, I'm really gonna have to watch yar back now."

Frank smiled, shaking Desmond's hand. "Thank's Des, cause I've already told Greta and her father that you're my best man."

Frank O'Connor married Greta Schmidt in mid-June 1919. The church bells rang as the normally stern Gregor Schmidt smiled and walked his lovely daughter down the aisle. She wore a slim, beige, ankle-length, dress with delicate, matching shoes and an elaborate beige clutch hat. Her flawless complexion turned a deep red when Gregor placed her delicate hand in Frank's, hard, blistered fingers.

And Frank, wearing a black suit, with his shaggy brown hair cut short and his narrow mustache trimmed neatly, could easily have passed for a silent film star.

It seemed like forever to Frank until Monsignor Murdock pronounced them man and wife and told Frank to kiss his bride. The newly married couple walked hand-in-hand back through the empty church to the vestibule where Desmond congratulated them. Greta reached for Desmond's hand. "Tank you vor being our best man. You are Frank's only family und now you are my family."

Desmond smiled at Greta. "Promise me that you will be a fine wife to Frank because he is the only truly good man that I've met in this world."

"Yah, Frank is gud man und I vill take care of him, alvays. I promise."

The newlyweds, accompanied by the small wedding party, walked through The Glen Center to the Schmidt's corner row house where white ribbons adorned the front porch. The curtains were pulled back to show off windows that sparkled like fine crystal. Vases filled with fresh cut flowers from Greta's garden graced the highly polished end tables in the living room as well as the buffet in the dining room. The table was fully set with Greta's mother's Bavarian china placed carefully on top of a hand-embroidered table cloth.

"Come in, yah, please, come in." Gregor bowed, a broad smile on his usually dour face.

Desmond sat across from Frank and Greta, between Hilda, Greta's cousin, the Maid of Honor, and the widower, Mr. Flannagan. Monsignor Murdock claimed the foot of the table.

Gregor brought a tray of sliced, cold meats from the kitchen, placing it in the center of the table. Greta followed him with a tray of potato salad and rye bread.

Lighting two thin white candles on the sideboard, Gregor pointed to a double tiered white cake surrounded by pink rose petals, announcing, "Yah, look here, my daughter, she bake her own vedding cake." Then Gregor took his seat signaling the monsignor to give the blessing.

"Bless us O Lord and these Thy Gifts . . .

As they all began to eat, Monsignor Murdock said, "You are a lucky man, Frank O'Connor."

"I am, indeed." Frank responded.

Desmond stood to make the toast. "To Mr. and Mrs. Frank O'Connor. May they be happy every day and live to see their grandchildren's children. And Frank, me friend, I'll always have yar back."

The small group applauded as Frank kissed Greta. Gregor wiped the tears from his plump cheeks.

Desmond refilled his water glass from a pitcher while the corpulent Monsignor reached for a third helping of cold roast beef. And when the guests left, Greta handed each of them a slice of wedding cake wrapped in white tissue paper, tied with pink ribbon.

The next morning was Sunday but Gregor went to his butcher shop to work on inventory, leaving Greta and Frank alone for a short time. On Monday, Frank returned to work at the carpentry shop and Greta joined her father behind the counter at the butcher shop.

They worked six days a week for the next fourteen months - until August 15, 1920, when Greta gave birth to a beautiful baby girl whom they named, Catherine.

And in September, Desmond once again stood beside Greta's cousin, Hilda, in St. Joseph's Church, this time as Catherine's godfather.

After the christening, another celebration took place at the Schmidt row house on the corner of Broadway and Garden Street. The back yard overflowed with friends and neighbours, except for the family that lived in the row house right next door. It seemed that Mr. and Mrs. O'Toole and their daughter, Hannah, refused all invitations, preferring to keep to themselves.

But Isaac Weinberg and his wife, who lived in the row house on the other side of the O'Toole's, came to the christening party and marvelled at the bedroom and back porch that Frank had added to the original row house.

"You're an artisan, Frank, better than any builder in the area."

Greta proudly showed off the hand-carved crib that Frank made for little Catherine.

Gregor hired a recent immigrant, a young boy from Germany, to replace Greta at the butcher shop. And Flannagan's Carpentry Shop took on an apprentice carpenter to help Frank with the overflow of work.

Life in The Glen was good, very good indeed.

Chapter 6

A steady flow of immigrants, attracted by cheaper rents than in New York City, moved to The Glen. The carpet and elevator factories functioned at full capacity with three daily shifts and their fat payrolls supported the shops in The Glen Center. Conversations in Polish, Czech, Italian and Yiddish were commonplace in The Glen.

Milk from Foley's Dairy in Tarrytown arrived fresh at every front door in The Glen and, neat little trucks from Duggan's Bakery in the Bronx sold fresh bread products door-to-door. Swedish immigrants, fresh off the boat, opened a produce market on Broadway just a few doors from Schmidt's Butcher Shop. And even with The Prohibition, O'Brien's Pub remained the heart and hub of The Glen Center.

Trolley cars rattled down tracks in the middle of Broadway but still more and more cars appeared on the streets of The Glen. With few garages, all the additional cars parked along the curbs seemed to make the roads shrink and appear smaller.

Orders for Frank's furniture began to come from the big New York City stores. Housewives from The Glen crowded into Gregor's butcher shop along with the kitchen maids from the elegant homes up on Park Place. Gregor had to devise a number system to ensure that his customers were served in the right order.

Desmond, now the eyes and ears of Boss Garrigan, made rounds on the streets of The Glen Center every day. He'd often stop by Flannagan's to talk with Frank. "Hey me friend, you're quite busy aren't ya?"

"Des, how are you? Listen now, you've got to come by the house to see your goddaughter or she won't even recognize you."

"I know that I've been lax in me godfather duties. I'll try to get there but I'm busy like everyone else. Give little Catherine this for me." He handed Frank a shiny, new silver dollar.

Frank laughed. "If you keep giving Catherine silver dollars, she'll be too rich to bother with either of us working stiffs. Des, we all miss you, and, besides, you look like you could use a square meal."

"I could, indeed, Frank, and we all know that your wife is the best cook in the state. I'll get there soon. Ya know Garrigan's runnin' for Mayor of The Glen now."

"So I hear, Des."

"Well Frank, there's little or no room left to build so he's got to do something. And every apartment in the Glen Center is rented, filled with people from God knows where. Their food smells as strange as the words that come from their lips. I don't know what this country is comin' to, lettin' just anyone come here."

"Des, those poor souls are coming here for the same reasons we did, to find work so they can feed their families and survive."

"Aye, is that why we came?" Desmond joked, as he left the shop.

Boss Garrigan won the race for mayor while Desmond, as his right hand man, got busier and busier. He was a fixer, an enforcer and a mediator, as well as the most feared man in The Glen. He did a fine job for Garrigan and the Boss knew it.

Unlike Brooklyn and the Bronx, the streets in The Glen were safe. Random crime did not exist. But organized crimes like gambling thrived, well managed by the two men who occupied the front window of Mario's Restaurant.

They also collected from the newspaper/candy store manager who openly sold bets on the horses and the daily numbers. In addition, every business in The Glen paid Garrigan for a sort of "anti-crime" insurance policy.

Of course, there was the occasional drunk staggering around the streets after leaving O'Brien's Pub. And then there were those screams heard from the row houses or apartments above the stores. But those were family matters - not real crimes - and certainly not the business of the police.

As Prohibition became the law of the land, it caused many changes even in The Glen. Garrigan convinced Sean O'Brien to renovate the Pub, moving the grand mahogany bar to a back room and replacing it with a small sandwich bar. The interior of O'Brien's appeared to be a very small luncheonette now but, behind the new back wall, construction crews remodelled the old Pub into a private club.

Garrigan asked Desmond to see if Frank O'Connor would head up the renovation project for the Pub, "I'll pay him twice what he gets for that furniture and he won't have to use his hands at all – just manage the job and make it right. Frank has a keen eye for things and I want O'Brien's Back Room to be the best in the country."

So Desmond stopped by the carpentry shop. "You should be joinin' Garrigan on this job, Frank. He'll pay you top dollar to be in charge of the project to update O'Brien's Pub. He wants it to be truly grand."

"No, Des, that kind of job is not for me. I'm a free spirit as you well know."

Other men who refused offers from Boss Garrigan were found bloody and bruised in a dark alley. Some even disappeared permanently. But Desmond, true to his word, always had Frank's back.

When the renovations at O'Brien's were complete, the back wall of O'Brien's Sandwich and Coffee Shop had a green door with a brass knocker and a peep hole on its back wall. Customers would knock to gain access to the private back room where the old mahogany bar now stood, fully stocked with whiskey and cold beer flowing freely from the polished copper taps.

Thanks to Prohibition, Garrigan now earned money every time someone in The Glen downed a brew.

O'Brien bragged, "Thanks to Garrigan, I've enough whiskey in my cellar to last for ten years." But no one in The Glen could figure out how O'Brien's kept the beer flowing from its taps.

Federal agents sniffed around, asking questions, but Desmond usually got rid of them with a payoff. There was, however, this one young fed who would not go away. He doggedly asked too many questions and even took a room at Leary's Boarding House where Desmond lived, brazenly questioning Desmond at the dinner table.

"You've a nerve disturbin' me when I'm trying to enjoy this fine corned beef and cabbage dinner," Desmond growled. "And anyway, what do ya care if someone wants to enjoy a beer with a chaser or a few shots a whiskey? What are ya, some holy roller or Bible thumper?"

"Selling alcohol is against the law Mr. Lynch," the young fed replied.

"And whose law is it against? It used to be alright and it will be again one day," Desmond said with a broad smile on his face.

"Why, even God himself made some very fine tastin' wine out of water at a wedding according to the 'good book.' And those old time commandments don't say nothin' about not drinkin' beer." As he spoke, Desmond placed a roll of hundred dollar bills on the dining room table.

"Are you bribing a federal agent, Mr. Lynch?"

"Certainly not!" Desmond answered, standing up and walking out of the room, leaving the money behind.

The young agent did not touch the money. But he continued to nose around The Glen, asking questions.

Old man O'Brien complained to Boss Garrigan, "That fed is determined to figure out how the beer gets to my pub."

Garrigan passed the problem along to Desmond, "Take care of the fed. I don't care how you do it."

It was no surprise to anyone when the nosey young agent disappeared. Rumors spread. People said that two of Desmond's punks dragged the agent out of Leary's Boarding House in the wee hours of the morning, with his hands tied behind his back, intimating that Desmond killed him.

But Desmond told everyone a very different story.

"I took the young man to the old Glen Brewery – the one that closed its doors the very day that Prohibition became law. So I says to him, 'young fella, I hear that you want to know how O'Brien's gets the beer flowin' from its taps?' And it's such a tasty brew at that. Me, I'm not a drinkin' man, but I hear that everyone loves it. And the young fella asks me if the brewery is still workin'? So I says, just let me show you."

Desmond described how he took the federal agent around to the back of the brewery building and removed the boards across the old back door. "I brung him inside and he sees a full crew working in the old brewery. And then the young fed kept asking me, 'But how do you get the beer into O'Brien's?"

"So I tells him, "Well me boy, that's the genius of it. We pump it through these nice clean new fire hoses that run through The Glen's sewer system right into O'Brien's Pub and right up to the copper taps on the bar.' And the young fella jumps up saying, 'So that's why I could never find a delivery truck.' And then he says that's all he wanted to know and the next day he left town to go back home to his Mamma somewhere in Kansas, wherever that is. And he took all that money that I left on the table at the boarding house and a lot more with him. I bet he never seen so many hundred dollar bills at one time before."

Everyone in The Glen believed Desmond's version of events but some of the federal agents did not. They came looking for the young man, asking questions of everyone in The Glen.

Perhaps those agents eventually took a payoff themselves. Or maybe they just could not "prove" foul play. But after a time, the feds went away and things in The Glen carried on as usual.

O'Brien's Pub functioned unmolested by federal agents until Prohibition ended in 1933 when the Twenty-first Amendment repealed the Eighteenth Amendment.

Desmond's work load lightened after Prohibition ended. He continued to live at Leary's Boarding House, going off to Henrietta's Brothel in the north Bronx almost every night where he paid for companionship and affection.

And, despite the fact that Desmond and Frank lived very different lives, they remained the best of friends.

Chapter 7

Boss Garrigan, now mayor of The Glen was called "King" Garrigan behind his back because he always wore expensive suits, white gloves and a black felt fedora hat to cover his bald head. He was driven everywhere by a uniformed chauffer in a sleek, black Lincoln Zephyr.

Desmond's loyalty to Garrigan was beyond question. Yet, Garrigan's demeanor made it clear that he did not consider Desmond an equal. But Desmond didn't mind. He had one friend, Frank O'Connor, and a job that paid very well. His stomach was full, his needs were met and he enjoyed being the most notorious and feared Irish gangster outside of Hell's Kitchen.

Still, Desmond worried a bit, when, out of the blue, Garrigan invited him to lunch at O'Brien's Pub. He dressed in his best suit and had his shoes polished by the son of the Italian shoe cobbler at his shop on Broadway.

When Desmond arrived at O'Brien's, Garrigan was comfortably settled into a booth and did not stand when Desmond joined him. "Ah, Desmond, glad you could make it. Sit down."

"I hope everything's alright, Mr. Garrigan. I mean with the job I'm doin' for ya," Des asked as he slid into the cushioned booth bench. It was always dark in the back of O'Brien's, even at mid-day, and the soft yellow lights along the wall cast eerie shadows on the faces of the two men.

"Forget the Mister and call me 'Boss' like everyone else. And you're doing a fine job. You're a hard worker and you keep your mouth shut. My only concern about you, Desmond, is that you're not married. You know, being mayor and all, people expect me to hire family men."

"Well, I've not been lucky enough to find a woman to marry. I work all the time and I'm not the best looking chap."

"But you're a real man, Desmond. You can provide for a woman and protect her. That's why it was no surprise to me when a fine, upstanding woman of my acquaintance asked about you. She's interested in making a match between you and her daughter. And that daughter is a pretty young thing."

"Young, you say. Well I'm not so young anymore." Desmond muttered. "Oh, I like the ladies. That I do. But I only know the ones at Henrietta's in the Bronx. But I treat them real good - with respect - no rough stuff like some a the boys."

The skin on Garrigan's pudgy face sagged from years of cigar smoking. He leaned in, reaching over the table to put his hand on Desmond's. "Well now, this young lady, Miss Hannah O'Toole, is not like the women at Henrietta's. She's a fine lady, that's for sure. But her poor Da passed away and left her Ma with a mountain of debt. Mrs. O'Toole's been searching for a strong man like yourself to take care of her daughter. She asked me about your character and I gave you high praise, indeed."

"Boss, that's kind of you. I've seen Miss Hannah O'Toole walkin' around the Glen with her Ma. She's real pretty and not so very much younger than meself – but a bit stuck up. She's never even so much as bid me a hello."

Boss Garrigan pointed his tobacco-stained finger at Desmond. "She's a looker for sure but she's not perfect. Let's just say that she's not as sociable as she should be. And none of us is gettin' any younger."

"Aye, that's a fact," Desmond agreed.

Garrigan began to pontificate, "Now, I'm not talkin' about that lovey-dovey stuff in those cheap novels. What I'm talking about is a union, a marriage, blessed by the Church that would be legitimate and stable – for you, for the community and for the next generation. You want children, don't you?"

Desmond thought carefully for a minute, aware that Garrigan, married for over twenty years, had no children.

"I'd like to have children but I'm more interested right now in a loving companion and a comfortable home."

"Loving companionship? Like that Frank O'Connor? Why everyone knows he married that pretty little Kraut just to get her father's row house and money. The old butcher probably still has the first dollar he ever earned."

Desmond changed the subject. "It would be nice to meet Miss O'Toole. I've often said hello to her but she's never even looked back at me."

"She's shy, and a bit willful. What our little Miss Hannah O'Toole needs is a strong man to take charge of her life and care for her."

"Is that a fact?"

"It is the plain truth. And after you're married, and you give Hannah a child, why she'll be tied to you forever. She'd not be able to leave you, even if she wanted to. And why would she want to?"

Desmond thought things over carefully. He acknowledged the he was lonely and he truly did want a home of his own to share with a woman who was not a paid companion. He looked directly at Garrigan. "Okay, I'd like to bid for Hannah O'Toole's hand in marriage – if she'll have me."

"Oh she'll have you alright and lucky she is to get you. If you could see your way clear to pay the sum that is owed by Hannah's mother, then the old lady will arrange the weddin' straight away." Garrigan was third generation American but he feigned an Irish brogue whenever he closed a deal like this.

"Mrs. O'Toole's debts will be paid in full by tomorrow at this time." Desmond promised.

Boss Garrigan shook Desmond's hand. "Aye this is a grand day and a great deal! Mrs. O'Toole will keep her home. Hannah will be taken care of and you get a pretty wife. My, but 'tis a shame you'll have to live with the old hag for now. But when Mrs. O'Toole passes on, that row house of hers right next door to Frank and Greta O'Connor will be all yours, me boy. I do right by them that's loyal to me. That I do."

Chapter 8

Desmond did not meet or speak to Hannah before their wedding, which took place on Saturday, October 16, 1928 in St. Joseph's Church. But he had been assured over and over by Mrs. O'Toole and Boss Garrigan that Hannah was delighted with the arrangement and very anxious to be his wife.

Desmond, ecstatic, paid for and made all the arrangements for the wedding, ordering flowers in tall metal vases to be placed on St. Joseph's white marble altar, with small bouquets in wicker baskets for all the other statues of saints. He presented Monsignor Murdock with a generous donation and hired the best organist in the county to play the Ave Maria.

Age had bestowed great favor on Desmond. Quite odd looking as a boy, his once thick carrot-colored hair was now faded prematurely to a mellow grey and his well-trimmed beard added a dignified sophistication to his once comical facial features. Standing beside Frank at the altar in a very expensive, tailor-made suit, his blue eyes riveted on Hannah as she walked toward him, Desmond could almost be called "handsome."

But Hannah didn't seem to see Desmond. Her pale blue eyes seemed blank and she did not smile. Still, she looked quite lovely in a slim pink suit, pink blouse and a small pill box hat with a pink veil that fell over her face. Her pale blonde hair hung loose touching her shoulders. Mrs. O'Toole held tight to her daughter's hand, coaching Hannah through the short ceremony, making sure that she made the correct responses so that her daughter's marriage would be legal in the eyes of the Church and the State of New York.

Eight year old Catherine O'Connor stood behind Hannah, gripping a basket of pink rose petals, ready to toss them over the bride the moment Monsignor Murdock declared her to be Mrs. Desmond Lynch.

Boss Garrigan and his wife, conspicuous by their absence, sent effusive regrets along with a generous cash gift.

After the ceremony, Desmond leaned over to kiss Hannah but she turned away. Misreading her refusal as shyness, Desmond whispered, "Aye, me darlin' wife, you're a chaste woman so we'll wait for privacy before I kiss you again. Just know that you've made me the happiest of men on this fine day."

Outside on the steps of the church, Frank and Greta congratulated the bride and groom but Hannah barely acknowledged them. She didn't even blink when little Catherine showered her with rose petals.

Danny Shay, one of Desmond's most trusted men, drove them back to Garden Street in a huge rented limousine. He parked in front of the O'Toole's row house that stood second from the corner, right next door to Frank and Greta's home.

On the street, Frank bowed slightly to Hannah. "Please, come into our home. Greta has prepared food and a very special wedding cake."

Mrs. O'Toole quickly replied, "How very kind of you, but no. Hannah appears to be tired. It's not every day a woman marries, you know. I think it best that Hannah take a nap after all this excitement."

Disappointment flashed momentarily across Desmond's face but he quickly masked it with a smile. "Sorry Frank, and Greta, but thanks to you just the same."

Frank stammered, "It's fine, really. I'll bring the cake over later and you can enjoy it at your leisure – perhaps even this evening." Rubbing Greta's shoulder, he continued, "Congratulations both of you – and you as well Mrs. O'Toole. We wish you all every happiness."

Desmond shook Frank's hand. "We're next door neighbours now, as well as friends."

"Right you are, Des, and now we'll be hearing each other's lives like a radio soap opera through that thin common wall."

"Well it's bound to be more private than sleeping on the floor of O'Brien's Pub." Desmond smiled, as if not having a wedding luncheon was alright with him. It wasn't.

"Frank, I'm so happy to have a wife and hopefully soon a family of me own."

Desmond got down on one knee to slip a silver dollar into Catherine's little hand and whisper to her, "Maybe I'll even be lucky enough to have a lovely daughter like you one day."

"Thank you, Uncle Desmond," Catherine answered as she smiled up at him.

Chapter 9

It all came tumbling down in 1929. The stock market crashed, the banks collapsed and hopes for a bright future died. There was a run on The Glen Center Bank. Depositors demanded to withdraw their savings and did so in large numbers – until the cash ran out and the bank closed its doors, leaving a mob of angry, desperate, terrified people standing in the street. The mood grew ugly and then violent.

They crowded into O'Brien's Pub where no one even bothered to hide the sale of liquor and beer.

It was bad, really bad, and everyone knew it. Every day the news seemed to get worse.

Cancelled orders forced the carpet and the elevator factories into one shift per day instead of three. Without those two huge payrolls, The Glen's economy imploded.

Frank didn't get paid for furniture that he'd already delivered. Flannagan's Carpentry Shop hemorrhaged money. Orders Frank was working on were cancelled and there were no new orders.

"Mr. Flannagan, I think we've lost nearly all of the credit that we extended. I am so sorry."

"I know, Frank. It's not your fault. But I can't keep the shop open like this. I can't pay the rent. My daughter wants me to move in with them and give her whatever cash I have left. They're literally starving."

"Well, your family comes first," Frank consoled his mentor. He took his tools home to the basement of his row house where he worked every day. Knowing that the market for fine hand-made furniture no longer existed, Frank remodelled his own row house and created a few special pieces of furniture for himself and a few pieces for Desmond's home as well.

Gregor Schmidt opened his butcher shop at the same time each morning as if nothing had happened. He even went so far as to lower his meat prices just to keep his loyal customers from starving. This went on for months as he worked every day just making ends meet with not even a nickel of profit. But when his meat distributor went out of business, Gregor had no choice but to close the butcher shop.

He paid his final rent check to The Garrigan Company and cleaned the wood counters, the display cases and refrigerators. He polished his knives and packed them into a huge wooden crate.

Tears welled up in Gregor's eyes when his young assistant bid him goodbye.

"Tank you Mr. Schmidt. I learned so much from you und you ver a gud and fair boss. I vill miss dis shop very much – and you, sir."

Gregor now stood alone in the empty, clean shop, looking around and thinking of how hard he had worked all those years to build up the business. He had money – cash in boxes hidden in the basement – only Greta knew where and how much. But it would not last forever. Maybe things would turn around.

He carried his box of knives outside and rested it on the sidewalk as he locked the door to his shop for the last time. A sharp pain ran through his forehead. It radiated to the back of his neck and his left arm went stiff. He tried to cry out but nothing came from his vocal chords.

It was mid-afternoon and there were only a few people walking on Broadway. Gregor, turned his head, thinking that he heard someone call his name - and then everything went black.

The police called Frank at home and he ran the two blocks to the butcher shop. It was too late. Gregor lay slumped over on his stomach, his face contorted in a grotesque expression, the key to the shop still clutched tightly in his stiff hand.

Greta took the news of her father's death hard. They had been very close since her mother's untimely death in Germany all those years ago. Gregor had been a good father, a gentle man and an excellent provider. After his initial objection to Greta's marriage to Frank, Gregor had come to love his son-in-law and he adored his granddaughter.

Greta decided to have a Mass said for her father but no viewing at the funeral parlor. She purchased a small plot for six at the Gates of Paradise Cemetery and placed a granite stone on the grave which read, "In memory of Gregor Schmidt, 1880 to 1931, a loving father and grandfather."

While they were still at the cemetery, right after burying her father, Greta told Frank that all of their money, as well as Gregor's money, was safe - all in cash, stuffed into metal boxes and hidden behind bricks in the basement wall.

"If ve are very careful," Greta said, "ve can live for quite a vile on dis money."

Frank marveled at his wife's shrewdness. "You are a genius and you've truly saved us."

He took Greta's trembling body in his arms and murmured, "Greta, I fear that life in The Glen will be very hard for a long, long time to come."

Unfortunately, Desmond Lynch was not as lucky with his finances. He followed Boss Garrigan's advice, putting most of his savings into the stock market and he lost everything. But Desmond had no intention of jumping off a bridge like so many others. He came from bad times and did not fear starting all over again. Desmond went back to the streets, once again as an "enforcer," a collector of bad debts, "Sure you'd be surprised how much money people can come up, when their very lives depend on it," he commented sarcastically about the dire financial times. Desmond worked long hours once again, glad to be away from home. It seemed that Hannah, always listless and exhausted, provided him little companionship and no comfort. They slept in separate bedrooms, their marriage never even consummated.

Lonely, ashamed and starved for affection, Desmond began to frequent Henrietta's Brothel in the Bronx again. He claimed a fragile, young girl named Peggy as his own. She had thin, straw colored hair, hardly ever spoke and never smiled, but she took the place of a wife for Desmond. In return, he treated her with respect and kindness, paying her well for her service and loyalty.

Henrietta was a shrewd business woman and she liked Desmond Lynch even more than she feared him. She understood, without being told, what his home-life was like and was glad that the fragile Peggy, the youngest girl in her employ, had a steady customer who treated her well.

"Ah Desmond, I'm sorry for your troubles. But, you know, there's other men with wives like yours."

Desmond stuffed a wad of cash into her mammoth bosom. "Thanks Henrietta. Now if anyone bothers you or if you need anything at all, you come to me for help. Ya hear?"

"Thanks Desmond, I need friends like you with the dangers in this business and times being so harsh."

Desmond looked into her eyes as he whispered, "I know me wife is not a real woman but I like goin' to Mass at St. Joseph's on Sunday morning with her on me arm and her Ma walkin' behind us. It's the only time when those 'so-called' decent people give me a bit a respect."

Desmond's expression changed and he grabbed Henrietta's arm. "But no one is to know about me family situation. Do you hear me? I can put up with me marriage the way it is as long as no one knows the truth."

Henrietta smiled. "Discretion is the biggest part of my livelihood. And anyway, Desmond, no one in their right mind would ever cross you."

"Aye, that's a fine point you make," he said, placing yet another twenty dollar bill into the deep divide between her milky white breasts.

"The Great Depression" dragged on. Homes foreclosed; families lived in tents in the parks; packs of dogs, once loving pets, roamed the streets, attacking people out of sheer hunger and an instinct to survive.

The immigrant community suffered in America what they had come so far to escape, their only consolation being that times were even worse in the places they left behind. When Congress repealed The Prohibition Amendment in 1933, Desmond commented to Boss Garrigan, "Them government types must think that people livin' in a depression time must need a bit a whiskey and beer to drink. But we'll be losin' some money with the drink goin' legal again."

"We will, but only for a while. I've got some ideas so don't you worry about your livelihood, Desmond." Garrigan spoke with a thick cigar stuck between his tar-stained teeth.

O'Brien's Pub took down the dividing wall. It seemed that the Pub was the only thriving business in The Glen. They offered tap beer for half price as a public service to their customers – all having hard times. And Mrs. O'Brien allowed homeless families to sleep on the floor over the bar without charging them a penny.

City jobs disappeared along with tax revenues. A Federal Job Works Program hired men who left their families behind to live and work in camps, building roads and bridges across the nation.

"These are sorry times for sure," Garrigan whispered to Desmond.

"Aye, there's almost nothin' left to steal."

The streets of The Glen became littered and dirty. The grocery store moved their produce indoors to stop the constant pilfering. Pickpockets roamed the streets stealing anything they could get their hands on.

And The Glen was no longer immune from random violence. The entire city reeled in shock over two bloody murders of wives by their husbands.

People talked of nothing else when an all-male jury at the County Courthouse in White Plains found one killer "not guilty by reason of insanity."

These were the very first "known murders" in The Glen where an actual body was found. But many suspected that those who went missing over the years were murder victims as well. It was just that there had been no body to bury. "They were probably dumped in the Hudson, weighted down with cement." The new young bartender at O'Brien's was heard to say.

Even elegant Park Place began to look shabby. The wrought iron gates surrounding the fine homes, now chipped, were in need of repair and the fine lawns were no longer well-manicured.

Frank ran into Desmond on Broadway late one afternoon. "What's this world coming to when a man stabs his wife on Broadway in The Glen?"

Desmond scoffed, "I don't believe for a minute that the husband done it. I think it was a bunch a them rough "*Pollocks*" from the Bronx or it could a been one of them colored people from the shanties down by the railroad."

"But Des, I heard that there were witnesses – at least to one of the murders."

"You can't even understand what those foreigners say. They don't speak proper English. And if the husband done it, then 'twas just bad blood between a husband and wife that got out of hand and not a real murder."

"A murder is a murder," Frank said, shocked.

"Well, the poor dumb bastard is in the crazy house and he'll never get out. All over a family disagreement! 'Tis a shame indeed."

Frank worried about Desmond's own home life after that conversation. But he knew better than to try to dissuade Desmond about anything, so he just walked on, shaken by the callousness of his best friend's remarks.

With times so bad in The Glen, Garrigan needed a new strategy to get votes, so he and Desmond began to attend wakes and funerals in order to win back the trust of the people. They'd give out quarters on the street and show up unannounced at front doors with bread and milk for struggling families.

"The way we run the city is changing, Desmond. We're gonna have to be seen and heard a lot more now, but in a personal way," Garrigan said. "And there's no need to keep meticulous records anymore. Cash is the only thing that matters now."

Chapter 10

It was September 1934 when fourteen year old Catherine O'Connor, on full academic scholarship, began high school at the prestigious Sacred Heart Academy in Scarsdale, New York. She commuted on the New York Central Railroad from the modest, working-class city of The Glen to the up-scale suburb of Scarsdale.

Bright and beautiful, young Catherine made friends easily and she was accepted by her wealthy, sometimes snobbish classmates. Margaret Kelly, who lived only a few doors from Sacred Heart Academy on Scarsdale's main street immediately became Catherine's best friend and invited Catherine to her home often. But Catherine never invited Margaret to the row house in The Glen.

It was at one of the Kelly's regular Saturday afternoon "get-togethers" that Catherine first met the handsome college freshman, Michael Brandon. An only child, like Catherine, Michael lived in a huge Tudor home on the next block directly behind the Kelly's home and commuted by car to Fordham University in the Bronx.

Catherine stared at the tall, handsome college freshman. She grabbed Margaret's arm and pulled her aside. "Tell me all about Michael Brandon. He's so, so handsome."

"Why, Cath, don't tell me you've got a crush on him?"

"Maybe!" Catherine smiled, her soft brown eyes sparkling. Tall for her age, with her mother's perfect skin and even features, she was the prettiest girl at Sacred Heart Academy as well as one of the brightest. "I adore those dark blue eyes of his - and that thick black hair"

"Michael's really cute but he's kind of stuck on himself. If I were you, Catherine, I'd stick to high school boys – like Tommy Flynn. He has such a crush on you." Margaret spoke in light tones but her comment was meant as a serious warning.

Catherine blushed deeply, her eyes still riveted on Michael Brandon.

The weeks and months passed and Catherine met Michael quite often at the Kelly home. They'd smile at each other and have a few passing words – nothing more meaningful than that.

The following September, at the end of the first day of Catherine's sophomore year, she ran down the front steps of Sacred Heart Academy to see Michael Brandon leaning against his father's long, sleek black Buick, parked at the curb. He smiled, calling out, "Hey Cath, can I give you a ride home?"

Catherine, her face beet red, walked up to Michael. "Okay," she stammered, shyly. "But you'll have to drop me off at The Glen Center and I'll walk the rest of the way home."

"Why can't I take you right to your door?"

"I don't think my dad would approve of me riding in your car?"

"Why not?" Michael teased. "I'm a good driver."

"It's not your driving. It's that he doesn't know you."

"Hop in pretty girl. One of these days, I'll have to meet your dad and make a good impression on him. Then I'm sure that he'll let me take you for rides."

Catherine smiled.

Michael stared at Catherine causing her to feel shivers inside. Even in a plain green jumper and beige cotton blouse, the daily uniform for Sacred Heart Academy, Catherine O'Connor somehow managed to look stunning.

Michael took her books, tossed them onto the back seat and opened the front passenger door for Catherine. He grinned, bowing slightly.

She laughed as she slid gracefully into the front seat.

It was a spectacular fall day with the sun gleaming through trees, their leaves just beginning to morph into autumn colors.

Michael drove south to a small park and pulled into a secluded spot that overlooked the Hudson River. "My folks used to bring me here for picnics," he said, looking into Catherine's eyes.

She smiled. "It's marvelous. Look at how wide the Hudson is - and the view of the rocky ledges of the Palisades is spectacular."

"It's nice to be alone here, away from all those critical eyes and gossiping tongues," Michael said as he pulled a bottle of beer from a brown paper bag, offering Catherine a sip.

She shook her head, no. He drank the whole bottle in a few gulps.

They talked for almost two hours until it was almost dark. Then Michael dropped Catherine off on Broadway in The Glen, two blocks from her parents' row house.

After that very first afternoon, Michael picked Catherine up every day after school. And he'd always have a few beers in the car with him. Eventually, Catherine tried the frothy cold brew and enjoyed the way it made her feel. They'd go to the same spot near the river where they'd talk and kiss. Before long, they got into some really serious necking.

Catherine tried to keep Michael's hands in safe places and restrict his kisses to her lips, but she was young and had strong feelings for him.

"I love you Catherine. Please, don't stop me now," Michael said, his voice heavy with passion. He opened and unzipped his pants, lifting Catherine onto his lap. His hand went underneath her skirt, pulling her panties aside. His fingers skillfully touched her clitoris, igniting sensations that pulsated through her entire body.

"Are you okay?" Michael asked.

"Yes," Catherine whispered.

"I want you so much, Cath. I'm so in love with you."

"Oh, Michael, I've never felt like this. I'm so scared but I don't want you to stop."

He unbuttoned her jumper, her blouse, unhooked her bra and kissed her bare breasts tenderly until she whispered, "I love you, Michael." Gently, he pushed himself up and deep inside of her. She moaned in pleasure and in pain. They clung to each other, clamoring for more, knowing that their lives had changed forever.

Their relationship continued to advance sexually. They made love every afternoon after school but didn't actually date and never saw each other on weekends.

Saturdays and Sundays were endless for Catherine. She lived for her clandestine meetings with Michael after school. And the weekdays in class were soon only a prelude to being with him. Catherine no longer heard the nuns teaching. She thought only of Michael. Before long she drank as much beer as he did. It made her dizzy. She lost all inhibitions, allowing Michael to do whatever he wanted with her perfect, young body. Catherine wanted nothing but to be in Michael's arms and experience the total abandon of lying beneath him in the backseat of his car.

At home, she avoided conversations with her mother and father, spending most of her time alone in her room. She became furtive, withdrawn, losing interest in everything except Michael.

The winter passed and in May, at the end of her sophomore year, Catherine tearfully confessed to her mother that she was deeply in love with Michael Brandon and probably pregnant with his child.

Too shocked to even speak, Greta ran to tell Frank. Fearing her husband's wrath, she tearfully told him everything.

Frank's reaction was shock and then sadness but not anger.

He went to his daughter's room. "We've never even met this young man," Frank said looking into Catherine's eyes. "I am hurt by your betrayal of me and your mother. We should have been told that you were seeing this boy. We love you, and we trusted you."

"Oh Daddy, Michael is older; he's in college and I thought you wouldn't approve. I knew you'd make me stop seeing him."

"Well, I don't approve of his age, or of his sneaking around with you."

"Daddy, he's smart and charming and handsome and I love him and he wants us to get married right away."

"The first thing you will do is invite this young man and his parents to come here to our home - tomorrow evening."

Frank left his daughter's room to go downstairs to talk with Greta. "I'd like to beat that young man. Our Catherine is only a child. But I will not hurt her any more than she's already been hurt.

"And I won't have our family torn apart the way families were in Ireland when a girl got herself in a 'family way.' Catherine doesn't have to marry Brandon. We can raise this child as our own."

"But she vants to marry him. She says she loves him," Greta cried. "Und now she von't even graduate high school."

"We'll deal with this just the way we've dealt with everything, with love and decency," Frank said, taking Greta in his arms.

The next evening, Mr. and Mrs. Brandon of Scarsdale, with their son, Michael, arrived at the O'Connor's row house at six-thirty. Michael and his mother had picked Mr. Brandon up at the railroad station where he came direct from his job in New York City.

Frank and Greta stared at the Brandon family. Michael, tall, like his father, had similar features, except that Mr. Brandon, now balding, sported blue and red blood vessels on his swollen nose along with puffy bags beneath both eyes.

Mrs. Brandon, wrinkled and very thin, wore a blue suit, high heels and a mink stole - even though the evening was quite warm.

"Come in! May I take your wrap, Mrs. Brandon?" Frank asked.

"No, I'll just keep it on but thank you."

"Well, sit down. I'm Frank and this is my wife Greta, and our daughter Catherine."

Mr. and Mrs. Brandon nodded to the O'Connors but did not respond or offer their own first names.

"Would you care for some tea?" Frank asked.

"I'll have a scotch and water," Mr. Brandon barked, as if speaking to a waiter.

"Sorry, but we don't keep liquor in the house."

Mr. Brandon cleared his throat and mumbled, "Well, this is going to be even worse than I thought."

Michael sat next to his parents, staring down at his hands.

Catherine sat on a dining room chair across from them, looking at Michael through red, swollen eyes.

Mr. Brandon took over as if they were in his home. "This is terrible news for us. A marriage right now will ruin Michael's chance for a career. And Catherine is hardly what we expected for a daughter-in-law. But I am willing to pay to have her go away until after the birth and put the child up for adoption."

"No one is going to adopt my grandchild, except, perhaps, me," Frank spoke firmly so there would be no mistaking his meaning.

"But Catherine and I want to get married," Michael spoke out for the first time.

"Well, my daughter is really too young to get married," Frank insisted.

Catherine began to weep. "Please Daddy, I don't want to go on living without Michael."

The room fell quiet.

Finally Mrs. Brandon spoke. "We will have to allow this marriage and hope for the best. Make it a quiet wedding, this Saturday, in your church here. We can't have our friends know about the ceremony. Catherine and Michael can live with us and we'll support them while Michael finishes up at Fordham."

"We'll see," Frank spit the words out while he looked over at Greta as she fumbled with the pocket of her cotton house dress, searching desperately for her handkerchief. "I made dinner if anyone is hungry," she offered.

"No, we have plans for this evening and Michael needs to drive us home," Mrs. Brandon responded, standing up. "Come along Michael." She took her son's hand. "You'll see more than enough of Catherine after the wedding on Saturday."

The Brandons left Frank and Greta's row house without even a handshake.

Catherine ran up to her room and slammed the door so hard that the house shook.

"I need some fresh air." Frank walked out the front door.

Greta went into the kitchen. Weeping, she cleared the table and put away the food.

Frank sat on his front porch steps with his head in his hands. He didn't even bother to look up when a car pulled alongside the curb to drop off Desmond Lynch next door.

Desmond, shocked to see his old friend in that position, walked over to join him. "It's been months, me friend, since we talked. What's going on?"

Frank told Desmond about Catherine's upcoming marriage.

"She's only a child. What are ye thinkin'?"

"There are circumstances," Frank replied.

"Aye, circumstances you say? Well we can beat the shit out a this kid, whoever he is." Desmond rubbed his thick, powerful hands together.

"He and Catherine claim they are madly in love and she doesn't want to live if we prevent the marriage. But there is something very wrong. I can feel it. His parents don't think much of Catherine or of us."

"Really? Well, we'll see about that. I have yar back, Frank. We need to make sure that me goddaughter is treated right."

Desmond sat down beside his friend, placing his hand on Frank's shoulder. Frank wept as he had wept only once before - as a child in Ireland, years and years ago, when his dear mother died.

It was a sad wedding with only the bride, the groom and their parents in attendance. The janitor and the church secretary signed the marriage certificate as witnesses.

After the ceremony, the Brandons refused an invitation to lunch at the O'Connor's house and they did not invite the O'Connors back to their home.

Mr. Brandon drove his big black Buick away from the church with Mrs. Brandon in the front seat while Catherine and Michael sat in the back together. Catherine peered out the back window and waved "goodbye" to her parents. She was sixteen years old, pregnant, married to a spoiled young man and going off to live in a house where she and her parents would never really be welcome.

A week after the ceremony, Desmond asked Tommy Shay, his trusted driver, to take him to the Brandon home in Scarsdale. As they pulled into the circular driveway in front of the big Tudor house, Desmond said, "I'll be but a few minutes, Tommy. So just leave the engine runnin'."

Desmond walked up to the front door and held his finger on the bell far too long.

Mr. Brandon came to the door with a full highball glass in his hand. "Yes, how can I help you?"

"This is the Brandon home, is it not?"

"Yes, it is. And we don't allow salesmen in this neighborhood."

"I'm Desmond Lynch, Catherine's godfather. I've come to give me girl a weddin' gift."

Mr. Brandon gasped when he heard the name "Desmond Lynch."

"You are askin' me in are ye not?" Desmond growled, as he pushed past him and stomped into the living room where Mrs. Brandon sat sprawled out on a velvet settee.

She looked up at Desmond. "And who are you?"

"Ah good evening Mrs. Brandon." Desmond smiled and bowed, using every ounce of his considerable charm. "Aye, 'tis a pleasure to meet you. I'm Desmond Lynch, Catherine's uncle and godfather."

Mr. Brandon, stood behind Desmond, turning pale and looking frightened.

"How do you do, Mr. Lynch. We weren't expecting company this evening." Mrs. Brandon sat up straight, smiling seductively. "Can I fix you a highball?"

"No, no, thank you, Ma'am. I never touch the stuff meself but I made a fine bit a money sellin' it during the Prohibition. But then I lost most of that money in the big crash. Makin' money is easy though, 'tis livin' a good life that's hard. Don't you agree?"

Mr. Brandon interrupted. "My son is not at home but Catherine is upstairs resting. Shall I get her?"

"No, now don't you be botherin' me darlin' girl. She needs her rest, her bein' knocked up and taken advantage of by that no-good son a yours." Desmond turned to face Brandon. "You tell your boy that I'll be watchin' him real close. So he'd better be sure to treat me goddaughter right."

Desmond dropped a rolled up wad of cash on the cocktail table. "This is just a wee gift for my dear Catherine. See that she gets it."

Desmond walked out of the living room and out of the house.

Mr. Brandon's entire body shook. "Do you know who that was? Desmond Lynch. My God, just what did that son of ours get us into?"

Chapter 11

Five months later, Catherine gave birth to an eight pound baby boy. She named him Keith Francis. And, of course, it being 1936, everyone counted backwards to the wedding day to determine if the child was conceived before or after the wedding.

The gossip mongers in both The Glen and Scarsdale enjoyed scandalous conversations about the timing of the wedding as well as Catherine's tender age.

When Michael came to the hospital to bring Catherine and their son home, it was obvious to Frank and Greta who were there visiting, that he had been drinking heavily.

Frank spoke softly, "Lad, you smell like an open bottle of rye. I don't think you should be drivin' at all."

"I'm fine and what I do is none of your business," Michael snapped.

"I don't give a damn what you do, but, when it affects my grandson and my daughter, then I'll have plenty to say. And I say that you're not fit to drive."

Their raised voices upset the entire maternity floor. A floor nurse called the policeman up from the lobby and he agreed that young Michael reeked of whiskey and should not drive.

Frank called a taxi while Greta escorted Catherine, in a wheel chair, holding her five day old son, to the hospital lobby. Frank secured his daughter and his grandson in a cab and paid the driver.

Michael ran to his car and started it, making a noisy exit from his parking space in front of the hospital. He sped away, almost knocking down a street lamp as he bounced over the curb onto the sidewalk.

At the big Tudor house, Mrs. Brandon helped Catherine up the stairs to the guest room that she and her husband had quickly converted into a nursery.

"Catherine, dear," Mrs. Brandon's said, "some neighbors will be dropping by later this afternoon to drink a toast to our new grandson. Do come down and join us when you're settled in."

"No, I'll stay here with little Keith. Thank you for fixing up this room for him. It's really lovely."

"Oh it's nothing. Every boy needs his own room."

Michael suddenly appeared at the doorway of the nursery, angry at having lost a major confrontation with Catherine's father. When Mrs. Brandon left the room, Michael grabbed Catherine's arm. "Put the kid to sleep and come downstairs. You don't have to act like a nun just because you have a baby."

"Michael, we're both parents now. You're drinking too much and I never get to spend time alone with you. You're always partying."

"Spend time alone with you?" Michael glared at her. "Why would I want to? You're a fat mess. And now the kid is going to be hanging on you all the time. You're not what you used to be."

"Neither are you," Catherine answered with fierce anger. "You're a disgusting drunk."

Michael's hand landed across Catherine's face with such force that she fell to the floor.

He stormed out of the nursery, slamming the door, waking up baby Keith.

As time passed Catherine lost her capacity to smile. She lived only to care for her son and nothing else. When Greta and Frank visited Catherine at the big Tudor house in Scarsdale, they came during the day when Michael and his father were at work. Mrs. Brandon slept until noon and then pampered herself in her private bathroom until what she called, "the cocktail hour."

Catherine put on a brave show of normalcy, telling her parents how much she liked having the nursery and the kitchen totally to herself.

A maid came once a week to clean the living room, den and the Brandon's bedroom and bath, but no one ever even went into the huge kitchen, except to get ice from the icebox. So Catherine entertained her parents in the kitchen and they used the back door only.

Greta or Frank would take turns holding little Keith while Catherine made them tea. They enjoyed seeing their daughter and grandson but always felt uneasy leaving them to take the trolley back home. Greta and Frank sensed that something was terribly wrong but they could not get Catherine to talk about it.

Greta begged her daughter to leave Michael and move back home to The Glen with them. But Catherine refused.

Michael's drinking got worse. He became more belligerent and violent. He'd scream at Catherine, "You trapped me into marrying you. And now, you smell like sour milk."

"Michael, please," Catherine pleaded, as she slipped Keith out of her arms into the crib. Her biggest fear was that Michael would hit her while she was holding their baby.

Catherine learned to be clever about hiding her bruises. To the outside world, everything seemed fine. Time passed and in early June of 1939, Catherine gave birth to a second child, a beautiful baby girl, Sarah Lynn Brandon.

But Michael, even with his fine education and his parents' powerful contacts, still could not manage to keep a job for more than a few months.

One night when Sarah was three months old, Michael came home late, even more angry than usual. His clothes were wrinkled and his eyes bloodshot. He yelled at Catherine, "I want you to pay some attention to me, to me, not just those little brats."

He grabbed Catherine's wrist.

"Michael please. Let me be. Go sleep it off. You'll feel better in the morning."

But his rage only escalated. He slapped Catherine over and over again. She fought back and their struggle woke little Keith in the next room.

At last, Michael just fell to the floor, completely passed out, allowing Catherine the chance to check on her children in the nursery next door.

"Oh no!" she cried out, seeing that Keith's bed and the crib were both empty.

She opened the closet door to find four year old Keith sitting on the closet floor, his newborn baby sister, Sarah, asleep on the floor behind him.

"Momma," Keith said, his dark blue eyes wide with fear, "I hid Sarah from Daddy."

"Oh Keith, you are such a brave little boy. I'm not ever going to let this happen again. Tomorrow, everything will be alright."

Catherine lifted Sarah into her arms and placed her in the crib. Then she helped Keith into bed and sat with him until he fell asleep.

When Keith finally drifted off, Catherine got dressed. She packed the children's things in a big white laundry bag.

At five o'clock in the morning Catherine crept down the stairs to the front hall, picked up the phone and asked the operator to connect her to her parents' home.

Frank answered, "Hello," sounding half asleep.

"Dad, I need to come home."

"I'll be there as soon as I can." Since Frank didn't own a car himself, he went next door just in time to meet Desmond who was being dropped off by Tommy Shay.

Desmond looked like a deer caught in the glare of headlights, a sheepish, guilty look spread over his face. He was just arriving home after spending the night at Henrietta's in the Bronx.

"Des, Catherine just telephoned me. She wants to leave that brute of a husband right this minute."

"It's fackin' time she came to her senses," Desmond exclaimed.

Tommy Shay drove Frank and Desmond to the Brandon's home in Scarsdale.

With her husband still passed out across the double bed and his parents snoring in their huge, master bedroom, Catherine quietly slipped out of the house with her two children. Desmond held the back door of the car open while Catherine slid into the back seat with Sarah in her arms. Keith hopped onto Frank's lap.

Placing the big white laundry bag in the trunk, Desmond looked up at the house, saw a curtain pulled back on the second floor and made an obscene gesture with his finger. Then he slipped into the front passenger seat and slammed the car door shut.

As Tommy Shay drove out of the Brandon's circular driveway, Desmond turned to Catherine, "I'll be droppin' by to see the Brandons later this week with some a me boys and we'll be gettin' the rest of your belongin's at that time, Catherine."

"Thank you Uncle Desmond"

Frank said, "Desmond, Tommy, I'm truly and forever in your debt for bringing my family back home to The Glen."

Chapter 12

On January 5, 1940, a wet snow began to fall just before noon. Greta O'Connor finished her baking and laid it out on the kitchen table to cool. Singing happily, she washed and dried the mixing bowls and cookie sheets. With her kitchen sparkling and neat once again, she called down to Frank in his basement workshop, "I'll be back in half hour. I vant to valk before da snow - it gets too deep." She pulled on her goulashes, donned a heavy blue coat and wrapped a white scarf tight around her head.

When she opened the front door, Greta noticed a mound of snow in the gutter. As she strained to get a closer look, she realized that it was a body.

"Frank, Frank, help me, come quick." Running to the curb, Greta immediately brushed snow from the face.

Frank ran out and stood behind her. "Who is it?"

"It's Hannah Lynch, she's vith child. Look ad her. See da spasms. Baby eez coming. See der in da snow dat eez her blood."

"Oh my God!" A woman shrieked from behind them. It was the Lynch's housekeeper - the latest in a long line of women Desmond hired to help his aging mother-in-law, Mrs. O'Toole care for his dazed, sickly wife.

"Oh, Mrs. O'Connor, you can't imagine what goes on in that house. Mrs. Lynch is a 'devil' - that she is for sure. Here I thought she was napping and she's out here in the snow. What will Mr. Lynch do to me when he finds out?"

Frank attempted to calm the hysterical housekeeper. "Go on back to the Lynch row house and take care of old Mrs. O'Toole. My wife and I will call an ambulance and we'll also get in touch with Mr. Lynch. No one will blame you for this. I promise."

Frank felt Hannah's face. "Greta, she's very cold."

They half carried, half dragged Hannah into the front hall of their home and placed her gently on the soft, clean carpet. Catherine, who was watching from the second floor window, came running down the stairs with blankets and towels.

Greta knelt beside Hannah, rubbing her cold feet.

Frank grabbed the telephone on the front hall table. He shouted into the mouthpiece, "Get off this party line. I have an emergency." Hanging up, he mumbled, "I don't know why these women are on the phone all day." He picked the receiver back up a few seconds later. "Send an ambulance to 10 Garden Street. We're right at the corner of Broadway. Hurry, please."

Young Keith watched everything from the top of the stairs. When Greta saw him, she said, "Keiz, go into Sarah's room. Dis eez not someting for cheeldren."

Keith froze but did not respond.

Greta spoke again, this time in German with a fierce tone in her usually gentle voice. Little Keith immediately ran into one of the upstairs bedrooms and closed the door.

The ambulance arrived, skidding and sliding on the snow-slick road. Two young men jumped out and ran into the row house carrying a stretcher.

Hannah, now conscious, moaned in pain.

Catherine grabbed her coat from the hall closet. "Mom, Dad, watch Sarah and Keith for me. I'll ride in the ambulance with poor Mrs. Lynch."

"That's kind of you Catherine," Frank said, picking up the telephone once again. He called The Glen Town Hall, "If you know the whereabouts of Desmond Lynch, you'd better tell him to get to St. Joseph's Hospital right away. His wife is gravely ill."

Chapter 13

January 6, 1940. At St. Joseph's Hospital, Hannah's difficult labor continued throughout the night. And at the first light of dawn, just when the Church bells rang out for the Feast of the Epiphany, Hannah Lynch gave birth to a baby girl. But, when the mid-wife tried to place the child in Hannah's arms, she turned away, refusing to even look at the infant.

The young doctor in charge left the Delivery Room to speak with Desmond Lynch who had slept all night on a couch in the waiting room. He touched Desmond's shoulder, waking him gently. "Mr. Lynch, sir, you have a daughter. She's very small. And, uh, well, we just don't know what's going to happen. And Mrs. Lynch, at her age, and with her other problems, we are concerned about her as well."

The young physician wasn't the least bit comfortable giving bad news to the infamous Irish gangster and he squirmed as he spoke, looking down at his shoes.

Desmond pulled his stiff body to a standing position and lied, skillfully, "Yes, I'm not surprised. My wife's near forty-six but she wanted a child so much."

"Sir, it might be wise to have the baby baptized."

"Yes, yes, good thinking. If something happens, I want me baby girl to be buried inside The Gates of Paradise Cemetery, in sanctified ground." Even Desmond, whose relationship with the Church was tentative at best, knew that infants who died without being baptized could not be buried in blessed ground with their families. A place for these unfortunate babies, said to bear the original sin of Adam and Eve, was just outside the cemetery gates.

Desmond called for the uniformed policeman on duty in the hospital lobby to come up to the waiting room.

"Officer, fetch Frank O'Connor and his daughter, Catherine, will you? I need them here to serve as godparents for my baby girl."

"Yes sir." The young cop ran off.

Desmond turned back to the doctor. "May I see my wife now?"

"Yes, come with me. But try to be brief. She's very weak."

"Aye, Hannah is always very weak," Desmond muttered. "She's always been a solitary soul but this deep decline is recent. I hoped that perhaps when the baby came, she might perk up. This child is the answer to her every dream – and mine as well, of course."

In truth, Desmond hadn't even know until this evening, when he arrived at the hospital, that Hannah was pregnant. He thought his wife incapable of conceiving. They didn't need or want a baby now, not with Hannah being too helpless to even dress herself and her mother too old to help.

Desmond went to his wife's bedside and, on cue, tears filled his eyes. "I'm sorry Hannah. I'm so very sorry. I'll take care of everything, just like I always do."

Hannah opened her pale blue eyes and looked directly at Desmond. Her usual blank stare replaced now by a threatening expression of deep hatred, she groaned, "Desmond Lynch you Devil - just let us both die."

Desmond whispered, "Me dear wife, be calm. We must name our sweet baby girl. What shall it be now, Bridget or Deidre or little Hanorah?"

Hannah used what strength she had left to raise her head from the pillow and spit in Desmond's face. Then she fell back and closed her eyes.

Desmond put his lips next to her ear, "Hannah, my dear, you must confess to the priest that you tried to kill your own baby by starving yourself. I know what I am – and it ain't much - but at least I never tried to kill me own flesh and blood."

Tears seeped from Hannah's closed eyes.

"So, who's the real devil here, me darlin' Hannah?"

Desmond felt a presence behind him. He turned to see Monsignor Murdock. "Have you and Hannah chosen a name yet?" The affable monsignor smiled as he asked, apparently clueless to the fact that neither Hannah nor Desmond were the least bit happy about being the parents of this beautiful baby girl.

"Yes," Desmond answered, covering up his emotions, "We will christen our baby daughter, Angela Marie Lynch."

Frank and Catherine arrived a few minutes later. The Monsignor suggested that he perform the baptism ceremony right there in Hannah's room.

Frank looked down at Desmond's tiny daughter snuggled in Catherine's arms. "Ah Des, this little angel is a blessing for you. She's truly beautiful."

Angela Marie screamed when Monsignor Murdock doused cold water over her head. Frank laughed, saying, "My goddaughter has strong lungs, eh?"

Catherine rocked the baby in her arms, kissing Angela's tiny head. "Hush my sweet baby, everything is going to be alright."

After the brief ceremony, Catherine handed little Angela Marie to Desmond. But when Desmond held her in his arms, the memory of that awful night when she was conceived flooded his mind and he began to tremble and sweat.

It had been a tiring day of collecting protection money along with bad debts, when, exhausted, Desmond finally came to his last stop in the alley behind O'Brien's Pub. It was a pre-arranged meeting with the aged owner of the Chinese Laundry, a man whose name Desmond did not even know, having referred to him for years as the "little Chink." Behind on his payments, the old Chinese man pleaded for more time but Desmond only scowled at him, not answering. And when Desmond reached into his pocket, the old man appeared to become terrified. He clutched his chest and fell over backwards, landing hard on the concrete walk of the alley.

Checking his pulse, Desmond realized the old man was dead. He'd killed men before but never like this.

Desmond felt something strange and foreboding come over him - the very unpleasant, and to Desmond, completely unfamiliar, feeling of shame and guilt. He thought he must truly be a monster to be able to scare a man to death by just looking at him.

Rushing into O'Brien's Pub, Desmond downed three whiskeys with beer chasers. Not being a drinking man, the whiskey hit him fast and hard.

Sean O'Brien whispered, "That body out back. I suppose I'll have to clean up after you."

"I never touched him. Just call the police."

"I'll do that after you get out of here."

A loud voice called out, "Can I buy you a drink, Mr. Lynch, Sir?"

It was young Michael Brandon, staggering and holding onto the bar stools to keep from falling.

"I don't drink with the likes of you." Desmond pushed Brandon aside, storming out of O'Brien's, plodding down the dark street to his row house. He went inside. Passing through the unlit living room, he could hear his mother-in-law, Mrs. O'Toole, snoring loudly from the back, first floor bedroom.

He dropped his overcoat on the living room floor and climbed the stairs. Instead of going directly to his own room, he opened the door to Hannah's room and slipped inside. He stared down at his sleeping wife. In the moonlight, her thin grey hair spread across the pillow looked blonde - the way it used to be. And she smelled of sweet lavender. Sleeping so peacefully, Hannah looked the way she did when he married her all those years ago.

Desmond leaned over and kissed her forehead. His heart ached with loneliness as he whispered, "I know you can't stand the sight of me and I figured out a long time ago that your mother only arranged our marriage so that me money would take care of you both."

He wept bitterly. The death of the Chinese man and the effects of the whiskey brought on a drunken, crying jag. "But I didn't care. I loved you so much. I'd have done anything for you."

Desmond felt an urgency in his loins that he could not control. Slipping out of his trousers, he climbed on top of Hannah.

She whimpered, "No, please no."

"I'm your husband. This is my right. I should have taken you years ago but I wanted you to want me as well."

Desmond pushed himself deep inside Hannah. Panting and twitching like a dog, he pushed and pulled in and out of her stiff, dry body as Hannah groaned in pain. She pounded her hands on his chest and stomach but the feel of her touch only aroused him more. When he was done spilling himself inside of her, he fell onto the bed beside her and passed out cold.

Hannah lay there motionless, weeping quietly.

The next thing Desmond knew, Mrs. O'Toole stood looming over him. She dragged him out of Hannah's bed, forcing him to run, naked from the waist down, to his own room across the hall.

It was the first and only time their marriage was consummated and the only time Desmond ever lay beside his wife in bed.

And now, nine months later, he held the punishment for his sin in his arms – this baby girl - small and fair – and completely unwanted.

Frank, Catherine and the Monsignor stared at Desmond, watching him drift away in his thoughts as tears ran down his cheeks.

Frank said, "Ah Des, don't be ashamed. Those are tears of joy. We all understand."

Desmond replied weakly, "I'm terrible afraid that she'll be sickly like Hannah."

"Oh no, Uncle Desmond, she's tiny but she's strong," Catherine said.

Their kindness only made Desmond more afraid that everyone would find out that he'd forced himself on a sick woman. He pictured everyone in The Glen accusing him. Suddenly, he felt sick for the first time in his life. He handed Angela over to Catherine and ran to a bathroom in the hospital corridor where he vomited until there was nothing left but yellow bile.

This feeling of weakness and being sick was completely foreign to Desmond. He stared at his own reflection in the bathroom mirror and cursed himself and the God that he rarely, if ever, acknowledged, "How could you let Hannah conceive this child?" He cried out.

Desmond ran out of the hospital straight to the church where he demanded that the new priest hear his confession. It was his first confession since he left the Workhouse in Dublin as a young boy. "Father, forgive me," he pleaded. "I forced myself on my sick wife. I never thought she could conceive but she did. I don't know what to do with this baby. Oh Father, help me, just this once."

The priest answered, "My son, it's a wife's duty to give the comfort of her body to her husband. You have not sinned. But you will sin if you do not accept a child sent by God."

"My wife hates me so much that she tried to starve herself and kill the child."

"Oh my! Well, if there is no other way, and the child's life is in danger, then you can put the baby in the foundling orphanage. She may be adopted by a prosperous family of faith. And, if not, then she will be cared for there."

"Father, there will be terrible gossip about me and me wife and the baby."

And there was, especially at O'Brien's Pub. "Sure somebody got poor Hannah in a family way," jeered an old man as he swallowed his third glass of beer.

Another mocked, "Yeah, maybe it was the Holy Ghost that done it to that old bag a bones, eh?"

The bartender chimed in, "Maybe old Hannah has a secret boyfriend."

Derisive laughter filled the Pub.

The shock of Hannah's giving birth literally killed Mrs. O'Toole. She suffered a stroke while Hannah and little Angela Marie were still in the hospital. Desmond buried his mother-in-law in a plot that he purchased at the Gates of Paradise Cemetery.

Frank and Greta O'Connor and Boss Garrigan were the only ones to join Desmond at the cemetery for Mrs. O'Toole's burial.

Frank put his hand on Desmond's shoulder. "Come by the house for dinner tonight, Desmond. Please don't stay home alone in that empty house."

Boss Garrigan stayed with Desmond at the cemetery after Frank and Greta left. "So the row house is yours now, Desmond. I told you the old hag couldn't live forever. I did right by you, that I did. And I hear that your little daughter is a beauty. I'd just about given up on you. Thought you'd never have a child. I even wondered if you ever got any from Hannah. But I should have known better, Desmond, you stud?"

"All this talk about Hannah havin' a baby at such an old age has people makin' me out to be a monster. I'm givin' the baby up to the Foundling Home."

Garrigan frowned. "People will talk more if you do that, Desmond. But if you put Hannah in St. Teresa's Nursing home and hire someone to take care of the child, they'll sympathize with your plight and think of you as a hero."

Desmond's facial expression returned to normal for the first time in days. He smiled. "I could pay Frank's wife and daughter to take care of Angela. He's in need of money with that drunken son-in-law leavin' him and Greta to care for Catherine and her two children."

"Brilliant idea, Desmond. The gossip mongers will be calling you a saint; a man with a sick wife, and a baby to raise, and here he is helping out his old friend besides."

"Brilliant you say?"

"Yes, brilliant," Garrigan said. "I'm surprised you thought of it. Will Frank's family do it?"

"Frank's a proud man so he won't want it to look like I'm giving him money. But I know he needs it." Desmond replied.

"Everyone needs money - that's how we control them." Garrigan winked.

"I'll be takin' Hannah to St. Teresa's later on this very day."

"Good," Garrigan said. He slipped an envelope into Desmond's hand. "Here's a little something for the baby girl."

Later that afternoon, Desmond rode in the ambulance with Hannah from St. Joseph's Hospital to St. Teresa's Nursing Home.

Hannah appeared to be lost somewhere inside herself. She was barely conscious.

Desmond took his wife's delicate hand in his, kissed it and whispered, "Hannah, me love, all you ever wanted was to be left alone. Well now, my dear wife, you shall have your wish."

Chapter 14

With Hannah safely tucked away in St. Teresa's Home, Desmond turned to his best friend, Frank, for help with his newborn baby girl. Greta greeted Desmond at the front door. As always, she looked perky and neat in a crisp house dress, her grey-blonde hair neatly braided and wrapped around her head. "Yah, Desmond, ees so gud to see you. Come in. How is da baby girl?"

"Thanks Greta. You look well, as usual," he said feeling that same twinge of envy whenever he entered Greta's comfortable parlor. "I need to talk with Frank."

"Yah sure. Sit down, please," she said pointing to the couch. "I get him vor you."

Desmond made himself comfortable on the soft couch, inhaling the smell of fresh-baked cinnamon bread.

Frank emerged from the basement workshop, followed by his grandson.

"Good morning, Desmond, what's up?"

Desmond hesitated, looking down.

Frank nodded, rubbing Keith's thick black hair. "Go on into the kitchen and help your Granna, okay?"

Desmond smiled as Keith obediently left the room. "He's a handsome boy but he favors the Brandons. He doesn't look a bit like you or Greta or even Catherine."

"Aye, that's true. But he's my grandson all the same and I'm a happy man having him live here with us."

Greta bustled into the room with a tray of coffee and sliced bread. She placed it on the coffee table in front of the men.

"Thanks Greta," Desmond said.

Greta nodded, smiled and left the room.

Frank poured the steaming coffee into cups, handing one to Desmond. "How are things at City Hall?"

"Ah, you know, Frank, The Glen is crowded with people from strange places, the names of which I can't even pronounce. What's this country coming to, letting all them foreigners come here to live."

"They're no different from you and me. Remember how hard it was when we first came?" Frank looked uncomfortable with the subject, remembering how Greta had been called a "Nazi" at the Post Office just yesterday.

"How's little Angela doing?" Frank asked. "She's a feisty little one just like you, Des. I'm so happy for you – having a family of your own now."

"I don't know about that." Desmond shrugged. "I just committed Hannah to long-term care at St. Teresa's Nursing Home. The doctors say she'll never come home again. But Angela Marie will come home today. That's why I'm here. I'd like to pay – a tidy sum, mind you – your wife and daughter to take care of me daughter."

Surprised, Frank stood up. "Sounds like a fine idea to me but I need to talk it over with Greta and Catherine. Wait here, I'll be right back."

Frank returned with Catherine at his side. She smiled and hugged Desmond. "Oh, Uncle Desmond, we would love to take care of Annie. That's what we call your little Angela Marie. And she'll have Sarah and Keith to entertain her. Oh what joy there will be with three children in the house."

Frank said, "Let's go right now to the hospital and pick her up. We'll take Sarah's carriage and come back here together." He held a pile of what Desmond thought was neatly folded laundry in his hand. "Look, Greta has these clothes that used to be Sarah's. They're all clean and ready for your Annie."

"Frank, you're the best friend any man could have."

At Saint Joseph's Hospital, Frank and Desmond watched the nurses dress little Annie. Frank carried his goddaughter down to the lobby and placed her in the carriage, covering her with a pink, hand-crocheted afghan.

Desmond pushed the carriage through The Glen Center while everyone they passed called out to him and wished him well.

The traffic cop yelled, "Hey, Mr. Lynch, God bless your new baby girl." He stopped traffic in both directions to allow them to cross the street.

When they walked past Mario's Restaurant, one of the men who always sat at the front window came out to shake Desmond's hand. "For the baby," he said, slipping an envelope into the carriage.

At the row house, Frank said, "Don't rush off. Stay and enjoy Annie's first day at home. Greta is making a special meal in your honor."

Greta fed Annie a special, home-made formula that she gulped down, burping out loud when Greta raised her up to her shoulder.

Keith comforted little Sarah who cried, fitfully, staring at Annie's bottle until Catherine got one for her. The wooden play pen, now a permanent fixture in the living room, held both baby girls. And after being fed and changed, they napped together.

"Aye, 'twas a fine meal and a fine day," Desmond said. "Thank you all but I need to get back on the job. I'll be droppin' by often to see me girl here and to pay you."

"Well, now we've got something that will make you come to visit us," Frank said, putting his hand on Desmond's shoulder as he walked him to the front door.

Life at the O'Connor row house got even more frantic and happier. Little Annie fell into the house routine. Greta and Catherine took care of the three children and Frank pitched in when and where he could. They all made sure that both Annie and Sarah were held and hugged often.

Catherine often whispered to Annie, "I thank God for sending you to us. You are our little angel."

Keith sang out, "She's Annie the Angel." And Sarah stared and smiled at Annie, as if she were a mirror image of herself or a twin. Frank built a double crib for the baby girls to share, placing it in the downstairs bedroom right next to his and Greta's bed.

Catherine used her old room upstairs and Keith slept in the room next to her. The money that Desmond paid them arrived at the right time - just as Greta's savings from the basement had dwindled to a dangerous low. Desmond paid for Annie's care every week but rarely spent time with his infant daughter.

Time passed. Desmond seemed to forget about his daughter except for the money he gave Frank every week.

Annie grew and thrived along with Sarah. The O'Connor home was a happy one indeed.

Eleven months later, in December, Desmond stopped by at Frank's request to see for himself how Annie was standing up and trying to walk.

"My but you two women amaze me, managing this house and all three children. I'm truly in your debt for the fine care that you give my little Angela, ah I mean, Annie." He stared nervously as Annie pulled herself up by holding onto the coffee table and then swayed, almost falling back down.

Frank commented, "She falls back but gets right up again and the name Annie seems to fit her cheerful disposition."

"I like it." Desmond smiled.

Sarah, six months older, walked and moved around the living room, always encouraging Annie to follow.

Desmond laughed. "Me girl's got spirit, alright. I didn't think she'd make it."

Catherine bristled at how casually Desmond spoke of Annie not surviving. "I always knew that Annie would thrive and grow. She is as strong as she is beautiful."

Leaving Frank's house, Desmond went straight to Henrietta's Brothel in the Bronx to fill the emptiness he felt deep inside. The shame and guilt about Hannah made him want to distance himself from little Annie. And, as the months passed, he suppressed any love or pride he felt for his daughter, fearing that it would make him vulnerable. He never visited Annie. And as time passed, the emptiness that plagued Desmond grew stronger.

The O'Connor house was a happy home except for the fact that Michael Brandon showed up often at the row house, unannounced, always drunk, and demanding to see "his family."

Chapter 15

It was December 6, 1941. A frigid morning rain turned to sleet in the afternoon. And by evening a heavy wet snow fell silently. The barren trees, heavy with ice, looked like monsters with outstretched arms ready to snatch anyone foolish enough to venture out on such a terrible night. Even Desmond had the good sense to stay at home and not visit Henrietta's Brothel. He retired early, falling into a deep sleep by ten.

Just before midnight he woke up to loud shouting and banging sounds coming through the common wall from Frank and Greta's row house.

"I want my family back," A male's voice pleaded.

"How did you get in here?" Catherine yelled.

Desmond got up and dressed quickly.

A drunk and mean Michael Brandon was in Catherine's room, on top of her, his face so close that she could smell the whiskey on his breath.

She pushed him away, kicking and screaming.

Brandon hit Catherine over and over again.

Greta and Frank also woke up to Catherine's cries for help. Sarah and Annie, awake and frightened, stood up in the double crib, holding onto the railing, wailing in terror.

"Get out of here and leave us alone," Catherine yelled.

Little Keith ran next door to his mother's room. "Leave my mother alone," he shouted and grabbed at his father hands, trying to stop him from hitting his mother.

Desperate, the little boy sunk his teeth into his father's hand.

Brandon yelped like a dog. Cursing his young son, he lifted Keith up over his head.

The frenzied six year old wiggled and screamed.

"I'll shut you up," Brandon shouted.

Catherine pleaded, "No, please don't hurt Keith. Don't hurt your own son."

Smiling as saliva dripped from his mouth onto to his chin, Brandon threw Keith across the room. His little body slammed into the wall and slid down onto the floor.

As the child's twisted, limp body lay crumpled in a heap, a silence more terrible than any noise could ever be, engulfed the room.

By the time Frank got to Catherine's room, she was kneeling over Keith's motionless body.

Desmond ran into Frank's row house, almost colliding with Brandon as he tried to escape. They scuffled and Desmond pushed Brandon to the ground but the younger man pulled loose from Desmond's grasp and ran, disappearing into the swirls of heavy, thick snow.

Desmond reached for his pistol and shot twice into the darkness and snow.

From behind, Desmond heard Frank's agonizing howl, like the bleating of a wounded animal. Frank came down the stairs toward him with little Keith's body cradled in his arms. "He's still breathing. I have to get him to the hospital." Frank said, his voice shaking.

Barefoot, wearing only pajamas, Frank ran out of the house praying out loud for God to spare his grandson's life.

Sarah and Annie were too young to actually remember what happened on that terrible night but the terror they endured, mixed with stories that they later heard, left deep, terrible scars on their souls.

"Help me, Uncle Desmond," Catherine said, her face bloody, her nightgown torn. She struggled to get into her coat. Desmond knelt down and pushed boots onto Catherine's bare feet. Together they ran out into the snow. Half way down Broadway, Desmond said, "Look Catherine, a police car is picking them up."

"Thank God," Catherine said, her breathing labored. They trudged the rest of the way up the hill to St. Joseph's Hospital, slipping and falling and cursing their slowness. It seemed like an eternity before they got to the hospital lobby where Desmond went straight to the Reception Desk.

Catherine looked around. A tall, black man in a white jacket approached her. "I'm Dr. Smith. Are you the boy's mother?" he asked, staring at her bruised face.

"Yes. Where is my son?"

"He's in a treatment room down the hall."

"I need to see him. He's only six years old," Catherine mumbled.

"He may have a concussion and a broken shoulder."

Desmond turned and walked over to Catherine. "The boy's name is Keith and this is Catherine Brandon. Her father, Frank, brought the boy in. Where's Frank?" Desmond looked around.

When Dr. Smith didn't answer, Desmond grabbed the collar of the man's white jacket. "Where is he, you black bastard?"

Dr. Smith pushed Desmond's hands away, "The man who carried the injured boy into the hospital, well, he, he collapsed. It must have been a heart attack. I am truly sorry."

Desmond spoke to Dr. Smith in a contemptuous tone, "A colored doctor? Here in The Glen? Well, you can tend to your own kind but I'm gettin' another doctor for Frank right this minute."

Dr. Smith repeated, "I'm so sorry."

But Desmond yelled at the top of his lungs. "Get me a doctor."

Frank O'Connor passed away less an hour past midnight – during the first hour of a terrible day - December 7, 1941.

Desmond felt that same emptiness and panic he felt when his mother died all those years ago at the Workhouse in Dublin. Frank was his only friend; the only person who had ever shown him any true kindness; the only man for whom he had any respect.

Desmond glared at Catherine. "Michael Brandon killed Frank as surely as if he shot him. 'Twas you who brought that scum into Frank's life. You fornicated with the devil and betrayed your own father and blood being what it is, that bastard son of yours will grow to be a devil as well."

Catherine looked at Desmond in horror. "How can you say such things about my son? Frank's grandson? You're my godfather, a man I call my Uncle?"

Dr. Smith intervened, "Enough now. A man is dead and a boy is badly injured. I don't know what happened here but I've already called the police."

"The police you say? Don't you know who I am? I run the police. Your black ass has had it. You helped kill Frank."

Catherine put her hand on Desmond's arm. "Stop it. Now. I know how much my father meant to you but we have little Keith and my mother and the girls to think of."

But it was too late. Desmond's heart turned to stone that night. And Catherine would never again call him "Uncle Desmond."

Chapter 16

Frank's passing went almost unnoticed by the people of The Glen during those frantic days following the sneak attack on Pearl Harbor.

Greta, inconsolable, put all her energy into caring for Sarah and little Annie. Catherine, her face still bruised and swollen, showed remarkable strength and resolve by taking care of all the funeral arrangements for her father and visiting Keith at St. Joseph's Hospital.

Esther Weinberg, who was staying with her cousins in the row house on the other side of Desmond's, spent hours with Keith at the hospital and brought him home by taxi. She took care of all three children on the morning of Frank's funeral.

Monsignor Murdock eulogized Frank O'Connor as a "gifted artist, a truly kind and good man, a loving husband, father and grandfather as well as the truest and most loyal of friends."

Desmond did not attend the Funeral Mass for Frank but he did go to his burial where he stood alone at the gravesite, several yards behind Greta and Catherine, weeping openly. He did not apologize to Catherine because he truly believed that she had initiated the chain of events that ultimately caused Frank's untimely death by bringing Michael Brandon into their lives.

Desmond, never a forgiving man, could not stand the sight of Keith because of the child's strong physical resemblance to his drunken father. Still, he felt an obligation to Frank's widow and so he continued the arrangement for Annie's care, knowing that Greta and Catherine needed the money.

Desmond threw himself into his work, spending even longer hours on the streets of The Glen, and, rarely, if ever, visiting his little daughter.

Keith's healthy, young body healed but the horror of that night and the loss of his beloved grandfather left its mark on his life and on his soul.

Life in The Glen went on, changing rapidly as War War II consumed everyone's time and attention. Garrigan put Desmond in charge of the food and gas rationing in The Glen which then led to his managing the inevitable black market that sprung up, seemingly overnight.

Organizing the local VFW to a high level of efficiency, Desmond called on veterans of World War I to escort young soldiers to the train station as they went off to war and to meet the bodies of the fallen when they were returned.

"With most of the men gone, we'll be busier than ever keeping things in order," Boss Garrigan confided to Desmond. "And you'll be coordinating everything for me. I'm not just the mayor; I'm like a father to these people. By the way, Des, how's your family?"

"Hannah's the same. I guess she'll always be that way. And I hear tell that my little Annie is havin' a grand time chasing about after Sarah."

"It's nice to hear that Annie is healthy and not a worry to you. Tensions are running high all over the country - even here in The Glen - so we need to keep things peaceful." Garrigan lowered his voice, "By the way, I'm hearing some strange stories about your neighbor's cousin – a woman from Europe - staying with those Jews in the row house next to you."

Desmond nodded. "Aye, that would be Esther Weinberg - a strange one to be sure."

"People seem to think that she's crazy," Garrigan said more as a question than a statement of fact.

"She may well be. Came here a few years ago through Canada from Switzerland. Isaac Weinberg's done right by her. But he bought her that damn violin that screeches day in and day out. And Isaac's wife buys her nice clothes but Esther just walks around The Glen in the same old dress with her hair hangin' over her face."

"Well, just between you and me, she has some powerful friends. They say she was a famous musician in Europe. Any idea why she's so strange?"

"I haven't a clue but that damn violin is a nuisance, if you ask me. I can hear it through the common wall between our row houses. And I don't like the looks of her with those eyes – blank – just like Hannah's. Don't know if she can even see with that mop of hair hanging over her face. People say something bad happened to her in Europe."

"Well, keep an eye on her for me. Don't want those powerful people to hear about anything happening to her during our watch."

"Aye, I'll do that," Desmond said. "She's safe in The Glen for sure."

The only person in The Glen, outside of Isaac and his wife, who actually ever spoke to Esther Weinberg, was Catherine. The two women enjoyed walking together. Esther would push Annie in her carriage, walking beside Catherine, who pushed Sarah's stroller. Keith, six years old now, was in school at St. Joe's Elementary.

"Esther, it's so nice of you push Annie so that both girls can enjoy this lovely fresh air," Catherine said.

Esther nodded. "Eez my pleasure. Dis leetle Ansha eez so lovely."

Catherine agreed. "Yes, and she is as loving as she is beautiful. Say, Esther, would you consider coming over to play the violin for the girls?"

"I vould luv to," Esther replied.

"Come this afternoon after their nap. It will be such a treat for all of us."

Esther pushed her hair back and smiled at Catherine.

They walked to the top of the hill, past St. Joseph's complex of hospital, church and elementary school, and continued into the prestigious Park Place where the elegant homes of the wealthy enjoyed a beautiful view of the Hudson River to the west and looked down onto The Glen to the east.

Catherine pointed at Boss Garrigan's home. "Isn't it lovely, set back like that behind that wrought iron fence? Talk is that he hardly ever spends time there."

"Some, zey have everything, others nothing," Esther replied and then whispered to herself, "Drek."

Catherine had no idea what "drek" was but she nodded in agreement.

Esther chatted much more than usual that day. She confessed to Catherine that she felt drawn to little Annie, "Zer is sometink about little Ansha, und her vith no moder or fader to love her. People, zey are such fools."

"Yes, it is not easy to understand why Desmond seems unable to love or spend time with Annie. But then so much about him is mysterious."

As the friendship between the two women grew, Esther began brushing her thick brown hair away from her face, revealing lovely even features and enormous brown eyes.

"Esther you are quite beautiful," Catherine said.

Slowly, the terrified expression on Esther's face faded and she began to wear the clothes that her cousin s wife purchased for her. Catherine and Esther continued to spend time together, talking of many things, but never about what happened to Esther in Europe.

Chapter 17

The entire country supported the war effort and deep patriotic fervor ran high. It was not a good time to be German or Japanese.

"Cazerine, I vill not do shopping anymore but I vill make up to you and do everyzing at home. Okay? Ze do not understand that I am American and not German in my heart," Greta said, recalling the terrible things she had recently overheard people say about her German accent.

"If Daddy were still here, he'd set them straight and you wouldn't have to live in fear." Catherine hugged her mother.

Keith understood. "If anyone says anything bad about my Granna, I'll fight them." As he spoke, his handsome face furrowed into an angry pout and he held up his right hand, curled into a ferocious fist.

"It will do no good to fight," Catherine told him.

"Yes it will. It'll make them stop," Keith said.

Sarah stood behind Keith and yelled, "Yes, me too."

And Annie, sitting on the floor, said, "S" emphatically.

Greta smiled. "Stop dis talk of fighting und I veel give my sveet darlings some cookies."

As the war went on and anti-German sentiment got worse, Greta never left the house. Catherine shopped and ran the errands, always fearing that she would run into her violent husband on the street.

But Brandon seemed to have disappeared completely. There were rumors that he was seen staggering out of O'Brien's late at night. And a regular at the bar told Catherine that Brandon had been stabbed in a brawl in The Bronx.

But the most consistent rumors were that Brandon had enlisted in the Armed Forces. Several business people in The Glen swore that they saw Brandon at the recruitment office, in uniform, and that he told them he was shipping out to Europe with the Tenth Mountain Division.

One of Brandon's buddies from Fordham University, who was just about to be sent to England with the Army Air Core, met Catherine in the bakery and told her that Michael had been drafted. "Best thing for him. Might stop his drinking."

"You're sure?" Catherine asked.

"I'm sure. He may be a lush but he's able bodied enough to fight. And his dad can't get him out of it because every man his age is serving. And, Catherine, his mother is real sick. The whiskey finally caught up with her. She's a mess."

"I'm sorry to hear that Mrs. Brandon is so sick, really. And thanks for telling me about Michael," Catherine said. "Good luck to you in England. I hope you come back safe from this awful war."

She walked home feeling as if a huge weight had been lifted from her shoulders and told Keith that his father was far away fighting in the war. "He can't possibly show up here to hurt any of us."

Confiding in Esther, Catherine said, "Every other able bodied man his age is in the Armed Forces. He must have been drafted. Although I can't picture him being disciplined enough to be a good soldier."

"Eez enough if he is bad soldier. At least he's far away. I hear dat many fighting in zos Italian mountains have perished."

The Glen's two factories converted from making carpets and elevators to churning out fuselage and engine parts with the mothers and housewives in The Glen taking over the factory jobs and working all three shifts.

Catherine signed on to work the night shift at the old elevator factory leaving Greta alone with the three children from mid-afternoon until past midnight. Still Catherine's fear of Michael Brandon was so strong that every afternoon when she left her mother and the children behind at the row house, she prayed that he really was fighting in the Italian mountains and could not possibly show up at her home.

Keith truly understood that, while the war caused terrible suffering to children in Europe, it brought safety and peace to his life in The Glen. The lives of the children in Europe got worse as the lives of the even the poorest American children improved as they slept in warm beds and, even with rationing, had more than enough to eat.

Gasoline went to the war effort so there were few cars on the streets of The Glen. And this meant that the children could play in the streets. They had mock victory parades, marching down the middle of the road, carrying home-made flags and singing "God Bless America," like Kate Smith.

Annie and Sarah followed Keith around like little shadows. They'd watch Keith and the boys his age tumble into the coal chutes of the row houses, sliding into the basements and landing on a huge pile of coal. And they'd always be sure to pocket a piece of coal for marking games on the cement sidewalks.

One day Annie decided to slide down a coal chute. She ran ahead of Keith and the others.

Not realizing that she had to check to be sure the coal pile was high enough, she threw herself into the chute, tumbling down into the basement, landing on the cellar floor because the supply of coal had dwindled to almost nothing.

She fell much too far, too fast and landed too hard.

The other children heard her cry out in pain. Sarah ran to the chute and stared down into the basement with a look of pure terror on her sweet face. Keith jumped down after Annie. He scooped her up into his arms and carried her up the cellar stairs, running all the way home and carrying Annie as if she were a rag doll.

Annie was black from the coal, her knees and hands scraped and bleeding.

"Granna, Granna, help quick. Annie's hurt bad," Keith said, bolting through the front door of the row house. He didn't even notice Desmond Lynch sitting on the couch sipping coffee.

"Bring Anika into da kitchen. Sit her on da side of da sink." Greta was quick but calm. She washed Annie's skin and put iodine on the cuts while uttering words of comfort, some in German and some in English. Satisfied that Annie had suffered no broken bones, she scolded her softly, "You are von lucky leetle girl and you must not ever do dat again. Promise me pleez, Ansha?"

Keith and Sarah watched, their eyes wide in fear.

Greta shook her finger at all of them. "Und now dis is de last time anyvone vill slide on de coal chute, Yah?"

"Yes Granna."

Desmond watched and his anger grew and grew until it boiled over. He grabbed Annie. "Stand here, young lady." He pulled her coal stained underpants down and wacked her bare bottom hard with his open hand.

Annie wailed in pain, dropping her cookie.

Keith's face turned deep red. "Stop it, she's already hurting enough."

Greta grabbed Keith by the ear. "Go up da stairs now."

"They should all feel the sting of a belt for doing such a stupid thing," Desmond said.

"Pleez, zis weel nut 'appen again. You 'ave my vord. Und I vill punish Keith for speaking out like dat - und Sarah as vell." Greta burst into tears barely able to speak coherently.

Desmond moved closer to Greta, saying, "You tell that grandson of yours that he'd better watch out. From now on, Annie is to play only with Sarah and not with him. I'm paying you to keep my daughter safe. Do you understand?"

Greta nodded.

Annie, Sarah and Keith, unaware of any other way of life other than living in a world dominated by a war being fought in a far away land, were told over and over, "Do not waste that food. Think of the starving children in Europe." And then they were left to ponder how cleaning their plates would somehow make food appear on the plates of children in war-torn Europe.

Sarah and Annie prayed for those sad children whose pictures they saw on the front page of the newspapers and magazines. But they could not fully understand and their real focus was on their own lives in The Glen.

When Sarah and Annie were ready to start school, Catherine and Greta sighed in relief. Nine year old Keith, handsome in his school uniform, a white shirt with blue tie and long navy blue pants, impatiently paced back and forth as Catherine and Greta fussed over the girls' hair.

"Listen up girls," Keith said, knowingly. "Those Nuns may look like big black birds but they're just old ladies who dress funny. So don't let them scare you. But they don't like a lot of talking so try to be quiet – that way they won't have a reason to smack you. That will be real hard for you, Annie, but please try hard to be quiet."

Annie already had the reputation of being a non-stop chatterbox. But Sarah was a quiet, serene and proper young lady.

Catherine styled Sarah's long black hair in two thick braids and tied then with blue ribbons while Greta struggled to brush the knots out of Annie's thick blonde curls. Still, Annie's thick hair tumbled down over her face.

In desperation, Greta clipped Annie's hair back with a silver barrette. "Anika, pleez - not to take zis out of your hair. Zis vas my Mama's, so don't lose it."

Annie hugged Greta. "Thank you Granna. I love the barrette because it is yours and I promise not to lose it."

"Und I luv you, my little Anika."

"You both look lovely in your new blue jumpers," Catherine said.

"Let's go," Keith said. "I'll keep an eye on them."

The girls set out for school with Keith walking behind them, watching every move they made.

In the afternoons after school, when the weather prevented the children from playing outside, they'd sit at the kitchen table doing homework while Greta made chicken noodle soup, baked bread and sang songs in German.

Keith absorbed the language like a sponge. He even understood some Polish, Czech and Yiddish by just hearing them spoken on the streets of The Glen.

At least once a week there was a mandatory air raid drill in the early evening. Families closed their drapes, turned off all the lights and sat quietly in silence until the sirens wailed an "all clear." Annie and Sarah tried their best to stay quiet in the dark but their giggles often grew into loud laughter. And they'd try to peek out from behind the shades to see what was happening on the dark street.

"Be quiet. Sarah, stop opening the curtain. And, Annie, your voice is too loud. Come on, now, this is important. You have to know what to do in case of a real attack." Keith ordered the two girls.

Sarah pouted. "Oh be quiet, Keith, you are not the boss of me."

But Annie never argued with Keith because she always wanted to please him.

Greta broke up the arguments between Keith and Sarah. "My sveet leetle vons, you vill pleez be still und say prayers for ze poor cheeldren who are living in ze Var."

"Do you think my father is shooting the enemy right now, Granna?" Keith asked.

"If he has to, zen he must do zat," Greta answered, kissing Keith's forehead.

"I used to be so afraid when my father came here, just like I'm afraid a little bit now during the raids," Keith said.

Greta hugged him, "Dun't be afraid, my boy. Ve need to be ready but der are no bombs coming here because ve are so very far avay from ze real var."

"I'm glad my father is in the war and that he can't come here to hurt us. I hope he never comes back. Is that bad of me, to not want him to ever come back?" Keith asked. "No," Greta said. "You are a gud boy." And so it was that while the war brought suffering to children in other parts of the world, it brought quiet and peace to three small children in The Glen.

Chapter 18

When World War II ended, the fighting men returned home. They married, fathered babies, purchased new houses, furniture, cars, washing machines and radios. Fueled by consumer needs and demands made by a new military/industrial base, the economy of the United States grew at a startling rate, creating a large middle class.

Catherine's factory job ended abruptly when the manufacture of carpet and elevators resumed and the men who came home from the war took their jobs back.

The old neighbourhoods with apartments and row houses in Brooklyn, the Bronx and The Glen now seemed to be relics of the past. Clusters of new cookie-cutter homes sprung up in the suburbs of Long Island and New Jersey.

The Weinberg family sold the row house next to Desmond Lynch and relocated to Levittown, Long Island to be close to their son who worked at The Grumman Aircraft Corporation. Esther Weinberg got a job performing at the New York Symphony in Manhattan and took an apartment on the upper East Side of Manhattan.

At the dinner table one evening, Annie said, "I hate it that Miss Weinberg is moving. I'll miss her and her lovely music so much."

"We'll all miss her." Catherine smiled, wiping drops of butter from Annie's little chin. Lately, there seemed to be a great deal of neighbourhood news to discuss at dinner. "But Miss Weinberg is a gifted musician so it is only right that she live in the city to be near her work."

Keith added, "I saw Miss Weinberg today and she had on the highest heels, real big." He held his fingers apart to illustrate.

"Who vants more noodles?" Greta asked.

"Oh no Mom, you have filled us all up with your wonderful dinner," Catherine said.

Keith cleared the table, using his time in the kitchen with Greta to chat in German.

"Keiz you have amazing gift vor language," Greta said, gazing at him with deep pride in her eyes.

"Thanks," he answered as he delegated little jobs to Sarah and Annie who always clamored to be included in anything that Keith did. "Sarah, get the dessert plates and put them on the table. Annie, you get the dessert forks and put them on the left side of the plates. This side." He touched Annie's left shoulder.

"I know my left from right," Annie replied, quite insulted.

"May I have your attention, please!" Catherine teased. "Our dear friend Esther, Miss Weinberg to you children, gave us tickets to the New York Symphony Matinee on Saturday and promised to take us backstage for a special tour."

"Can I wear my new dress, Mamma?" Sarah asked.

"Wow, that's great," Keith commented.

Annie jumped with excitement. "I can't wait for Saturday." And indeed all three children, the long wait for Saturday made the week seem almost endless.

They woke early on the big day, dressed in their best clothes and went down to the kitchen where Keith fixed them a breakfast of dry cereal with orange juice and toast.

When Greta joined them, she called up to Catherine, "Luk how seese leetle angels are vaiting for us, all dressed."

There was a knock on the front door.

Sarah opened it. "Hello, Mr. Lynch."

Annie yelled out "Daddy" and ran to Desmond, hugging him around his knees.

Desmond ignored the hug, gently pushed her away and walked into the living room with an envelope holding the payment for Annie's care. He placed the envelope on an end table and said, "Well now, don't you all look fine this morning? Annie, it's lucky that you're dressed so nicely because I'm here to take you to visit your mother at the nursing home, and later on, we're invited to a lawn party at the Garrigan's home."

Annie's face fell as she looked sadly over at Sarah and Keith.

Desmond took Annie's hand and led her out of the house. "I'll bring her back tomorrow evening after supper, if that's alright with you?"

Greta nodded.

Catherine said from midway up the stairs, "That's fine. We're happy to have Annie back at any time."

Desmond barely looked at Catherine, completely avoiding eye contact with Keith.

Sarah and Keith watched Annie walk away with Desmond, her blonde curls bouncing as she ran to keep up with him.

"He never even bothers to visit Annie. Why does he have to take her today?" Catherine commented.

"Vat can ve do? He is da fader, und better for leetle Ansha dat ve do not upset him."

"That's for sure." Catherine's tone was pure sarcasm.

When Annie turned back to wave at them, Sarah burst into tears.

"It's okay Sarah. We'll take Annie to see Miss Weinberg another time." Catherine hugged her daughter.

Keith stared silently out the window, watching Annie and Desmond walk away.

As Desmond and Annie passed through The Glen Center, strangers commented about Annie's blonde curls and her likeness to Shirley Temple. And passengers complimented Desmond on Annie's good looks as they rode the trolley to St. Teresa's Nursing Home in Fleetwood.

When they got to Hannah's room, Annie climbed onto her mother's bed and tried to hug her. Desmond scooped Annie off the bed and placed her in a wooden chair by the window. "Stop it now and don't disturb your mother."

Annie whimpered, her arms held out to her father, imploring Desmond to pick her up.

"Stop it now, Annie. Now wait here while I go down to the main office for a few minutes."

But sitting still and being quiet were two things that Annie found very hard to do. She put her hands together and prayed the way the nuns taught her. "God, could you make my Daddy hug me sometimes and tell him that I try to be a good girl." Wiping her tears away, she blew her nose into the skirt of her new dress.

When Desmond returned, Annie, crumpled and wrinkled, had fallen asleep in the chair. He picked her up and carried her outside to a waiting taxi.

Annie woke up in the cab. "I'm thirsty."

"You'll have plenty to eat and drink at Mr. Garrigan's."

When the cab stopped in front of the Garrigan house, Annie climbed onto the big stepping stone while Desmond paid the cabbie's fare. "Get down off that dirty rock," Desmond yelled.

Annie followed Desmond through the wrought iron gates and around to the back yard where bridge tables were set up near the flower beds and a buffet table overflowed with food. Being the only child there, Annie became the center of attention.

"Oh my, Mr. Lynch, but your daughter is so cute."

"Just look at those blonde curls and big green eyes."

"And dimples, such dimples, just like Shirley Temple. Can you dance like Shirley Temple?"

"No, I can't dance," Annie shouted, running off to hide behind a tree.

Desmond enjoyed the compliments from the women but soon left Annie to join a heated political discussion with a group of men standing around the beer keg. That's when Annie spied the Garrigan's brown cocker spaniel puppy. The two became instant friends, chasing each other in the soft, freshly mowed grass.

When Desmond saw Annie rolling in the grass with the puppy licking her face, he grabbed her tiny wrist and yanked her to her feet. "Look at you, grass stains on your dress, your face filthy. Don't they teach you any manners?"

Annie cried and her tears mixed with the dirt and grass on her cheeks. When she wiped her face, everything smudged and got worse.

"We'll have to leave. I can't have you running around looking like this," Desmond muttered.

He made Annie walk all the way down the hill to O'Brien's Pub in The Glen Center where he picked out a booth in the back. Annie tired now and still thirsty, tried to lift a huge, filled to the brim, glass of milk to her lips. But the tall glass tipped onto her dinner plate, spilling milk on her lap, forcing her dinner plate to slide off the table, dumping gravy, sliced chicken and peas all over the floor.

"Annie, you are the worst child in the world," Desmond scolded.

Annie cried. "I feel sick." She vomited, projecting a white stream of liquid from her mouth across the table onto Desmond.

Terrified now, she wailed, "I want to go home."

Everyone in the pub turned to stare.

"Lord, I don't know how Catherine and Greta put up with you. And them with two other children as well." Desmond left money on the bar, picked Annie up and carried her back to the row house on the corner of Broadway and Garden Street. Catherine, Greta and the children had just returned from the city when Desmond rang the bell.

When Catherine saw Annie, she had to choke back laughter.

Desmond blustered, "I hope this doesn't inconvenience you but something came up and I can't keep Annie until tomorrow as I planned."

"Oh, no it's fine. Mom and I are always happy to have our little Annie back."

Catherine put her arms out to take Annie but Desmond shook his head and placed Annie on the floor.

Catherine said, "Go upstairs darling, and Granna will help you get ready for bed."

Desmond, sighed wearily. "As you can see Annie is wearing everything she ate and rolled in or sat in. She's a wild one."

"She's a spirited child with a big heart," Catherine said, looking away, always wary of Desmond's temper. "Would you care for some tea?"

"No, no. I've had more than enough of everything for one day."

"Well, I need to ask you about something?"

"What is it?"

"It's about my husband. As you know he was with that division that suffered so many casualties in the mountains of Italy. But, when I went to the VA Claims office, they told me that there is no record of an enlistment or a draft regarding a Michael Brandon from this area."

Desmond's face flushed. "Ah, Catherine, there were so many paperwork mistakes during the War."

"But if there should be some kind of death benefit, I need to pursue it for Sarah and Keith. And I'll need some sort of death certificate."

"Yes, of course. I'll look into it for you. Give me a week or so."

"That's very kind of you."

"Not at all! I owe it to Frank to be sure that his family gets what's coming to them."

Chapter 19

Isaac Weinberg's row house sold quickly, remaining empty for months but no one seemed to know anything about the new owners, not even Desmond Lynch. Until one morning, a moving truck pulled up in front of the empty house. Neighbours found excuses to peek out their windows. Before long almost every resident on the block stood silently watching the colored family help the moving men carry their possessions into their new home.

Catherine came out onto her front porch and saw Desmond standing on his porch next door, watching every move the black family made. He looked like a wild cat about to pounce.

Catherine called inside to Greta, "Look Mom, it's Dr. Smith - that doctor from St. Joseph's Hospital - you know the one I told you about – the man who treated Keith and Daddy that awful night."

Desmond's face flushed deep red with rage, "How could the Weinberg's sell to coloreds? They were good neighbors except for their crazy cousin Esther. But to sell to coloreds! Once one a them buys a house, everyone sells out cheap and soon the whole neighbourhood is a slum. Block Busting they call it."

Catherine answered, "But it's the real estate speculators who scare the white homeowners and cause the prices to drop - not the new owners."

Desmond didn't even hear her. "This is a disgrace," he huffed.

Catherine asked Desmond, "Have you had any news about my husband's VA benefits?"

"No, I'm still waitin' for an answer."

"Annie is out on the back porch with Sarah. Do you want to visit with her?"

"Maybe tomorrow," Desmond answered, going inside and slamming his front door.

The Smith family began remodelling the row house immediately.

They had a medical office constructed on the first floor and remodelled the second floor and attic into comfortable family living quarters.

Catherine wanted to speak with her new neighbours but they did not move in for several weeks until the construction was done. So when Catherine noticed that the Smith family was actually living in the house, she planned her welcome visit. Greta baked and Catherine took the children with her to deliver a heaping tray of cookies and fresh breads.

Dr. Smith answered the door.

"Hello, Dr. Smith, I don't know if you remember me," Catherine said smiling.

"Yes, of course I do. I'm only sorry we met at such an awful time. Come in please. Ah, Keith, how's that shoulder doing?"

"It's fine, Sir."

"He's okay now, but losing his grandfather, well that's something he'll never get over. And this is Keith's little sister Sarah, and Annie, Desmond Lynch's daughter."

Dr. Smith squatted on his knees to shake hands with the two little girls. He introduced his wife, Elaina, and she called out for seventeen year old Reggie and ten year old Bernadette to come downstairs to join them.

Catherine gave Elaina the tray. "My mother baked. She's the best cook in The Glen but she doesn't go out much."

"Come in and sit down. This is our new waiting room," Elaina said.

Annie and Sarah plopped down on the new carpet with Bernadette, while Catherine, Keith, Reggie, Dr. and Mrs. Smith settled into the new leather waiting room couches.

Elaina smiled. "Bernadette will be going to St. Joseph's Elementary, perhaps a year ahead of Sarah and Annie. Reggie goes to St. Simons in Scarsdale."

Dr. Smith added, "We've been living in an apartment in the Bronx ever since we moved from Brooklyn. I did my residency at Kings County and I think St. Joseph's Hospital could use a modernized Emergency Room program like that."

Catherine agreed. "Yes, I've heard about Kings County. Boss Garrigan speaks often about starting an Emergency Room program here at St. Joseph's."

"Garrigan seems to have a hand in everything here in The Glen," Dr. Smith commented with a slight smile.

"Oh that he does and his ambitions go all the way to the state capital in Albany. And, of course you know Annie's father, Desmond Lynch, pretty much runs The Glen for him."

Elaina whispered, "I don't think Mr. Lynch likes having us live next door." She glanced over at little Annie to be sure the children didn't hear. The three girls were engrossed in their own conversation, already giggling like old friends.

Keith heard what Elaina Smith said and moved to sit down on the floor behind Annie, always protective of her whenever someone made remarks about her father.

Later that evening Desmond stopped over at Catherine's row house. Annie ran up to hug him.

"Now stop it girl. I've business to discuss with Mrs. Brandon."

Catherine smiled at Annie, "Go on upstairs with Keith and Sarah."

Annie ran up the stairs, disappearing into one of the bedrooms.

A few minutes later, Sarah peeked out of the room, stuck her tongue out and slammed the door.

Desmond saw nothing, and ignored the slamming door and the giggles. He concentrated on what he came to say. "Well Catherine, it's been a few weeks since you asked me to look into the Veteran's benefits issue. The fact is that a lot of soldiers will never be found and their fate will never really be known. There are no records of Michael Brendan's death but we did find enlistment papers that were never processed correctly."

"Oh dear," Catherine said, disappointed.

"Aye, wait now. The Veteran's Administration agreed to settle your claim with one lump sum payment. But you must agree to drop all future claims."

Catherine replied, "Then Michael must have been overseas with the Army."

"I'm bettin' that he was and the VA thinks so as well."

Catherine's relief was obvious.

Desmond went on.

"It's a bit less than you would normally get as the widow of a soldier, but it's not a bad deal considering that there's really no proof that Brandon died for his country."

Catherine was silent, thinking.

Desmond continued. "If I were you, I'd take the settlement because if you press the issue too hard, the VA may find additional paperwork - perhaps a dishonourable discharge or something worse. As you well know, he was a bad penny. Not knowing exactly what happened just might be a blessin' in disguise."

Catherine agreed. She knew that her husband's drinking could easily have gotten him thrown out of the military or worse.

Desmond gave her a money order in the amount of $5000.

"Actually, this is a grand sum and we can use it. Thank you," Catherine said.

"I'm always happy to help Frank's family." Desmond patted Catherine's hand. "So this whole business of your drunken husband is behind you now."

Catherine nodded. "Yes. For so long I feared that he would come back."

"Oh, I doubt that he's comin' back," Desmond said.

Catherine thought it was odd that it was a money order instead of a government check but she was not about to question Desmond any further. She hated even asking him to look into the matter after the way he behaved the night her father died. She cashed the money order, deposited it in the bank and pushed all her questions about government insurance and her husband's death out of her mind.

Chapter 20

In the 1950's, Americans started to see themselves as the "haves" of the world, the fortunate citizens of a triumphant country whose destiny it was to be prosperous. They were no longer "the ragged extras, discarded by their motherlands." Americans became confident, sometimes even arrogant, feeling quite superior to those who lived in post-war rubble. As new homes and roads appeared on the American landscape, white families spread out to the suburbs and black families moved into the cities. Leary's Boarding House became a house of worship with a huge neon sign on top of its big front porch that flashed in red and yellow, "The God Is Love Church." Many of the old businesses in The Glen Center closed leaving store fronts empty with "For Rent" signs taped to the display windows.

A family of gypsy fortune tellers took over one of the smaller store fronts and hung a huge crayon printed sign offering anyone a glimpse of their future for fifty cents. The matriarch of the family, stooped over with arthritis, with wild grey hair and yellow teeth, was the clairvoyant of the clan and the only one who made eye contact or spoke. She dressed in layers of brightly colored material that somehow managed to adhere to her body. She and her multi-generation family lived right there in the store, behind a thick black curtain.

Greta warned Catherine and the children, "Do not go near de gypsies. Ze will steal money and jewelry and kidnap ze cheeldren to sell dem for slaves. Dey did such tings in Europe. I know."

Keith may not have completely believed his grandmother but decided that it was not worth the chance to even walk on that side of the street when passing the gypsy's storefront.

But Sarah and Annie went into fits of giggles at the sight of the old gypsy woman and they'd press their noses against the glass to peek into the store when she was giving a reading to a customer.

There seemed to be no end to the line of people who sought to learn their future. Sometimes, when Annie and Sarah were not with Keith, the gypsy woman would signal to them, beckoning them to come inside. But Sarah would grab Annie and they'd run off.

Until one day, Annie took two quarters from her little amber glass piggy bank and walked down Broadway all by herself. She went right to the gypsy fortune teller's shop and walked inside.

"Ah, so, the pretty little girl wants to know her future?"

"I do," Annie answered, frightened, regretting now that she had entered the dirty storefront that reeked of garlic and boiling cabbage.

"Sit down, my sweet, and put your little hands on the table so I can read your palms."

Annie could hear people behind the curtain talking and arguing, half in English and half in a strange foreign tongue.

The old woman took Annie's little hand in hers and held it in a tight grip. "Ah, I see that you are smart and get good grades in school. But you take a lot of chances. You should be more cautious."

Annie thought for sure now that she was about to be kidnapped.

The old woman's voice was deep and creepy, "My dear, I see here that there is much trouble and a lot of danger for you in the future. And I warn you again that you must be more cautious. You are too bold. And I see a very bad man who wants to hurt you but his face is not clear to me."

Annie pulled her hand away and got up to leave, saying, "I think you tell everyone the same fortune and that you are just trying to scare me. It's not worth the fifty cents."

The old woman looked sad. "I can tell you more but not if you do not believe me. Go home my pretty little girl and be careful. The world is more dangerous than you know."

Annie put what the gypsy said out of her mind. She skipped home wondering if she should tell Sarah about her little adventure. But she knew that Sarah would never do what she did so maybe Annie thought, she'd just keep this little adventure to herself.

Modern supermarkets began to open in strip malls near the new housing developments in the suburbs. But the big stores did not invest in places like The Glen or Newark, not in neighbourhoods where the population was a mix of races.

The Glen changed so much that even O'Brien's Pub closed its doors. Young Colin O'Brien took over from his grandfather and decided to open what he described as a "trendy new seafood restaurant and bar" on the north shore of Long Island. He confided to Desmond, "That damn television makes people stay home of an evening. And now there's two of them damned liquor stores selling whiskey - and even beer in cardboard holders of six - to take home. People drink in their living rooms. That's what working people in places like The Glen want today."

"Yeah, I know. Some of them people swallow a whole bottle of booz like it was a shot glass," Desmond said, "and they drink their beer in front a that stupid little screen."

"What's this country coming to when the picture of someone you don't even know, yapping in a little box, takes the place of your buddies at the bar. It's disgusting. But it's the new world," Colin said as he shook Desmond's hand, got into his new car, and drove away from the old pub for the last time.

Desmond and Garrigan had to run The Glen differently now. They tried to charm the black residents the best they could. And when Puerto Rican families moved into the apartments above the stores, Desmond didn't know how to handle them. He did not know how to even speak to them.

But Garrigan ordered Desmond to include them. "They're citizens of this country and every one of them can vote so you be sure to get them registered and thinking that we're on their side. Smile, Desmond, smile, and learn a bit a Spanish will ya."

"What is this, you say they're citizens without the language and they're able to vote already?"

"Seems we got ownership of their little island home from Spain when we won a war way back when. So these people are all born full-fledged citizens. And when they come here, they have the right to vote. And I need their votes. Life is changing, Des, and we have to change with it."

Chapter 21

In September of 1953, Keith Brandon went off to high school at St. Simon's School in Scarsdale, commuting by train every day. He played basketball, joined the debating team and went to the social mixers and dances at the "all girl" parochial high schools. Annie and Sarah hardly ever got to spend time with Keith now.

Reggie Smith commuted by train but going in the opposite direction, to Fordham Law School in the Bronx. He and Keith often walked together to the station. Bernadette Smith, a grade ahead of Annie and Sarah, walked through The Glen Center, to and from St. Joe's Elementary, with Annie and Sarah every day.

In November, Hannah Lynch passed away peacefully in her sleep, leaving everyone who knew her relieved that her sad life of suffering finally ended. A huge crowd turned out for Hannah's Wake to pay their respects to Desmond Lynch.

Desmond made Annie stand beside him, next to her mother's closed casket in the main room of O'Farrell's Funeral Home. As Desmond accepted condolences, he whispered to Annie, "I'm proud of the way you're acting this sad day. She was your mother and, no matter that she wasn't much of one, still blood is blood."

Annie nodded, not sure what Desmond was talking about. "I wish she'd talked to me sometimes. But I think of Catherine as my mother."

"Well, we can't choose our parents but we can choose our friends," Desmond said.

"I'm not sure what you mean," Annie responded.

But Desmond was busy now accepting condolences from people he'd known for years and years in The Glen.

After Hannah's burial at the Gates of Paradise Cemetery, Desmond made an announcement.

"Seems so strange not havin' O'Brien's Pub in The Glen to go to anymore. The world has sure changed."

"But, please, all of you, join me and me daughter, Annie, at the Wild Geese Inn right down the road for a brew and some food before goin' back about your business of the day. I'm grateful to ya all for bein' here with me at me poor wife's funeral."

Most everyone came to the Wild Geese Inn. They all talked about Hannah's sad life and how Desmond, her loyal husband, paid for her care all those years. Some old-time residents of The Glen drove all the way from Long Island and New Jersey to pay their last respects to Hannah and to show their deep admiration for Desmond. He had many loyal followers – people whom he'd helped during hard times.

Boss Garrigan worked the crowd, shaking hands and talking politics to his constituents.

When Catherine approached Desmond to say goodbye, he took her aside. "Catherine, you and your mother have taken excellent care of my Annie for years now and you never complained once, even though she can be a handful."

"We adore Annie," Catherine replied, tensing up as she always did whenever she spoke with Desmond.

"Well she's a big girl now, not a baby, and she doesn't need constant care anymore. Annie should be comin' home to her own house after school and sleepin' in her own bed at night. I know that Sarah is a good influence on Annie's wild nature so, of course, I want them to continue to be friends. But I'll be carin' for Annie now and spendin' more time with her – and reignin' in that wild spirit of hers."

Catherine choked back tears of bitter disappointment along with her fear for Annie's welfare. She smiled, covering up her emotions. "Well I hope Annie can at least have dinner with us when you're not at home. I hate to think of her spending her evenings all alone."

"Once in a while, of course, she can have dinner with ya, but not every night," Desmond said.

Catherine nodded. Her hands shook with fear and helplessness. There was nothing she could do. Annie was Desmond's daughter, not hers, even though she loved Annie as much as her own daughter. And Catherine dreaded telling the sad news to Greta who adored Annie.

Chapter 22

The demographics of The Glen changed daily – or so it seemed – becoming one third white and one third black and the rest Puerto Rican. Negroes owned half the row houses and Puerto Ricans occupied all the apartments.

Racial tensions ran high. Fights often broke out between the Negroes and the Puerto Ricans. And white gangs from the Mount Vernon and Pelham roamed the streets of The Glen looking for fights with anyone they could find.

Keith was known to get along with everyone and was one of the few young boys who could walk safely through the streets alone. Everyone else needed a few buddies or a whole gang just to walk the streets of The Glen.

But one afternoon as Keith walked from the train station through The Glen Center to his row house, he heard screams coming from the alley behind the produce market. He ran to see what was wrong and found three white boys he did not know. Two held Sarah and Annie while the third boy knelt over Bernadette who was on the ground.

"What's going on here?" Keith yelled.

The huge boy holding Annie by the wrists let her go. When Keith turned to ask if Annie was okay, the boy sucker punched him in the kidney. Keith fell to his knees. The boy who had been holding Sarah jumped Keith as well.

Keith yelled, "Annie, run for help!"

Annie ran toward the street, screaming at the top of her lungs. She went right to the traffic cop on the corner. "Help me, help me. They tried to hurt Bernadette and now they're trying to kill Keith."

Sarah, her hands free now, found a long piece of wood. "Get off my brother!" She smashed the huge boy hard on the back of his head. That caused enough of a distraction to give Keith a chance to land a hard right to the other boy's jaw.

The third boy left Bernadette and jumped Keith from behind. Keith kept swinging but soon all three were on top of him. They got him down on the ground and kicked him hard while Sarah tried to pull them away.

Suddenly there was a loud whistle and Annie's screaming could be heard again. The boys took off, running through the produce store and out onto the crowded main street. The young policeman came over to Keith to see if he was alright.

"I'm okay," Keith said, standing up, bruised and bleeding.

"Take it easy. You're hurt worse than you think but you sure held your own."

Sarah and Annie helped Bernadette stand up. She was okay but really scared. Her jacket was pulled off and her uniform was torn.

Annie excitedly told the policeman, "They called Bernadette some really bad names and they told us to shut up. They hit me in the stomach and that's when I started screaming. Is Keith going to be okay?"

Two more policemen rushed into the alley. They transported Keith and the girls to Dr. Smith's office where the waiting room was packed with patients. But Doctor Smith tended to Keith and the three girls right away. He examined Keith while his wife, Elaina, a registered nurse, checked out the girls.

Reggie rushed into the examining room, "You're a hero Keith. You took a bad beating but you saved Bernadette from something terrible. You're quite a young man and I thank you."

Desmond assigned extra police to Broadway. He didn't want that kind of trouble in The Glen. But they never found the three boys. Desmond said it was better that they didn't make an arrest. He didn't want Annie or Sarah to have to testify and said that he'd be sure nothing like that happened ever again. "I took care of them scumbags. They'll not be back." He even grudgingly commented, "Yeah, Keith Brandon handled himself real well that one time."

Desmond began taking Annie to the nine o'clock Mass at Saint Joseph's every Sunday morning, proud to show off his beautiful daughter.

"You look a bit like your Ma, Annie, but you're stronger and full of spirit."

"Thanks, Daddy." Annie smiled. It was the first compliment her father ever gave her. "But I think I'm strong like you."

As they passed by the "God Is Love" Church, they heard clapping and rhythmic singing. Annie tugged at Desmond's arm. "Please, Daddy, can we go there next Sunday to listen to the music?"

"Don't be ridiculous, Annie. That would be a sin. Haven't the nuns taught you that all that shoutin' and clappin' is heathen?"

"No, they never said that."

"Well, I'm telling you now."

"Why are you always so mad at me Daddy?" Annie asked. "My friends think it's because you're so much older than their fathers."

Desmond's face flushed. "Don't be disrespectful, young lady. I can still take me belt to you. And don't be talkin' about me and me private family business with your school chums. I get mad at you because you're a foolish girl and you're always wantin' to do what young ladies should not do."

During the Mass, Annie looked over at Sarah, standing beside Keith, wishing with all her heart that she could be with them as she used to be.

Old Monsignor Murdock gave a very different sermon that Sunday. "My dear parishioners, there is a terrible disease called Polio threatening our country. Its origin is unknown and we don't know how it spreads. I ask for your prayers that we may discover the cause and a way to stop it."

The monsignor's well-intentioned sermon, meant as a warning, caused a panic. Parishioners ran out of church straight home, to lock their doors and close the curtains on the windows as if that would keep the dreaded germs away. Some even blamed the blacks for bringing the polio up from the south.

Polio continued to strike randomly. Some recovered, others were left with a crippled limb and some had to live in an iron lung just to be able to breathe. Some even died.

On a Monday morning in April, when Sarah and Annie met outside their neighboring row houses to walk to school, Sarah said, "We need not wait for Bernadette this morning. She's very sick."

Annie knew instantly that it was the Polio.

When they arrived at school, they discovered that their classroom was less than half full.

Desmond rushed home that afternoon to warn Annie not to go near Bernadette. "I never liked you spending so much time with that colored girl anyway but now, you see, she's got the Polio. All those sick people in and out of her father's office right in their home, look at what it got them. Some doctor he is. He can't even protect his own daughter."

"Bernadette can't help being sick. A lot of people are sick," Annie reasoned, with tears in her eyes.

"Don't talk back to me," Desmond said, "What I'm saying is for your own good. So stay in this house and I'll get your homework from the nuns. You are to not to talk to anyone. Do you hear me?"

Annie nodded.

But every day, when Annie was sure that her father was well out of sight and away from the row house, she went next door to spend time with Bernadette. Sarah, and Keith, joined her there after school.

Bernadette rallied during their visits. But the Polio progressed, getting stronger as Bernadette grew weaker. Dr. Smith arranged to have an iron lung brought to his row house. But eventually even that was not enough to keep her breathing. At only fifteen years of age, Bernadette Smith lost her battle, leaving Dr. and Elaina Smith defeated and heartbroken. Her older brother, Reggie wept openly for weeks.

"Why would God let her die like that? Bernadette wanted to help everyone. She wanted to be a doctor like her father," Annie cried, struggling with the cruel, senseless loss.

Desmond offered Annie no comfort. "Sure life is cruel, Annie. But Bernadette was not like you – she was colored. You gotta accept that life is unfair and grab whatever advantage you can."

Annie didn't understand and went up to her room alone. She'd often sneak next door to be with Sarah. Catherine listened to the girls and tried to help them cope with the loss of their dear friend. Keith gave up his extra activities at school to come home early in the afternoons just to be with Sarah and Annie to add whatever comfort he could.

Chapter 23

In 1953 Sarah and Annie graduated from St. Joe's elementary school and went off to attend Sacred Heart Academy in Scarsdale. Desmond sent Annie there because it was all girls and he did not approve of the dating and dancing and general reckless behavior of the students in the regional public high school. Sacred Heart Academy charged a hefty tuition but

Sarah received a full scholarship from "an anonymous donor" in honor of her late grandfather. Catherine knew that Desmond Lynch was the donor. But she accepted the scholarship for Sarah's sake – and to keep Sarah and Annie together. And, in truth, the scholarship was a great help, except for the fact that it highlighted Desmond's contempt for Keith. But Keith, aware of how much Desmond disliked him, ignored the slights and showed Desmond nothing but great respect in return.

In the 1950's, it was fun to be a teenager in America. Frivolous music and crazy dances were all the rage.

And now, most families owned a television set and the "Evening News" took on a whole new meaning.

There were weekly television shows that portrayed the "average or perfect example" of an American family and these depictions relegated reality to a dismal, inferior level. The children of television families had a stay-at-home mother, a father with a high-paying job and they lived in an ideal neighborhood with a white picket fence surrounding a picture perfect house.

Sarah and Keith, with an abusive drunk for a father and a "German" grandmother, were not the typical American family. And Annie Lynch who had lived with neighbours because her mother was too sick to care for her and had a gangster father too busy to even visit her, fell into that same "misfit" category.

But Keith, Sarah and Annie were happy. They studied hard and had great fun, even if they were nothing like the television examples of American youth.

Sarah, tall for her age, had dark blue eyes, pitch black hair, and grew more beautiful and stately every day.

Annie, average in height, had an angelic face surrounded by blonde curly hair that looked very much like a halo. Her body was curvaceous. But despite Annie's very feminine looks, she remained an impulsive tomboy and her huge green eyes took in everything that went on around her.

But Annie's and Sarah's differences only made them love each other more. They were closer than sisters.

Their classmates at Sacred Heart Academy only tolerated Annie and Sarah, occasionally inviting them to parties and calling them "a low element from The Glen" behind their backs.

Still Sarah enjoyed the socials at Sacred Heart and always had more than her share of dance partners. "Oh Annie, you love to dance so much. Why don't you join in and have some fun while we're here."

But Annie had no interest in dancing with the boys. Only Keith Brandon held her interest and she prayed every day that he would see her as grown up and not the little girl he'd always known. She watched as Keith took girls his own age to his junior and senior proms but nothing could diminish her devotion to him.

When Keith graduated from St. Simon's with high honors, his counsellors and teachers suggested that he enlist in the Army before the GI Benefits ran out, rather than wait to be drafted. Keith hated the idea of leaving his family but even Catherine believed that it was the right option for Keith. And it was the only way that he could possibly afford a college education. A few days after his graduation, Keith reluctantly enlisted in the Army.

On Keith's last night at home, Catherine and Greta held a farewell dinner, inviting Keith's closest friends from St. Simon's. Sarah invited Annie to join them.

Desmond did not want Annie to go but he eventually gave in, admonishing Annie to be home by nine o'clock.

When one of Keith's school buddies saw Annie, he pulled Keith aside. "That friend of Sarah's is gorgeous. What a body! What basumbas! I gotta get to know her. Tell me everything you can about her, quick."

"Shut up," Keith said. "She's just a kid."

"Are you blind? That is not the body of a kid."

"Don't even think about it. Annie's off limits," Keith insisted and pushed his friend against the wall.

"I know what's going on. You want her for yourself. Why don't you just be honest instead of acting like she's some sort of saint or something?" Keith's angry friend said as he pushed back.

"Hey, what's going on here?" Catherine asked. The boys smoothed over their tensions and sat down to dinner. It was a great meal with lots of pleasant conversation.

Just before nine, Annie said her goodbyes. She stood on her toes to kiss Keith's cheek and he reached out to give her a friendly hug. When their bodies touched, they felt a charge of electricity that made them both blush.

Keith said, "Hey, I know it's only next door but let me walk you home, okay?"

"Sure." Annie said.

Keith took her hand the minute they were outside and they walked right next door onto her front porch. Standing together in the shadows, Keith pulled Annie close, leaned down and kissed her lips.

Annie kissed him back.

Keith whispered, "I don't want to take advantage of our special friendship. Are you sure you're okay with me kissing you like this?"

"Keith, I've wanted you to kiss me for so long. Promise that you'll write to me. Send the letters to Sarah so my father won't see them."

Annie's row house was dark and they both knew that Desmond was not at home.

Keith kissed her again and again, moving from her lips down over her neck, whispering, "I'll write to you every day, Annie."

Keith waited on the porch until Annie went inside, closed the door and slipped the lock into place.

Inside, Annie leaned against the front door, feeling Keith's presence on the other side. She knew that her lifelong friendship with him was over, replaced by something incredibly powerful, mysterious and totally irrevocable

Chapter 24

Keith kept his word, writing to Annie every night after his long days of gruelling basic training. He sent Annie letters in an envelope along with notes to his mother and sister.

Sarah gave Annie a new letter every afternoon and she loved the idea of a match between Annie and her brother. "Annie, if you marry Keith someday, then you and I will truly be sisters."

Annie smiled, too cautious to hope for much. "I'm just grateful for every new letter. Oh, Sarah, I've always loved Keith."

Sarah smiled. "I know."

And although Keith's letters were short, they were just what Annie wanted and needed. The letters evolved gradually, morphing into intimate love letters.

My Dearest Annie,

I think of you the first thing in the morning and all day long, no matter how crazy things get here. And I look forward to lights out so that I can be free to picture your face in my mind.

I've known you forever and yet there is so much I don't know about you. Tell me one thing from the deepest part of your soul in a letter every day. What are your hopes for the future? What do you really want out of life?

I dream about you every night. Your sweet kisses have bewitched me. All I want is to hold you in my arms and feel your soft curls brush against my face.
All My Love,
Keith

Annie's letters were long. She told Keith everything, holding back nothing. And all the while, Desmond had no idea that Annie was even in touch with Keith Brandon.

When Keith came home for a week after basic training, Annie somehow arranged to eat dinner with him and his family every night.

Catherine put the new television that Keith purchased for them in a spot where it could be seen from the dining room table as well as from the couch in the living room. And it was during one of Greta's wonderful dinners that they learned about the Salk vaccine on the six o'clock news.

It was the miracle that the country had prayed for. And it represented yet another great victory for a country that seemed destined for the world spotlight.

The mood in The Glen and in the entire country was euphoric.

Dr. Smith pledged to give every child in The Glen a vaccination free of charge as his way of memorializing his daughter, Bernadette.

Having Keith at home made Annie happier than anything could. She grew adept at the art of deception, telling her father elaborate lies about school activities that she needed to attend in order to sneak off and be with Keith. She even skipped school completely for two days, spending the entire time with Keith. They took the Day Liner Riverboat from the Yonkers dock up the Hudson River to Bear Mountain. While the boat glided along past the lovely landscape on both sides of the great Hudson River, they found a spot outside on the deck where they were shielded from other's view and they clung to each other, kissing. The cool river breezes blew over their hot flesh as they became completely lost in each other as only young lovers can.

"Keith I love you so very much," Annie whispered.

"And I love you. But you're still so young. I don't want you to miss out on your prom or any of the things you need to do. If it's real, then our feelings will last."

Annie unbuttoned the top of her blouse.

But Keith took her hands in his. "No, Annie. You're too special and our love is too special."

They danced to the music coming from the juke box inside the main hall of the day liner - "In the Still of the Night," "Young Love," and "Earth Angel."

Their bodies were close and their feelings ran deep.

"Wait for me, Annie?" Keith asked.

"I love you Keith. There could never be anyone else."

Desmond was busy that week working on Boss Garrigan's campaign for The State Senate.

Boss Garrigan delegated almost every important detail to Desmond. "Des, this campaign will force me to halt a lot of my business activities. You're my right hand man but times are changing and I have got to get away from our old ways of doing business. I hope you saved up some money because you might even need to get a regular job. The days of protection and gambling money are gone."

"Boss, I don't know what kind a work I'd be able to do."

"I'll find something for ya but it won't be a cash cow like before."

Desmond walked home to his row house in time for dinner for the first time in months. Surprised that Annie wasn't at home, he read the note that she'd left on the kitchen table telling him she was next door having dinner with Sarah's family.

Angry, Desmond said to himself, "Well that'll be comin' to an end soon 'cause I'll be havin' dinner with me own daughter every evening soon." He ripped up the note and opened a can of Campbell's soup, heating it in a saucepan on the stove. Then he carried his soup into the living room and turned on the television.

It was after nine when Keith walked Annie home.

Desmond opened the front door just as they arrived. "Sure, 'tis about time you're home from dinner, Annie me girl."

"It's Keith's last night on leave so Greta made a special meal and Keith walked me home even though it's just right next door." Annie smiled.

Desmond looked at his daughter, thinking how she had her mother's delicate facial features but was tough, strong and healthy, like him. And, like him, Annie could tell a very convincing lie.

"Good evening, Sir." Keith extended his hand but Desmond ignored it.

"Hello, Keith," Desmond answered. "Go home now and spend some time with your family. Annie shouldn't be interfering with a family when they have such a short time to be together."

"But Annie is family, as are you, Sir. I remember how my grandfather loved you like a brother."

"Aye, Frank was even more than a brother to me. And I'll never get over his dying so young. But that's all in the past now. Good night, Keith, and good luck to ye."

"Good night, Sir. Good night, Annie."

Annie nodded, afraid that she would burst into tears if she spoke.

Keith left for Fort Riley, Kansas early the next morning. From there, he would go on to join the occupation forces in West Germany and it would be a very long time before Annie would be in his arms again.

Chapter 25

The long, painful separation seemed to make Annie and Keith fall more deeply in love.

Sarah and Annie graduated from Sacred Heart Academy. Catherine scraped enough money together to enroll Sarah in the Katherine Gibbs Secretarial School in New York City.

But despite Annie's superior grades and the fact that she desperately wanted to go to college, Desmond believed that higher education for women was a waste of time and money. He now worked a legitimate job as a supervisor for Garrigan's construction company and it proved to be a lot less lucrative than collecting high-interest, illegal loans and gambling debts.

Garrigan went on to the State Senate. But he visited his root constituents in The Glen often. And whenever he met Desmond, he'd always ask about Annie.

"She's number one in her class and she wanted to go to St. Vincent's College in the Bronx but I think what she really needs is a good, solid marriage," Desmond said.

Boss Garrigan smiled. "You know Desmond, Fiona Fogerty has a son studying pre-med. Now he'd make a fine husband for Annie. And I plan to throw a lot of things Liam's way."

"That's just what I want for my Annie – a solid marriage to a man with a profession – a man of means, not the son of drunk like that Keith Brandon," Desmond replied. "But me daughter, Annie, can be a handful. I'm finding it very hard to deal with a young girl of such spirit at my age. She fights me on everything"

Boss Garrigan cleared his throat, harsh and scratchy from years of cigar smoking.

Coughing and sputtering, Garrigan manipulated Desmond as he spoke, "I hear tell that Annie is sweet on that Keith Brandon. But she's a rare beauty, indeed, and she'll need to trade on her looks while she's still in the bloom of youth. And that Brandon boy is nothing but a poor soul with no money and no future."

"Brandon's away in the Army and she knows I don't approve of him. He's got too much of his father in him."

"He also has that high and mighty attitude from his grandfather." Garrigan had never liked Frank O'Connor.

"Frank was like a brother to me. If Catherine hadn't run off with Michael Brandon, me good friend would still be alive. And that Keith looks just like his father. He'll never be with my Annie, never. I took care of his old man and I can take care of him."

"Let's not go digging up old skeletons."

"I know, I know. I hated the fact that Catherine's evil husband was thought fit enough to serve our country."

"That's all in the past now. It's the future we need to plan. And I propose a match between your Annie and young Liam Fogerty – a future physician."

"Annie can be fierce. She might scare Liam off with her smart mouth."

"It's a shame she had no mother to teach her the things that women need to know."

"I did my best," Desmond said, "I'm a simple man and not very good with women. But what in particular do you mean?"

"That in the dark of night, all men are the same. All a woman has to do is close her eyes and spread her legs and it won't matter if it's Keith Brandon or Liam. But in the cold light of day, it's Liam who will provide Annie with all the comforts of life, like a fine home and security."

"Annie's head is filled with all that romantic foolishness. She buys those 45 records with mushy love words and wild drum beats. It's not at all like the music of the twenties." Desmond shook his head in disgust.

"Annie needs to obey her father."

"You're right and I won't let me girl run off with the likes of Keith Brandon like Frank's daughter, Catherine, ran off with his no-good father."

Garrigan smiled. "I'll talk to Liam's mother, Fiona. I plan to be very generous to young Liam and his wife because of my close friendship with Liam's father – the poor man - he died much too young."

Desmond nodded. "Fine. You talk to Liam's mother and I'll take care of Annie. Don't you worry about a thing!"

Garrigan spoke low, barely above a whisper, "Make sure that Annie understands the whole situation and all the implications of her behaviour. After all, a father knows what's best for his own daughter. Sometimes a few lashes of a belt across a woman's back can enhance her understanding."

Desmond looked down. "I've never really beat Annie like that."

"Well that explains a lot." Garrigan scoffed.

Chapter 26

It was five in the morning when Sarah woke up to Catherine's cries for help, "Call Dr. Smith and hurry!"

As Sarah ran to the phone, Catherine realized that it was too late. Her dear mother, Greta, had slipped away, peacefully and quietly, in her sleep, not enduring even a moment of pain or suffering.

Sarah ran next door to get Annie. "It's Granna. She's gone. Oh, Annie, she died in her sleep."

"I'll come right over."

Catherine hugged Annie when she arrived. "Granna loved you as her own, just as I do. I'm sure they'll allow Keith to come home for the funeral."

Annie trembled, overwhelmed with the pain of losing Greta, whom she adored, and the anticipation of seeing Keith again.

After Dr. Smith pronounced Greta dead and the hearse took her body to the funeral home, Catherine calmed down enough to make plans.

"What do you think, girls?" Catherine asked. "Granna's been housebound for so many years and she doesn't really know very many people, so I'm thinking that maybe a private funeral and burial, with just a few, invited people and no viewing. Does that sound appropriate to you?"

"I think that is exactly what Granna would want," Annie replied.

Sarah nodded, crying too hard to even speak.

Desmond was staying in New York City attending a builders' convention, purchasing wood and other supplies for Garrigan's Construction Company.

So Annie felt free to do as she pleased. She took the next few days off from her job at the Town Hall and spent all day with Catherine and Sarah, preparing dinner for them while they worked to finalize last minute details.

The next day, in the late afternoon, as Annie peeled vegetables under the running tap water, she didn't hear Keith open the front door. It wasn't until she shut the water off that she heard his footsteps and turned to see Keith standing there in front of her. His jet black hair was cropped short and his dark blue eyes appeared even more intense than she remembered. And he looked so handsome good his uniform that Annie's face flushed as she took in every detail.

Keith dropped his duffle bag.

Annie wiped her wet hands on her jeans and threw her arms around his neck.

Keith kissed her hard on the lips, lifting her light body up off the floor.

Taking a deep breath, she whispered, "I'm so glad to see you but not under these circumstances. I'm so sorry about your grandmother."

"I know you are. She was your grandmother too. She loved you so much."

They held each other close for a long time.

Annie made tea and they sat at the kitchen table to talk.

"You know, Annie, I visited the town where Granna was born. There's no family of hers left there now. I remember getting so angry because it was always so hard for Granna, being German and considered the enemy here in The Glen. But it would have been even worse for her there. You can't imagine what it's like over there. And now the Russians – you should see the things that they do."

Annie took Keith's hands in hers and kissed them.

When Catherine and Sarah got home there were hugs and tears as they greeted Keith. That evening, they all ate dinner together as a family once again - but without their beloved Granna.

After dinner, Sarah offered to take Catherine up to bed. "Mom is exhausted and she needs all her strength to get through the funeral."

Keith kissed his mother goodnight.

Annie washed the dishes as Keith dried and put them away. Checking his watch, he asked. "Do you have to get home?"

"No, my father's in the city at a builder's convention. I haven't told him about Granna. The funeral is private and I don't think your mom wants him there anyway."

Keith took Annie's hand and led her up the stairs to his room where he fell backwards onto his bed and pulled her down beside him. Exhausted, they laid together on top of the bedspread, wrapped in each other's arms, drifting off into a deep, peaceful sleep, fully dressed, not even moving until the first light of dawn.

The next morning a hired car picked them up and took them to St. Joseph's for the Funeral Mass. Dr. and Mrs. Smith, Reggie Smith and Esther Weinberg were the only invited guests.

Later, at The Gates of Paradise Cemetery, Monsignor Murdock led the small group in prayer as Greta Schmidt O'Connor was laid to rest with her beloved husband, Frank O'Connor and her father Gregor Schmidt.

The small group of mourners went to the nearby Wild Geese Tavern.

"My but that is an absolutely huge and very beautiful cemetery," Esther Weinberg said to Catherine, patting her hand.

"Mom purchased the plot when my father died."

"Do you know the story about the cemetery, Esther?" Sarah asked.

"No, I do not. But I know it is very valuable real estate."

Catherine gave Esther a knowing smile, "Yes it is. All that land was left to the Archdiocese by a wealthy Catholic family in 1910 before my father even came to this country and the Cardinals decided to split the estate into small burial parcels and sell them individually. And, of course, they hired Garrigan Construction Company to put in the roads and build the office building and the chapel. They marketed the burial plots from the pulpit every Sunday. And people clamoured to buy a final resting place for their loved ones in the place they truly thought of as The Gates to Paradise."

Dr. Smith added, "I hear tell that it was the single most successful real estate marketing venture in the history of the State. Just imagine, the land cost them nothing so the Church made a pure profit on every one of the burial plots."

Keith, holding Annie's hand under the table, spoke, "And just after World War I, the state built a railroad station right on the cemetery grounds to bring the caskets and mourners up from New York City. Quite an enterprise!"

"It takes a lot of power to get a railroad to build a station within a cemetery. Those poor immigrant families never owned their own homes but they were proud to be able to own a final resting place," Sarah commented.

"Amazing!" Esther said.

Reggie piped in, "So the poor buggers only realized the American dream of owning land after death. What pathos."

"And zey say that we Jews are the business people," Esther spoke now with only a very slight but still intriguing accent. She was the first solo violinist with the New York Symphony and she owned a comfortable apartment on the upper east side of Manhattan. The toast of New York City, Esther had a lot of friends and suitors but no steady man or husband. And she maintained her strong interest in Annie. She had even offered to pay for Annie's college tuition but Desmond dismissed her offer, telling her, "to mind her own business."

Keith, more talkative than usual, shared some of his experiences in the Army with the small group and Esther confirmed all of Keith's observations about the overall political situation in Europe.

Reggie Smith talked about his burgeoning law practice in the Bronx. "Hey, it's killing my love life to live at home with my parents but the rent is zero and the food is good. And it's what I need right now since most of my clients don't pay me."

Dr. Smith laughed. "It's great to have Reggie living at home. And we all feel closer to Bernadette in the row house." He kissed Elaina's hand whenever he spoke of their deceased daughter.

The group drank tea and coffee until the afternoon was gone. It was past four-thirty when they headed back to The Glen and Esther went back to the city for her evening performance.

Back at their row house, Sarah and Catherine went to their rooms to rest.

Keith asked Annie to go for a walk. They wandered through the streets of The Glen Center and boarded the trolley. Sitting close and holding hands, they rode all the way to the end of the line at River Walk along the Hudson

"Time goes by so fast when I'm with you," Keith said.

"Let's keep walking here by the river," Annie pleaded "I don't want to go home yet."

River Walk was the oldest section of Yonkers, with huge old Victorian houses, most of them now converted into small hotels, boarding houses or Bed and Breakfast Inns.

Annie sat down to rest on a stepping stone.

Keith sat close beside her, saying, "A long time ago, the fine ladies of Yonkers and New York City would step out of their ritzy horse-drawn carriages onto this huge stone."

"I can just picture them in their long gowns." Annie smiled.

"Let's go inside. I need to be alone with my girl for a little while – just to talk and maybe kiss you a few times without prying eyes. I know Granna wouldn't mind if we enjoyed our time together. It's almost like a gift from her."

"And I need to be alone with you," Annie agreed.

They walked through the double front doors into a huge parlor furnished with floral overstuffed furniture and lots of over-grown snake plants. An elegant white haired woman in her sixties behind the desk asked Keith to sign the guest book.

Keith scribbled, Sergeant and Mrs. Keith Brandon, next to the date.

"Sergeant Brandon, I'll have tea and scones sent to your room. It's on the second floor - in the back – number 210. There's a wonderful view of the river. Do you need help with your luggage?"

"No." Keith smiled. "Our bags were misplaced at the railroad station. A cab will drop them off later tonight."

"Well, I'll have them left outside your room as soon as they arrive."

Annie laughed. "How did you think of an answer so fast?"

"It's part of my job to be an accomplished liar," Keith answered, kissing Annie's forehead.

Their room had the same floral motif as the lobby. Annie sat at the wicker table in front of the window and Keith joined her. They ate the fresh baked scones and drank the hot tea with lemon and honey.

"Annie, you are the high point of my life. I miss you so much."

Annie replied, "I watched you all during the Mass this morning, memorizing your profile. I want to be able to visualize every detail of your face when you're gone. Oh, Keith, I can't stand it that you're leaving again."

"You're pouting. Just like when you were little, like an unhappy angel with that halo of blonde curls around your face.

"I'm not an angel, Keith."

"Sure you are." He leaned over, kissing her lips.

"No, I'm a grown woman who is deeply in love with you."

Keith kissed her over and over again. "This is all I want - just to be able to kiss my girl in private."

Annie whispered, "But I want more Keith." She led him over to the bed.

"Annie, will you come to Germany so we can get married as soon as you're eighteen? I'll send you a ticket and get you a place to stay." He slipped Greta's ruby engagement ring on her finger. "Granna wanted me to give this to my bride. And I'm sure she knew it would be you."

They were on the bed now, lying side by side. Annie rolled over on top of Keith. "If that's a marriage proposal, the answer is yes."

"I'm not good at saying things. But you must know how much I love you."

Annie unbuttoned her blouse and slipped it off.

Keith whispered, "I want you so much. But we have to wait."

"No Keith, it's too hard to wait."

He held her head in his hands, her blonde curls slipping through his fingers. "Annie, I just want to do what's right for you."

"This is right." She unbuttoned his shirt.

"Your father hates me and I'm so afraid that he will take you away from me."

"My father hates everyone. If he ever found us alone together like this, he would probably condemn us to hell and then force you to marry me. So, if that's the worst that can happen? Well for me – that's the best that can happen." Annie smiled and opened Keith's belt.

Keith peeled away Annie's clothes, kissing every inch of her young body, lingering on the places that made her wild with passion.

Annie was lost in a fog of pleasure. She enjoyed even the momentary sensation of pain when Keith pushed himself deep inside of her. She felt intimacy and a sense of belonging - complete for the very first time in her life. They gave themselves to each other again and again until at last they fell exhausted into a deep sleep.

It was three in the morning when they got back to Annie's row house.

"We'll be married in a few months," Keith said. "You need to get a passport and I'll send a plane ticket to Sarah. I have less than half a year left in the military and then we can come back home together – as a married couple."

Annie looked down at Greta's ring on her finger. "We're already married, Keith." She put her finger over Keith's lips. "Don't say goodbye to me. Promise me that you'll never say the word, "goodbye."

Keith kissed her one last time.

Alone now, in Desmond's dark, lonely row house, Annie could still feel the sensation of Keith's body deep inside of her.

She ran up to her room and threw herself down on her bed, weeping uncontrollably at the thought of being apart from Keith.

A soldier picked Keith up two hours later. Annie watched from her window as they drove off to Stewart Air Base in Newburgh where Keith told her they would catch a MATS flight back to Bamberg in West Germany.

The next day, Annie told Sarah everything. Sarah exclaimed, "We always were sisters but now it's official. I always knew that you and Keith were meant for each other. And so did my mother and my Granna."

Annie laughed. "I guess Keith was the last to find out."

"Men!" Sarah said.

Annie took off Greta's ring and gave it to Sarah. "Keep this safe for me. You know I can't let my father see it."

Sarah nodded and took the ring.

Annie went back to her job at the Town Hall. But the boring job and her mean-spirited supervisor seemed so much more tolerable now that she knew she would soon be with Keith.

Sarah resumed her studies at Kathryn Gibbs in Manhattan.

And everything appeared to be as it was before.

But, in reality, everything had changed.

Chapter 27

When Desmond got home that evening, he was livid. "You should have called me. Greta's husband was the only family I ever had. I was their best man and I should have been at her funeral. Annie, I don't know where your head is sometimes."

"I'm sorry. It was a private funeral and I didn't want you to rush home if you were not invited." Annie said, not meaning it.

Desmond shrugged. Then he rattled on and on about upcoming parties that he wanted Annie to attend, particularly a dinner party at Fiona Fogerty's home. And he mentioned Fiona's son, Liam Fogerty, at least five times.

Weeks passed. Annie applied for her passport. Everything was different now that she knew that Keith loved her as much as she loved him. All she wanted was to be with him and it didn't matter where, as long as they were together.

Early on a Friday morning in early November of 1957, Catherine answered the doorbell. Two soldiers in uniform greeted her. "Mrs. Brandon?"

"Yes. Come in."

"Thank you Ma'am."

"Please, sit down."

"We'll stand, thank you."

Catherine noticed a patch on their uniforms - the same one Keith wore.

"Mrs. Brandon, the Army regrets to inform you that your son, Keith Brandon, is missing. It is believed that he got lost and inadvertently drove across the border into East Germany. We don't know where he is or even if he is still alive. So, at this time, Sergeant Keith Brandon, is officially classified as missing."

Pain and shock rushed through Catherine's body as she fought to concentrate on the rest of their conversation.

Somehow she felt sure they promised to keep her informed and, shortly after that, they left. She tried to get in touch with Sarah but she wasn't at her desk. She called Annie and asked her to stop by after work.

Both girls rushed to Catherine's row house after work. "Oh my darlings, two young soldiers were here this morning." Catherine's hands shook. "Keith evidently got lost and drove across the border and now, well, the Army doesn't know where he is. They don't even know for sure if he is alive."

Sarah reacted with anger. "They're lying. Keith doesn't get lost – not ever."

Catherine said, "Darling please stay calm."

Annie sank to the floor onto her knees, weeping. She touched her stomach where Keith's child was growing deep inside of her, just beneath her pounding heart, certain now that she would not be flying to Germany to marry him.

Chapter 28

Thanksgiving Day 1957 came and went with no word about Keith. Catherine pleaded with her Congressman and Senators to help. Word of Sergeant Brandon's disappearance spread throughout The Glen but there was no official announcement or press release.

Catherine and Sarah were frantic. They spoke of nothing else.

When Desmond telephoned Annie at work, she thought it must be news about Keith. "What is it? What happened?" she asked, feeling nauseous.

"Nothing happened. Calm down, Annie. I just want you to meet me for dinner at that new place, Schraft's, in Fleetwood tonight. We'll have a bite to eat. You need to get out – you're lookin' pale. So bring a hearty appetite – well not too hearty cause you're puttin' on a bit of weight lately."

"Yes, I know," Annie answered, aware of her extra few pounds as well as her swollen, painful breasts. She knew that she'd have to do something soon if even her father, who barely ever looked at her, had noticed the changes in her body. Desperate to use the Pan Am ticket that Keith sent her, she carried it with her all the time. But without Keith, she didn't know if or how she'd be able to manage in Germany. She'd hidden her passport at the bottom of her underwear drawer.

Waves of nausea overcame Annie yet again and she ran to the ladies room. Just that morning the supervisor reprimanded her for going to the lavatory too often. And now, once again, her over made-up, pinched-faced supervisor glared at her, walked across the room and tapped Annie on the shoulder. "Miss Lynch, try to stay at your post. You are leaving it far too often. After all, you do have a break mid-morning and mid-afternoon."

Annie apologized profusely. She planned to tell Catherine about the baby that night but now this invitation to supper with her father made that impossible.

Sarah, of course, knew, without being told. Annie knew that Catherine would be kind. But the very thought of Desmond's reaction filled Annie with a fear so deep that she shuddered.

Annie's supervisor came back to berate her for mistakes. Annie apologized for being distracted. She felt so sick to her stomach that the supervisor's public reprimand brought her to tears. Things were spinning out of control.

After work, Annie took the trolley to the new Schraft's restaurant in Fleetwood. When she walked into the modern restaurant, she saw her father sitting in a booth with Boss Garrigan.

Both men stood to greet her. "Ah, Annie me girl, you're finally here," Desmond said.

Boss Garrigan pulled Annie into his arms, hugging her so close that her sensitive breasts pressed into his chest. Her face was pushed into Garrigan's woolen jacket that reeked of cigar smoke. The odor, combined with her own raging hormones and the tension of her terrible work day, and it all made her sick. She shrieked, "Stop it. Let me go. You smell awful and I hate it when you pull me so close."

Anger flashed across Garrigan's face.

Desmond, having spent his entire life sucking up to Boss Garrigan, stared at her, with an expression of pure horror on his face. "Annie, what's gotten into you?"

Garrigan's face twisted into a false smile. "Never mind, Des. I forget sometimes that Annie's a grown woman now. I still think of her as a beautiful child. I shan't be huggin' her anymore."

Both men sat down and Annie slid into the booth next to her father. Desmond sighed, shaking his head. "Annie, we're here tonight because the Boss here, and me, well we think that you are far too lovely and intelligent to work at that boring clerk job. Although the Boss here knows how grateful you are to him for gettin' you the job."

"I don't understand." Annie thought her father might be suggesting that she attend college next semester.

"We've been thinking long and hard about your future," Garrigan commented.

Desmond smiled, taking Annie's hand. "Annie girl, I'm sellin' the row house and most a that money will go to your dowry."

"My dowry? What is that?"

"I've made arrangements. You're going to be married to Liam Fogerty early in the New Year. You'll have an elegant and easy life."

"Have you lost your mind?" Annie's voice shook and she spoke too loud. "This isn't Ireland in the Middle Ages. This is America and it's 1957. This is just not done."

Everyone in the restaurant stared at them.

Desmond whispered, "Marriages are arranged everywhere, even today. Romance and all them stupid love songs are all nonsense. Marriage is a business whose product is the next generation. Liam will be an excellent provider and a successful doctor. Papers are signed, money has exchanged hands - it's a done deal."

"Are you saying that you sold me like a piece of livestock? No one makes deals using me. Not me. Not ever." Annie turned pale.

Boss Garrigan watched Annie and Desmond argue and he grinned.

"Liam is just beginning Medical School at Taylor University in Houston, and when he finishes, Boss Garrigan will set him up in his own medical center right here in Fleetwood. Your life is grandly laid out before you." Desmond reached for Annie's trembling hand and placed something small into it. "Liam and I agreed that you should have your mother's ring."

Annie pushed her father's hand away. The ring flew into the air, landing on the floor and rolling under the table.

"I will never marry Liam Fogerty," Annie insisted.

"Shut up, Annie. I'll handle you when we get home."

Garrigan glared at the people staring at them until they all looked away.

"Okay, let's go home then." Annie stormed out of Schraft's, past the elegant bar, filled with the after-work, happy-hour drinkers, mostly men wearing expensive suits.

Everyone stared at Annie as she stormed past them.

"Now there's a woman for you," a tall young man commented.

The bartender nodded. "She is a looker alright but what a wicked temper."

"A man can put up with a lot when a woman is that beautiful."

Garrigan looked down at Desmond who was now on his knees, searching under the table for his dead wife's wedding ring. "For heaven sakes, Desmond, get up."

"Aye, I found it. But I'm feeling every one of me fifty-eight years," Desmond said, sweating profusely as he pulled himself to his feet.

Garrigan smirked. "Can't you even manage a mere slip of a girl, Desmond?"

"I can manage me daughter alright. She'll feel the back of me hand tonight," Desmond mumbled as he apologized. "And she'll come round, you'll see. This was a surprise to Annie, her being a virtuous girl, taught by the nuns and all. Just discussing her being with a man probably frightened her – her bein' a young, innocent virgin."

"Any other girl would be grateful enough to kiss your feet and mine. Annie's like a wild horse that needs breaking."

Desmond stated firmly, "There will be no further embarrassment. And this marriage will take place. I'll see to it."

When Desmond got back to his dark row house, Annie was in bed, reeling with nausea and feeling very dizzy. He burst into Annie's room without knocking and snapped on the overhead light. "Are you mooning about that Keith Brandon?" he shouted. "Do you know what he's done? He deserted the Army proving me right. He's a coward just like his father before him."

"Keith Brandon is not a coward. And his father changed. He died for his country."

"I don't believe that malarkey for a minute."

Desmond began to rifle through Annie's dresser drawers, looking for correspondence from Keith Brandon, throwing the contents on the floor. When he saw the passport, he went into a rage. "What's this for?" He tore it into little pieces. Then he grabbed Annie's hand and pulled her to her feet. "Are you planning to run to Europe after that Brandon? That will never happen. And I want an apology for the way you acted tonight."

Afraid for her baby, Annie's bravado faded and she pleaded, "Please don't hurt me Daddy?"

"Here I am paying me life savings to give you a chance for a successful husband and good life and you humiliate me in public, in front a me own boss."

Desmond slid off his belt.

Annie's eyes were fearful as she ran out of the room and down the stairs.

Desmond caught up to her at the front door, grabbing her wrist.

It was all too much for Annie. She fell to the floor in a dead faint.

Desmond looked down at her. "I can't beat you and I can't deal with you anymore."

He walked out of the row house, leaving Annie crumpled and unconscious in the front hall.

Chapter 29

Annie woke up to see Sarah and Dr. Smith, on their knees, attending to her. Sarah had overheard the argument between Desmond and Annie through the common wall of the row house. When Desmond left, she rushed next door to Annie and found her on the floor.

She telephoned Dr. Smith and pleaded with him to come over. Doctors still had regularly scheduled evening office hours but Dr. Smith left a room full of waiting patients to attend to Annie.

"Don't try to move, Annie. An ambulance is on its way," Dr. Smith said softly. "You're just fine. But Sarah tells me you might be pregnant."

"Yes." Annie replied as tears ran down her cheeks.

Sarah spoke hesitantly, "Annie and my brother. She's been so sick lately, always throwing up."

The ambulance pulled up in front of Desmond's row house, with lights flashing but no siren. Dr. Smith patted Sarah on the shoulder. "Go on home, Sarah. Tell your mother that I'll stop by later to speak with her. I'm going to admit Annie to the hospital. Then we'll figure things out."

At St. Joseph's Hospital, Annie was taken to a private room while Dr. Smith paged Dr. Warner, St. Joseph's only obstetrician. When Warner finished examining Annie, he conferred with Dr. Smith in the hall. "She's three months at least and she's been through considerable trauma. A pregnancy out of wedlock for an Irish Catholic girl is the ultimate disgrace. And, you say that she's Desmond Lynch's daughter? My God, Smith, what have you gotten us into?"

"I know, I know. He's a dangerous man. But, listen, you're out of it. I'll take it from here."

Dr. Warner put his hand Smith's shoulder. "It's not just us I'm worried about. Who knows what Lynch will do to her?"

Smith nodded. "Lynch would force the father of the child to marry her but in this case that is impossible. Although, the young man would do the right thing, if he could."

"Are you talking about that soldier who is missing behind the Iron Curtain?"

"Yes, I'm sure Keith Brandon is the father."

Dr. Warner shook his head. "Well that eliminates the shotgun wedding but it still leaves the shotgun. By the way, the baby is fine. But Annie can't be upset anymore."

"I'm going to admit her for a day or two. She can rest and heal until I think of something."

"Good idea, Smith. And I'll back you up on anything you need."

A few hours later, Desmond Lynch thundered into the hospital. He caught up with Dr. Smith as he was making his rounds. "Who gave you permission to treat my daughter? Just because you live next door to us does not make you our doctor. We have our own kind. And that nurse said that my Annie is in a family way. Does everyone in the hospital know about this?"

"Only the medical personnel who need to know. It's a medical condition. And it makes the fact that you terrified your own daughter even more reprehensible."

"Where is she?"

"She's asleep and she can't have visitors."

"Tell me where me daughter is." Desmond's face got red.

"Let me pass. I have patients waiting back at my office. I'll call you in the morning and let you know how Annie is." Dr. Smith turned his back on Desmond and walked away. He went to Catherine's row house and told her everything.

Catherine stepped up. "Annie will live with us and we'll care for her. I raised her as my own child and I'll raise my grandchild as well."

"No, it's too close to Desmond. I'm really afraid of what Desmond might do."

Catherine thought of her dear friend Esther Weinberg in Manhattan and called her right away.

Esther eagerly offered to help Annie. "Ah, my sweet little Ansha. I vill send a car to the hospital first thing in the morning to bring her here. I know people in New York. Ze are even bigger fish than Lynch and Garrigan and they swim in a much bigger pond than The Glen."

Chapter 30

Desmond's face went deep red when a nurse told him that he could not go into Annie's room. Furious though he was, he backed down, not wanting to make a public scene. He knew it was better if as few people as possible were to know about his daughter's disgrace.

He asked where there was a telephone that he could use and dialed Boss Garrigan.

"Desmond, you're lucky to catch me at the office so late."

"I've bad news. The marriage between Liam and Annie is off. I've been betrayed by me own daughter. I thought Annie was an innocent virgin and it turns out that she's carrying a child."

"You are such a fool, Desmond. I told you there was talk about Annie and that Brandon boy."

"He's like his no-good father. He seduced my Annie and then left her."

"Annie doesn't seem like the kind of girl to do anything she doesn't want to do. And she deserves what she gets from Keith Brandon."

"What am I to do? I can't even force Brandon to marry her. Who knows where he is? Maybe this thing about him going missing is just a ploy to get out of his responsibility for the child."

"Stop whining, Desmond. I know a place for unwed mothers where Annie can stay out of sight until the baby is born and they'll find a fine Catholic family to adopt the child. But it will cost you plenty."

"I'll pay whatever it takes to get rid of the little bastard."

"You make arrangements to get Annie out of that hospital. Kidnap her, if you have to. I'll call St. Gerard's in Maine to make arrangements. She's a minor in that state until her twenty-first birthday so it is your decision, not hers, to put the baby up for adoption. Now, I've got to tell Liam and his mother that the wedding is off. That won't be easy."

It was around three in the morning when two men, complete strangers to Annie, snuck into her hospital room and woke her up. The shorter of the two, placed his hand over Annie's mouth while the other pinned her arms down. "Annie Lynch?"

She nodded.

"Be quiet and listen. We're taking you to your friend Sarah. So just keep quiet and everything will be alright."

"Is Sarah here with you?" Annie asked weakly.

"No. But you are in grave danger so we have to get out of here."

The taller man threw a blanket around Annie and lifted her up into his arms. They ran down the hall and entered the stairwell. At the ground level, they exited the hospital through a side door and walked several feet to a black car parked at the curb.

"Sarah, are you here?" Annie called when the big man pushed her into the back seat.

"Shut up, blondie, or you'll mess everything up."

Although Annie didn't recognize either of the men, they sounded an awful lot like the men who worked for her father. The shorter man got behind the wheel and started the car.

Annie memorized the shapes of the backs of their heads; the thickness of their necks; the color of their hair. She took short, deep breaths, forcing herself to stay calm for the sake of her baby.

They drove for hours, stopping only to buy gas. The taller man brought Annie a cup of water and a few saltine crackers. "You need to stay hydrated. Don't worry. You'll be with Sarah soon."

And at each stop, before they began to drive again, he escorted her to the gas station rest room. "Don't lock the door, don't even close it all the way," he ordered, staying by the door and closing it just enough to give her some slight privacy.

Annie tried to remember the landmarks that they passed. But the tall man noticed and said, "Get down. Stretch out on the back seat and stop looking around."

PART III

ST. GERARD'S CONVENT HOME FOR UNWED MOTHERS

ELLSVILLE, MAINE

Chapter 31

It was around three in the afternoon when they pulled up in front of a farmhouse. "Get out!" The driver bellowed at Annie without even turning to look at her.

Barefoot, wearing only the hospital gown with a blanket wrapped around her, Annie stepped out of the car into the freshly fallen snow. The car door slammed closed. Shivering in fear, she stood alone in the cold, when the car suddenly peeled away.

The farm house door opened and a giant of a man walked toward her. He didn't speak as he lifted her out of the snow and carried her up the steps onto the wrap-around porch.

She noticed a sign next to the front door. "St. Gerard's Convent, Ellsville, Maine."

The giant man set her down and held the front door open. Annie walked into the warm, comfortably furnished parlor. He led her up the stairs to the second floor and pointed for her to go into the first room on the right. It was a plain room with stark white walls, a single bed, one small window with a dark shade, an old oak bureau with a small glass lamp and one straight-back chair. A large wooden crucifix hung over the bed. The giant vanished without a sound but Annie soon heard footsteps on the wooden floors accompanied by a soft-swishing sound.

Two nuns entered the room. "Annie Lynch, my dear girl. Welcome to St. Gerard's. I'm Sister Muriel and this is Sister Rita, our Mother Superior. I understand that you've had a long journey so you must be hungry and tired."

"No I'm just cold," Annie answered, trembling.

Sister Muriel knelt down and tried to dry Annie's wet feet.

"No, don't touch me." Annie grabbed the towel and dried her own feet. "Where is Sarah? I want to see her right now."

"I don't know anything about a Sarah. But you're quite safe here," Sister Rita intervened, an authoritarian tone in her voice.

A very pregnant young girl, her sack dress bulging out in front, came into the room carrying a small tray. She smiled and placed it on Annie's lap.

Annie sipped the warm chicken broth.

Sister Rita pulled the straight-back chair up close to the bed. "So, how are you feeling, Annie?"

Annie stared at the nun but did not reply.

"I see. Okay, we'll talk later. You've been brought here to be cared for during your confinement. When you're stronger, you will participate in our convent life, helping with chores and attending chapel. However, your most important job is to eat and rest. Everything we do here is to insure that your baby is born healthy. And, of course, we provide spiritual support as well. You must attend mass and you are encouraged to confess your sins."

"If Sarah isn't here, then you kidnapped me. I was supposed to be taken to Sarah Brandon to stay with her and her mother."

"We do not kidnap people. Your care and board here is being paid for by a generous benefactor. Not every unwed mother has access to such excellent care. You should be grateful."

"Well I'm not grateful. I'm sure my father and Garrigan set this up. Sarah probably doesn't even know where I am."

Sister Rita continued her initiation speech, "One of our nuns is a midwife; two others are registered nurses and we have a doctor on call. When you deliver your child, he or she, will be adopted by a financially secure, Catholic family and raised in the Faith."

Annie's eyes opened wide. "I have no intention of giving up my baby." She tried to get out of bed but when she stood up, she swayed unsteadily and had to sit back down on the bed again.

"Annie, your baby's birth is months away. So for right now, why don't you just take care of that innocent child that's growing inside of you. We'll talk about the baby's future another time."

Sister Rita knelt down beside Annie's bed. "Dear Lord, please bless this young woman and give health to her unborn baby."

The two nuns left the room. Annie shivered and wept beneath the rough brown blanket as the afternoon light faded into dark shadows. She cried out loud. "God I miss Keith so much. Watch over him please. He must be in terrible danger because he would never willingly leave me like this."

Annie wondered if Dr. Smith knew about this place. And she got even more upset thinking how Sarah and Catherine would be frantic with worry about her. Finally, completely exhausted, she fell into a deep sleep.

Early the next morning, Sister Muriel came to help Annie get out of bed. She walked her down the hall to the bathroom. "Walking is good for you. You must be strong for the sake of your baby."

Alone in the bathroom, Annie opened the casement window and looked out at the rolling hills covered with a light layer of snow. Normally, she would say a prayer of thanksgiving when she looked at nature's beauty. But at the moment, she was much too angry at God.

Back in her room, she found a bowl of warm oatmeal with apples and raisins and a cup of hot chocolate on the dresser. She ate it all - for the sake of her baby. And as she ate the warm food, she made up her mind to cooperate with the nuns, at least for a while, until she got stronger. Then, she would figure out a way to escape.

Sister Muriel came back to check Annie's blood pressure and listen for the baby's heartbeat. "Dr. Harrison from town will be coming out next week to examine you," she said, smiling at Annie.

After a few days in her room, Annie felt strong enough to join the other expectant mothers for lunch in the dining room. And that same afternoon, Sister Rita summoned Annie to her office for a counseling session.

The Mother Superior's first question was about the father of Annie's child.

Annie answered honestly, "Keith is a soldier in Europe and he's missing. He doesn't even know about the baby. If he knew, he would never leave me - no matter what. His mother and his sister wanted to take care of me but my father sent those awful men to bring me here to this prison."

"Why would your father want you to be in a prison?"

"To keep me out of sight! My sins embarrass him. He's a dangerous gangster, you know. You should be very careful because everyone's afraid of him."

"Are you afraid of your father, Annie?"

Annie took a few minutes to think. "Yes, a little. I'm afraid of what he might do to Keith. And I don't know why my father doesn't like Keith or why he's always so unhappy. But I won't give up my baby no matter what he does or says."

Sister Rita leaned over and took Annie's hand. "I promise you that I'll make inquiries about your Keith Brandon and I shall also investigate the allegations of kidnapping that you made. But in return, you must promise me that you will eat and rest and take care of yourself. Now go and join the other girls."

Chapter 32

Annie decided to take care of herself and her unborn child. She participated fully in the structured life at the convent. Sister Rita assigned Annie to the kitchen where she helped Sister Vincent bake the convent bread.

If the girls felt up to it and the weather allowed, they would take walks after lunch and then rest in their rooms for an hour or so.

With the good food, the fresh air and lots of sleep, the color soon returned to Annie's cheeks and she started to gain weight. And Annie joyfully announced to everyone that she felt her baby move and kick inside of her for the first time.

But still Annie held back, not wanting to trust or get too close to any of the other girls or the nuns. Sister Muriel checked her blood pressure and the baby's heart beat every day. "Ah what a miracle life is. Your baby is growing and seems to be very active."

Annie, at eighteen, was older than most of the other girls. One girl, only fourteen told of being raped by a friend's father. Another, sixteen, related a tale of seduction by a friend of her mother. The man promised to take her away with him but then disappeared when he found out about the baby. Another beautiful young girl of sixteen shared her story of deep love for a boy at school. But his parents sent him away to live with relatives in Europe and paid her parents a large sum to send her to St. Gerard's so that her baby would be adopted.

At Annie's next counseling session, Sister Rita greeted her with a hug. "Oh my but you're looking wonderful, Annie."

"Sister Rita, may I use your telephone? I want to let Sarah know where I am and ask her if she has heard anything about Keith.

"I'm sorry, Annie, but that's not possible. Our girls have no communication with the outside world. Society can be cruel to unwed mothers and talking to someone outside might put one of our expectant mothers in real danger. Not many know of the true nature of our mission here. Please try to understand."

Annie looked down, an expression of bitter disappointment on her lovely face.

Sister Rita took her hand. "I've made inquiries about your Keith Brandon."

"You did?" Annie instinctively held her stomach, protecting her baby.

"First of all – there is an alarming lack of information regarding your young man or, to be more precise, a wall of secrecy. I believe that Sergeant Brandon is alive. If he were dead, there would be no point in all the subterfuge. And I learned also that everyone thinks highly of him. I believe, as you do, Annie, that such a young man would never abandon you or his mother and sister."

"Keith would never willingly leave us. And I know in my heart that he's alive. I would feel it if he were not."

"And I spoke at length with your father about your being brought here under nefarious circumstances. I implored him to allow you leave St. Gerard's – to be cared for by Keith's mother and his sister." Sister Rita shook her head. "But he refused and legally I can't go against his wishes. Even though you are now eighteen, you are still considered a minor in this state. And I'm sure that is why he sent you to this particular home for unwed mothers."

Annie's shoulders slumped, the hope in her eyes vanished. "Thank you. You kept your promise," she said, dejectedly.

"I will continue to try to find out more about Keith and I will do everything I can to help you keep your baby." Sister Rita smiled. "You'll see. I can be a strong ally and a fierce adversary."

Annie threw herself into the quiet, structured life at St. Gerard's. At night, when the weight of the baby stopped her from sleeping, she'd imagine that Keith was there, lying next to her. And she'd say his name over and over so that their baby would know it.

Other girls gave birth and left the convent. Annie thought often of those girls, living in a cruel world, pretending they never even had a baby. She vowed, "That will never happen to me; no one will take my baby."

Chapter 33

Months passed. It was mid-July and uncommonly hot for Maine – even for the height of summer. Annie was cleaning up the kitchen after breakfast when she felt a sudden weakness. She ran outside into the garden. A sharp, cutting pain swept through her body, so intense that it literally pulled her to the ground. She felt a thick wetness on the of her thighs.

"Help!" Annie tried to yell but only a whisper came out. She crawled toward the infirmary as the awful pulsating agony enveloped her entire body. Then she felt someone or something lift her off the ground.

She heard a voice at the end of a dark, dark tunnel say, "Put her on the table. I'll need the forceps."

Annie screamed, "No!" and then there was nothing, just a dense, whirling blackness. Annie's labor lasted only ten or fifteen terrible, treacherous minutes.

Annie heard a baby crying. As she opened her eyes, she saw Dr. Harrison talking to Sister Rafael and Sister Muriel. "What you did here is nothing short of a miracle."

"I think we may have had some Divine help," Sister Rafael said.

"Oh, I'm sure of it," Sister Muriel added.

Sister Rafael took Annie's hand. "Your son is beautiful but he does not look at all like you. He's got black hair and dark blue eyes."

Annie looked over at the portable bassinette but she couldn't see the baby inside. She tried to sit up. "Andrew," she said. "His name is Andrew."

The giant convent handyman came into the infirmary.

Annie remembered him being near her when she fell to the ground. She motioned for him to come closer. "It was you who carried me in here."

He nodded and smiled slightly.

"You saved my life," Annie said as she reached out and took his huge hand in hers. "Thank you."

Sister Rafael's sharp voice cut through the room like a knife, "Joseph, we're going to move Annie and the baby to the room behind the chapel." She pointed to the bassinette and Joseph quickly pushed it outside.

"Most of our girls are afraid of Joseph."

"Oh, no, I'm not. He saved my baby's life."

"Yes, he did." Sister Rafael said.

The nuns made Annie and Andrew comfortable in the room behind the Chapel. Joseph brought Annie's meals to her on a tray and Sister Muriel checked on her regularly.

After four days, Sister Rita came to see Annie and Andrew.

"Sister Rita, isn't my Andrew beautiful?"

"He's just gorgeous." The Mother Superior agreed but then her tone and demeanour changed as she said, "I've spoken with your father and he's coming here tomorrow. He claims that there may be a way for you to keep your son. Annie, you do know that I'm trying to do what I can to help you. As it is, my letting you stay here at the Convent with your baby is against convent policy."

"I know that you are taking risks to help me. And I'm very grateful. I planned to run away right after the birth but I didn't plan on the hemorrhaging and being so weak."

"Well I suggest that you listen to what your father proposes and we'll go from there. And I'm working on some other options as well; like placing Andrew in a temporary foster home until you can take care of him – but, if your father insists on adoption, then . . ."

"When my father sees Andrew and realizes that he is a grandfather, I'm sure that he will relent." Annie smiled. "How could he not?"

"We'll see, dear."

Later that day, Sister Rita escorted Desmond to Annie's room and left father, daughter and grandson alone together. Annie sat propped up in bed holding Andrew who was snuggled securely in a blue receiving blanket and wearing a blue cap. "Daddy, oh Daddy, look at your grandson. I knew you'd change your mind when the time came."

Desmond, stern and unsmiling said, "You look well, Annie, brazen as ever without even the sense to be ashamed."

"Maybe I'm just really tough, like you," Annie replied, smiling, trying hard to charm her stern father.

"You and that Mother Superior are a pair and she'll get a talking to from her superiors. I guarantee that."

"If you don't want your own grandson, then why are you here, Daddy?" Annie asked curtly. "Is there news about Keith?"

"No, that lout is still missing and, I hope, dead, by now. I came all this way to give you a chance since you want to keep that bastard baby so much. But I'll not have people talking about my daughter being an unwed mother. You'll need to be married if you want to keep the child."

"I don't understand."

"Liam Fogerty is willing to marry you and give that little bastard a name."

Annie looked sick.

Desmond shrugged. He looked older, his hair totally white and his shoulders rounded. "I don't know why he wants a 'used woman.' But I do know that, if you refuse him, then I will sign the adoption papers. There's a devout couple down in the lobby waiting to take him, even as we speak."

Little Andrew made smacking noises with his mouth, moving his head from side to side searching for Annie's breast.

Tears rolled down her cheeks as she spoke barely above a whisper, "Okay, I'll marry Liam Forgerty."

"Well that's the first sensible thing you've said in a very long time," Desmond commented as he walked out and closed the door behind him.

Annie lifted her bed jacket and put Andrew's tiny mouth to her breast as the hungry infant sucked ferociously. "It's okay, Andrew. We'll be just fine."

Chapter 34

Sister Muriel brought Annie a pink, tent-like dress with a little pink veil. "I'll take Andrew down to the chapel while you get dressed."

Annie slipped the pink dress on quickly and put the tiny veil on top of her thick blonde curls. She left her room behind the chapel for the first time and met Liam Fogerty in the hall.

He wore a navy suit with a crisp white shirt and a blue tie. Staring at Annie through his thick dark framed glasses, he inquired, "Annie, my love, how are you?"

"Liam, why are you doing this?"

"You mean why am I willing to marry you after you made your feelings for me known and then gave birth to another man's child? Hell, doesn't every marriage start out like this?"

"Why?"

"Well, it's not because I'm madly in love with you or anything like that."

"Obviously." Annie's sarcasm matched Liam's.

"This marriage can work for both of us. You want to keep your son and I need a family image until I get through med school. And there's money involved, support for both us, uh, I mean, all three of us."

"I can't be a real wife to you, Liam. Not ever."

Liam smirked. "Oh no, and I was so hoping you'd teach me some new sex moves."

Annie looked shocked.

"Come on, Annie – you're an unwed mother now so it's a little late for you to act like some innocent virgin."

"What are you getting at?" Annie said harshly.

"I have all the women I want. There's only one thing you have to do."

"And that is?"

"Pretend that you're madly in love with me in public and never, never humiliate me. In private, we will be nothing more than business partners – roommates so to speak."

"Why do you need an image?"

"I've made a few mistakes. That's all you need to know."

Sister Rita and Father Henley, from the local parish, joined them. "Are you both sure about this marriage?" Sister Rita asked.

Liam gave her a mocking answer, "Ah Sister, I've always been in love with Annie and I don't care how much she has sinned."

Sister Rita glared at Liam. "I can place Andrew in the infirmary and delay this marriage."

The clueless Father Henley sanctimoniously inquired, "Liam, can you truly accept another's child according to the example of St. Joseph?"

"Oh yes, Father Henley. I intend to be the ultimate surrogate father."

Sister Rita said, "I would prefer to postpone this wedding for at least a month."

But Liam got angry. "No, that's not possible. I'm missing critical classes right now and I must get back to med school in Houston - with my wife and son."

Sister Rita looked at Annie. "Are you sure, Annie?"

"I'm sure."

Inside the chapel, Desmond, his driver Tommy Shay, Boss Garrigan and Fiona Fogerty were settled into the front pew. Sister Rita joined Sister Muriel, holding Andrew, in the second row right behind them.

Despite the second-hand pink dress which was much too big, Annie looked beautiful.

The ceremony was brief, just an exchange of vows. When Father Henley pronounced Annie and Liam husband and wife, Liam leaned over kiss Annie but she swooned, almost falling to the floor in a deep faint.

Sister Rita broke Annie's fall. "My dear, are you alright?" She searched with her right arm deep inside her voluminous black skirts. "Ah, here they are," Sister Rita whispered as she retrieved the smelling salts.

Annie choked and coughed.

"Dear child, I fear that you are not strong enough to travel."

"No, I'm fine, really. With all the excitement, I forgot to eat breakfast. Don't worry. I'll be alright."

Sister Rita helped Annie into the parlor, sitting her in a comfortable chair. Then she went to the buffet table and brought her some tea sandwiches and a glass of water with lemon juice.

Desmond and Liam talked while Fiona and Boss Garrigan sampled the simple buffet, chatting amiably with the other nuns and Father Henley.

Liam approached Annie as soon as Sister Rita left her side. "You've already broken the terms of our agreement."

"What do you mean?" Annie asked looking up, her face a ghostly white.

"You humiliated me by fainting when I tried to kiss you. That hardly makes me look like loving husband."

"Oh no, Liam, my fainting had nothing to do with you," she replied, taking his hand in hers, feigning affection for others to see.

"That's better, Annie. But this first screw up will still cost you."

Desmond called Liam aside and gave him an envelope - a payoff - just like all the other payoffs Desmond had made over the years.

Annie looked over to see Liam's mother holding Andrew and she began to tremble. But she inched her way across the room to Desmond, "Daddy, please take me and my son home with you."

But Desmond answered contemptuously, "You made your bed, Annie, and now you must lie in it."

Sister Rita overhead what Desmond said but it was too late. Annie was now Mrs. Liam Fogerty and Andrew Fogerty was now legally Liam's son.

PART IV

TAYLOR UNIVERSITY

HOUSTON, TEXAS

Chapter 35

Annie, Liam and Andrew changed trains several times while enduring the 1600 mile, 26 hour journey.

And all the while, Annie and Andrew spent the entire trip in private compartments never even seeing Liam who spent all his time in the club cars, playing blackjack and drinking.

When at last they arrived, they walked fast through the Houston station. Liam leaned over to Annie and pointed at a female passenger. "Annie, see that old gal over there. She played blackjack with a bunch of us guys and literally cleaned me out. But, luckily, I used my wits and won it back. Traveling by train is really fun, don't you think, Annie?"

Annie nodded, too tired to answer honestly.

But there was something about the way Liam looked at the woman that made Annie uneasy.

As they stepped out of the air-conditioned station into the suffocating humidity of a Houston spring day enveloped Annie.

Liam hailed a cab to his apartment near the Taylor University Campus Hospital. The two-story, garden apartment complex consisted of three long buildings that surrounded a huge kidney shaped swimming pool.

Children splashed and giggled in the shallow water while adults swam in the deep end and others lounged around the pool, laughing and talking.

Liam led Annie up the concrete stairs and along the balcony protected by a wrought iron fence to a door marked "Fogerty."

Retrieving the key from his pocket, Liam unlocked the door and pushed it open. "I assume that you don't want me to carry you over the threshold," he said, sardonically.

While showing Annie around the small two bedroom, two bath apartment, Liam pulled off his tie and shirt and took a cold soda from the refrigerator.

The apartment was bare, the living room led to a small alcove with a bedroom and bath on either side. One bedroom had only an unmade double bed with clothes scattered on the floor. The other held a single bed, a crib, a big box and a baby carriage.

"I arranged for a crib and some stuff," Liam said. Pointing to the big box, he continued, "Your father shipped your clothes. You'll need to lose weight to get into them because there's no money in our budget for a new wardrobe."

"Thank you, Liam."

"What?"

"I mean it. Thank you for the carriage and the crib. That was good of you."

"Yeah, well, I need to get to the hospital. I'll have to make up for the time I lost so I won't be here for a while. But, when I am here, I'll be studying, so you'll have to keep Andrew quiet."

Liam stripped off the rest of his clothes and stood naked in front of Annie. "Don't look so concerned. I'm not going to jump your bones. I get all the sex I want from women who don't faint when I kiss them." He went into his bathroom, closed the door and turned on the shower.

Annie put Andrew on the cot to change him.

Freshly shaved and dressed in khaki pants and a white hospital jacket, Liam appeared at the door to Annie's room, looking amazingly rested. "There's some cash for food in the kitchen drawer to the right of the sink. You'll need to manage carefully. This is a business deal so do your part if you don't want anything to happen to your precious little Andrew."

Annie thought she heard wrong. "What was that you said Liam?"

"You heard me correctly. And clean this place up. It's a mess."

Liam left the tiny apartment slamming the door behind him.

As Annie nursed Andrew, she wept.

When Andrew fell asleep in her arms, Annie took him into her bathroom and laid him on the floor on top of some towels, too frightened to even leave him in the crib while she showered.

After her shower, she slipped on a nightgown from her box of clothes and walked around the apartment with Andrew sleeping on her shoulder.

The tiny kitchen had a small Formica table with two metal chairs, an avocado green stove with matching refrigerator that held nothing but four bottles of soda and some rancid Chinese take-out.

And then Annie saw it on the kitchen wall – the white rotary-dial telephone. Her heart pounded as she picked up the receiver, almost screaming with joy at the sound of the dial tone. She dialed zero. "Get me the long distance operator please."

When Annie heard Sarah say, "Hello," her heart almost stopped beating.

"Sarah, it's me, Annie."

"Annie, where are you? Give me the number you're calling from – quick - in case we get disconnected."

Annie read Sarah the number from the center of the dial and then tried to tell her all that had happened, "Sarah, I, I . . ."

"Annie, are you hurt? Where are you? I'll come to you."

"I have a son, Keith's son. He's sleeping in my arms right now."

She told Sarah everything.

And then she asked, "What have you heard about Keith?"

"Mom talks to people in Washington every day. But still there is no news."

"Can you ever forgive me for marrying Liam? His name is on Andrew's birth certificate. Our son's life is a lie."

"Mom and I went crazy with both you and Keith gone. The police even threatened Mom because she suggested that your Dad and Garrigan might have kidnapped you. Dr. Smith went crazy with worry. Oh, Annie, it's been so long."

Andrew began to stir. Soon he'd need to nurse again.

"I love you Sarah. I have to go now and feed Andrew. I'll call you again, soon."

The next day Annie struggled and finally got the stroller down the stairs. She asked two women who were talking at the bottom of the stairs for directions to the nearest food store.

"Hey, you're Liam's wife. Welcome, Darlin'! I'm Karen and I live right next door. My husband Fred is in Liam's study group."

"Hi, I'm Annie, Annie Lynch, I mean Annie Fogerty."

"Well, Annie, you wait here while I get my son into some dry clothes and we'll walk together over to the market." Karen's voice was gentle with a sweet, lyrical Texas drawl.

"That would be so great. I don't know anything about Houston," Annie answered, grateful for the company as well as the directions.

They walked to the Minimax Supermarket just three blocks away.

"Darlin', you just pick out what you want, pay for it and they'll deliver it within the hour."

"You're kidding? That's great."

"Liam didn't tell you anything, did he? That putz! You know I was the one who signed for those big boxes that came from New York. Fred put them inside Liam's messy apartment. And then we decided to put the crib and carriage together for you. Needless to say, we were shocked that Liam needed baby things. He never said a word about a wife and child."

"We decided quite suddenly - about the wedding – after the baby," Annie said cautiously, unsure of what Liam would tell people.

Karen looked long and hard at Annie, "You're lovely, you know, and not at all the kind of girl I pictured for Liam. I predict that you and I are going to be great friends."

"I think so too," Annie said as she smiled for the first time since the wedding. And after that, Annie and Karen truly were best friends.

Days passed and Liam didn't come back to the apartment. On Saturday morning, Annie heard the doorbell ring for the first time.

She opened the door to see Catherine and Sarah standing there.

"We took a red eye from New York to Dallas and then we got a commuter plane to Houston," Sarah gushed as she grabbed Annie in a tight hug. But Catherine pushed past them both and ran to the crib where Andrew slept. "Look at that dark hair, just like Keith and Sarah."

Annie wept with pure joy at the sight of them.

"Go ahead Annie and cry it all out," Catherine said. "If only we could have gotten to you before they did. Esther Weinberg planned to hide you in her New York apartment."

"You and Andrew are coming back to The Glen with us today," Sarah said.

But Annie shook her head, obviously afraid. "Let's not talk here. Liam might come back or even listen outside the door. We'll go down and sit by the pool. That way I can see if Liam is in the area."

"When does he usually come home?" Sarah asked.

"I don't know. He's been gone since the night we arrived. And with any luck, maybe he won't come back at all."

Sarah laughed. "That's Liam Fogerty for you. People are always happier when he's not around."

Annie whispered, "I think he's really dangerous. And I can't go back with you, not just yet. I have to figure some things out first."

"Okay," Catherine answered. "whatever you say. But you can and you will take this money so you'll be able to leave when you're ready."

Annie nodded and wiped her tears as she accepted the cash. "It's so complicated. Liam is legally Andrew's father now – his name is on Andrew's birth certificate. If I leave him, he can file for visitation rights with Andrew."

Then Annie told them how Liam threatened to hurt Andrew. "I need to plan things carefully because I just can't afford to make any more mistakes. I've messed things up enough already."

"Oh no, Annie, you have done nothing wrong," Catherine said.

The three women talked for hours – mostly about the search for Keith and all the people who were helping. They went to dinner at a local barbecue place and Andrew slept in his carriage as they ate. That evening, Annie put Andrew in his crib and spread blankets and sheets on the living room carpet so the three women could sleep together on the floor. It was the first night that Annie felt safe since leaving St. Gerard's.

But the next morning when it was still dark, the overhead light suddenly came on, glaring in their faces and waking them with a start. "Just what the hell is going on in my apartment?" Liam hissed, his faded blue eyes looking wide and huge behind the magnified lenses of his dark framed spectacles.

Annie jumped up. "Sarah and Catherine came to visit me."

"Well they'd better get out this morning. And you can leave with them, Annie. Go ahead – get the hell out of here. But my son stays here with me." Liam slammed the bedroom door behind him.

Around nine, Catherine and Sarah got ready to leave. Sarah arranged for a taxi to meet them at the entrance to the apartment complex.

Liam came out of his room. "I'm so glad to see you go that I'll even carry your bags down the stairs for you."

Andrew seemed to sense the tension, fussing and spitting up on Annie. She said, "You all go on. I'll be right behind you."

Liam carried two small bags to the curb at the apartment complex entrance, dropping them on the sidewalk. "Goodbye, ladies. Your precious Keith Brandon is probably dead but just on the off chance that he does show up one of these days, you be sure to tell him how beautiful **_my_ son** is."

Sarah gasped in horror as Liam so casually talked of Keith being dead. But Catherine just glared back at him.

Annie, with Andrew on her shoulder, arrived just after the dreadful remark.

And at that moment, the taxi pulled up to the curb. After a few quick hugs and sad goodbyes, Catherine and Sarah got in the taxi and it pulled away. Annie was alone again with Liam. He placed his arm around her and they walked back to the apartment. Liam smiled and greeted several neighbours along the way.

Back in the apartment again, Annie put Andrew in his crib. Liam came up behind her and grabbed her upper arms in a vise-like grip. He kissed the back of her neck and whispered, "If they ever come back, I will beat the shit out of you and drop that little runt of yours in the deep end of the pool."

Chapter 36

A terrified, Annie played her part. She was the perfect, loving wife of a busy medical student. And as much as everyone seemed to dislike Liam, they all liked Annie. People sometimes commented about Andrew's dark hair comparing it to Liam's fairness and Annie's blonde curls.

"Someone with dark hair in our gene pool from long ago, I guess," Annie would answer, laughing.

She could see by the angry expression on Liam's face that those remarks made Liam feel very uneasy – and ultimately angry. He often remarked, "You're doing your job well, Annie. I am viewed as a happily married man of virtue. But I hate that little bastard's dark hair."

As the weeks and months passed, Liam grew increasingly paranoid about how the Taylor University faculty and student body viewed him.

Annie never left Andrew alone with Liam. Whenever Liam came home, she'd take Andrew out by the pool to be with the neighbours. She felt safe with the neighbours around. Everyone living at the apartment complex had a connection of some sort to Taylor University. She put the money Catherine gave her in the bank and skimmed from the grocery money to add to it every week. And she applied for a passport for herself and Andrew. When it came by mail, she rushed out to put in a safety deposit box at the bank.

Early one morning Liam burst into the apartment and demanded that Annie make him breakfast.

"You're a great cook, Annie."

"Thanks."

"But you can't seem to manage money."

"What are you talking about?"

"Look at this telephone bill. You can't take care of my son if you are always on the phone. So I cancelled the long distance service."

Annie felt as if an arrow had just gone through her heart. But Sarah and Annie worked out a plan. Sarah would call Annie. If Liam happened to be home when she called, Annie would say, "No I don't use that product," and hang up immediately.

It became obvious to Annie that Liam was struggling with his studies. And, true to form, he blamed Annie and Andrew for his less than stellar grades.

Liam told Karen next door, "A wife and baby are a distraction. Annie tricked me into marrying her by getting pregnant. But still I flew back east to do the right thing because Annie was prepared to give our son up for adoption. I just couldn't go along with that."

Annie cringed hearing him say that. But she smoothed things over with a smile and a change of subject.

Karen commented to Annie one day when they were sitting by the pool, "Liam likes to make himself sound noble. But I've seen him . . . well, forget it."

"You've seen him do what? Go ahead, Karen, what were you going to say? You've seen him with other women?" Annie asked.

"You know?"

Annie nodded.

"And you don't care, do you?"

"No. I don't care."

"Do you want to talk about it?"

"No, Karen, I can't talk about it now. But I need your help. I read in the campus newspaper about a tuition-free Practical Nursing program at Taylor Hospital and it requires only morning classes for a year. I thought I might get an LPN license."

"Annie, I saw that notice. The admission test is tomorrow morning. Why don't you leave Andrew with me and give it a try?"

"Thanks, I really appreciate your help."

"That's what friends are for, Annie. And we are friends. And, you know, I can take care of Andrew in the morning while you're in training and you can take care of Eric in the evening when I'm at work."

"I didn't realize you worked in the evening," Annie said, surprised.

"I manage an upscale restaurant in The River District. Everyone at Taylor has dinner there at some time or other."

"Oh that would be a wonderful arrangement, Karen. But Liam won't like it."

"Probably not. But Liam will go along with it because he won't want Fred or anyone else to think that he's less than 'super-wonderful'." Karen imitated Liam's pompous mannerisms, as she spoke and made Annie laugh.

Annie was admitted into the LPN program. And, predictably, Liam resented Karen and Fred for intruding into his life. But the unexpected upside was that this baby sitting arrangement between Annie and Karen caused Liam to spend even less time at the apartment. The downside was that it caused Liam's hostility toward Annie and Andrew to escalate.

Chapter 37

Houston's tortuously hot, humid summer morphed into a warmer than usual fall. And it was now almost two years since Keith Brandon vanished.

Annie thought about Keith as she studied and cared for Andrew. She asked Liam if he wanted to visit his mother back east for Thanksgiving or Christmas, hoping she could see Catherine and Sarah and possibly even disappear to Esther Weinberg's apartment in Manhattan.

"I'm too busy to go home. Studying medicine is hard. I'm not majoring in emptying bedpans like you, Annie. But we do need to make a showing at the holiday functions here at Taylor."

Christmas at Taylor University Hospital meant faculty receptions and their annual Christmas Dance at The Rice Hotel in downtown Houston.

Liam seemed worried and confessed, "I need my teachers to pull for me so you'd better charm them Annie. Get a new dress and line up someone to watch the brat. Say, you look tired. Maybe you should give up those nursing classes."

"I'm fine and I will not give up the class. Don't worry - everything will go well for you at the holiday parties."

Annie wore a new black halter dress to the Christmas Ball. It showed off her tanned back. Her short-cropped blonde curls, bleached out by the Houston sun, damp from the humidity, nestled tight along the back of her long graceful neck. Everyone noticed as Liam showed her off like a prize race horse, holding extra tight as they danced almost every dance.

She hated the feel of Liam's body and the touch of his hands on her bare back.

"Remember this is strictly a business arrangement," Annie said, pulling away. "Let's go over and say hello to Dr. Debann. He's pretty high level, - isn't he?"

Liam followed, but then pulled Annie back before she could talk to the doctor. "Excuse me guys but I've been at the hospital so many hours this semester that I hardly ever get to see my beautiful wife. Let's dance, Annie darling."

"Can't we sit at least one dance out?" Annie pleaded, smiling sweetly.

But Liam pulled her close, whispering in her ear. "No we can't sit any dances out. But you might get an Academy Award for tonight's acting if you dance just a little closer to me. I want those old fogies to fantasize about me doing all sorts of things to your beautiful body."

Annie gasped in fear. She noticed that the pupils in Liam's eyes were huge and beads of sweat rolled down his face.

The festivities ended before midnight and the Rice Hotel emptied quickly. Everyone wanted to be fresh and ready for classes and rounds the next day. Fred and Karen walked back to the apartment complex with Annie and Keith.

When they arrived at the stairs leading to their second floor units, Karen's mother, who was babysitting for Andrew and Eric, came rushing down the stairs with little Andrew in her arms. "Thank God you're back! I tried to reach you at the hotel but they said you already left. Andrew is very sick."

Fred grabbed Andrew. "He's burning up and I don't like those blotches on his face. We better get him to the hospital right away."

Annie followed Fred who carried Andrew in his arms. They ran the two blocks to Taylor Hospital Emergency Room.

Andrew endured a spinal tap and blood tests before being placed in quarantine. He lay strapped to a board, with tubes forcing liquids and medication into his little body.

And Annie felt fear as she had never felt it before as she watched her baby son struggle to survive.

"Oh Keith," Annie cried to herself. "Our baby is so sick. Where are you?"

Karen came to the hospital twice a day bringing Annie fresh clothes and toiletries.

But Liam never came.

When Andrew was well enough to be moved onto the pediatric floor, Annie saw Liam in the hospital corridor. He glared at her, growling like a vicious dog, "Damn you, Annie! We missed the Christmas breakfast at the Dean's house because of that brat."

Annie turned and walked into the Ladies Room. While she was in the stall, two nurses came in and she overheard them gossiping. "That Fogerty is a piece of work hanging out at those strip clubs."

"Yeah, and he's high on something all the time."

Another time, as Annie walked the halls, she overheard two orderlies, "Fogerty is that intern who's humping the post-op nurse, that red-haired rich bitch."

"Yeah, and he's got a wife and baby."

Annie thought to herself, "Good for you Liam. Have all the women you want just as long as you leave me alone."

Andrew recovered completely. Annie went back to the nursing program, only missing a few days which she easily made up.

"Listen Annie," Karen said, "Mom has been taking care of Eric while you were with Andrew at the hospital and it worked out really well."

"Oh." Annie's face fell in disappointment. What would she do without the babysitting arrangement between herself and Karen.

"Hey don't get upset. My mom insists on watching Andrew in the morning – at least until you finish the LPN program."

"I couldn't impose on your mother like that."

"Eric loves Andrew and my son would be tough to handle without Andrew around to play with him. Come on, Annie, let the boys stay together with my mom."

Relieved, Annie smiled. "Okay but just until I finish up. And I'll babysit if you all want to get out together sometime."

"Great." Karen hugged Annie.

"What would I ever do without you, Karen?"
"Don't even think about trying to find out."

Chapter 38

A steady April rain fell on the morning when Liam stopped by the apartment to shower and change. Annie heard Liam at the door as she picked up the telephone on the first ring. Hearing Sarah's voice, she gave the usual signal, "I don't use that product."

But Sarah blurted out before Annie could hang up, "Keith is alive. Mom just found out that there are negotiations to get him released."

Liam walked toward Annie.

She put the white receiver back into its chrome holder, ending the call abruptly.

"Who was that?"

"Another one of those annoying sales calls!" Annie replied and then she ran to her tiny bathroom, locked the door and let the water run. Her hands trembled as she looked at herself in the mirror, took deep breaths and tried to calm herself.

When Annie came out of the bathroom, Liam stood in the living room waiting for her. He blocked her way back into the kitchen where Andrew sat in his high chair.

"Oh, Liam, I'm so sick to my stomach," Annie blurted out, "it's probably that nasty stomach virus that's going around the hospital."

Liam let her pass. "Well, in that case, I'm getting out of here. I don't need to be sick with qualifying exams coming up."

As the door closed behind Liam, Annie felt so faint that she had to hold on to the kitchen chair.

But as the news about Keith really sunk in, her initial moment of shock quickly turned into a joy so deep and satisfying that she laughed out loud.

Later that night, Sarah called again. "Keith is in a prison in Czechoslovakia. There are negotiations going on to get him released. He was sentenced to life as a spy but the negotiators feel that the charges will be dropped and that his release is only a matter of time."

The good news from Sarah seemed to be endless. In a call the next day, Sarah said, "Annie, a British priest, just released from that same prison telephoned Mom. He said that he met a young man at the prison who was fluent in English and German and that this young prisoner spoke endlessly about his fiancé and his family in The Glen."

"Keith mentioned me? Oh Sarah!"

Annie only had a few weeks of supervised nursing left before she took the qualifying exams for her LPN license. She purchased a ticket on the early morning Eastern Airlines flight from Hobby Airport to LaGuardia for May 15, 1960. She added the ticket to her money and passport in the bank safety deposit box. And a renewed strength flowed through her body and mind. Keith was alive and coming home. Annie felt that she could manage to do anything now.

Although Liam rarely spent any time at the apartment, he still insisted that Annie accompany him to any significant social events on campus. So when he came by the next afternoon, Annie was not alarmed. He slammed the door to the apartment and the noise startled Annie who was sitting on the couch reading to Andrew. Liam seemed to be angrier than usual.

He slapped Annie across the face. "Well, here's the lazy slut and her bastard son."

Andrew howled in terror and Annie knew in her heart that Liam suspected something. She wanted to leave that very day but she needed that nursing license in order to support herself and Andrew.

She took Andrew into their bedroom and closed the door. She could hear Liam showering and throwing things around in his room but she and Andrew stayed in their bedroom until she heard Liam leave the apartment.

Catherine and Sarah were ready for Annie's arrival on the 15th. They planned to meet her at LaGuardia and take Annie and Andrew to Esther's apartment in Manhattan.

When Annie passed the qualifying tests, everything fell into place. On the 14th of May, she pushed Andrew in his stroller to the Taylor Administrative Building to arrange for her diploma and LPN license to be sent to Esther's post office box in New York City.

As Annie walked into the office of The Dean of Nursing, Lillian Evans looked up at her. "Ann Fogerty. How nice to see you. Come in and let me have a look at your handsome son."

"Mrs. Evans, I came to drop off this form so that my license and diploma can be forwarded. There's a family emergency up north and I'm afraid that I'll have to miss the graduation ceremony."

"Oh no! I'm so sorry."

There was a knock on the door jamb. The two women and little Andrew turned to the open door. Dr. Jason DeBann, Director of Students, stood there. "Sorry to interrupt, ladies. Say, you're Dr. Fogerty's wife, aren't you?"

Annie nodded, hating it when people identified her in that way.

"We've never formally met but I know you by sight and by your fine nursing reputation. I'm Jason DeBann."

"I know who you are, Doctor. Everyone does."

DeBann, sixty, his skin leathery from years in the Texas sun, had blue eyes that sparkled with enthusiasm and charm. "And this is your boy?" He knelt on one knee to shake Andrew's hand.

Standing up, he leaned toward Annie and inquired, "I remember that he was very sick last December. How's he doing now?"

"He's just fine now. And I'm amazed that you remember him with all the patients you see."

"Well I have a special interest in him and in you. You know, I'm the one who's scheduled to present you with a well-deserved award at your graduation ceremony."

"An award?"

"Yes, recognition for your grades, your work, and your demeanour. Everything about your nursing is exemplary."

Annie bit her lip.

Lillian Evans interrupted, "I'm afraid Annie won't be at the ceremony. She has a family emergency back east."

"Oh, I'm sorry. Well, you go take care of your family. But when you come back I want you to continue in our Registered Nurse Program and then go on for a Bachelor of Science degree. And come to my office the very day you get back, ya hear, and we'll talk about getting you some scholarship money so you can finish your education."

"Yes, I'll do that. It is very kind of you, sir," Annie lied, knowing that she would not be coming back to Houston. She took Andrew up into her arms and left Mrs. Evans' office.

Outside in the hall Annie leaned against the wall for support, mumbling to herself, "Oh God, what if Dr. DeBann says something to Liam about the family emergency?" Her panic made Andrew cry.

"I'm sorry, Andrew, please don't be upset," she whispered, kissing him and hugging him tight.

Then Annie checked the Duty Roster and saw that Liam would be on duty all night. But he still might come to the apartment on his break so she'd have to be very careful. She stopped at the bank to get her money, passport and ticket and close out the safety deposit box.

Andrew fell asleep in his stroller on the walk back to the apartment so Annie carried him up the stairs. She stopped at Karen's apartment and knocked on the door.

When Karen flung the door open, Annie put her finger to her mouth. "Shhh, Andy's asleep but I need to talk to you."

"Come in, darlin'. Eric is down at the pool with my mom."

"I need a favor."

Karen raised one eyebrow. "Intrigue?" She closed the door gently so as not to wake Andrew. "Please tell me that you're having an affair with a dashing prince and that you're leaving Liam. Spill it, girl! You know I'll do anything for you!"

"I'm not having an affair but I am leaving Liam. I need you to keep this stuff for me." She handed Karen a plain paper bag. "It's money and stuff. I'll come by for it early in the morning on my way out. I don't dare chance Liam finding it in the apartment."

"Okay, darlin', you come over as early as you want." Karen's expression turned serious. She threw her arms around Annie. "Oh, darlin', I've noticed so many things. And I can't help myself anymore – hell, I'm just gonna be downright nosey. Is Andrew Liam's son?"

"No, Andrew is not Liam's son."

"That's what people are saying and the gossip is driving Liam even crazier than he normally is. Fred suspects that he is heavy into drugs. We've been worried sick about you and Andrew."

"Fred's instincts are right. And I intend to get Andrew as far away from Liam as possible."

"I've heard him yelling at you. These walls are paper thin, you know."

"It's a long story," Annie said. "When I realized that I was pregnant, Andrew's father was overseas and we couldn't get married. So my father forced me to make a deal with the devil or else he'd put Andrew up for adoption. He arranged this sham of a marriage so Liam could parade me around the Taylor campus and look like a family man."

"Well, everything is becoming clear now. You being married to Liam never made any sense. But you know, here at Taylor University, morality is as important as grades. And I hear that Liam is on the fence in the morality area. He seems to have quite a past."

Andrew stirred. "Momma."

"I have to go," Annie said. "He's hungry and thirsty." She kissed Karen on the cheek and went off with Andrew in her arms to their apartment.

Annie's whole body tensed. She knew as soon as she opened the front door that Liam had been home. There were dirty dishes in the kitchen sink and dirty laundry strewn about on the floor.

She fixed Andrew lunch and cleaned up quickly.

Then she and Andrew went down to the pool for a swim. It would be Andrew's last chance to splash about in the shallow water with his friends.

Later that evening, after a light dinner of scrambled eggs with cinnamon toast and sliced apples, Annie and Andrew went to sleep early.

It must have been around two in the morning when Annie woke up sensing a presence in her bedroom – an evil presence. Liam clamped his big, sweaty hand over her mouth and whispered, "Get up."

Annie reached for her robe but Liam yanked her by the arm, pulling her out of the bed. Grabbing both wrists, he dragged her out of the bedroom and closed the door. The room was dark except for the glow from the apartments' outdoor lighting that seeped into the room along the edges of the window shades.

Annie tried to pull out of Liam's grip. He pushed her and she fell onto her back on the floor. Leaping on top of her, straddling her body, he put his face up against hers. Then he covered her mouth with his hand. Biting his hand, Annie squirmed and struggled to get out from under him.

"Oh how sweet, Annie. Are you trying to give me little love bites." Liam mocked her and put his mouth roughly on top of hers, his tongue penetrating deep into her throat almost choking her. "If you don't stop moving, I will beat the shit out of that bastard in the next room."

Annie stopped struggling. "What do you want?"

Liam put his face close to hers. "I think what I want is rather obvious."

"No, we agreed that you would not touch me. This is a business arrangement."

"But you broke all the rules, Annie." Liam rubbed her breasts, squeezing her nipples hard as he spoke.

"I was here in the apartment today when a British priest called to talk to you – a real friendly sort of guy. He told me all about a prisoner in a communist jail. That fool priest actually asked me to have you call him. He said that he's heard a lot about you - from – guess who? – a man named Keith Brandon."

Annie forced herself to be calm. "So what! That's old news, Liam. I've known for a long time that Keith is in a prison behind the Iron Curtain."

"Really?" Liam took both of her wrists in one of his big hands and pinned them down onto the floor above her head. "Now, now, Annie, I told you that terrible things would happen to you if you ever humiliated me again."

"I didn't tell anyone about Keith. I didn't humiliate you, Liam."

"Liar! Dr. DeBann stopped by the Emergency Room to tell me how disappointed he is that my lovely wife can't be at her own graduation. And I'm sure he has it all figured out by now. It was obvious that I knew nothing about your upcoming trip or your so-called family emergency."

Annie's face flushed with fear. "I just don't want to go to the ceremony. I lied to get out of it."

"You said those things because you're planning to leave me. You know Annie, the only reason that you have your son is because I married you. You got what you wanted out of this deal but you didn't keep your end of the bargain. Instead, you made me look like a fool every chance you got."

"You're making yourself look like a fool, Liam. But I'm not leaving you. How can I?"

Annie pushed at Liam's body, trying to move, but he was too big and heavy. His grip on her hands cut off the circulation and the nylon carpet scratched against the skin on her back and her bare heels.

"I'm going to hurt you real bad, Annie. But, I'm such a good guy that I'm going to give you one chance to keep Andrew from getting hurt."

He let go of Annie's hands.

Annie stared up at him not moving.

Liam reached into his hospital jacket and took out a needle. Holding the needle close to Annie's face, he said, "See this? Now, if I inject you with this, I won't have to hold you down and I can do whatever I want to your lovely body."

Liam laughed and continued to threaten Annie. "But what fun would that be? I want to enjoy the terror in your eyes and see you writhe in pain. Now, I can inject Andrew with this and he's so small that it might just stop his little heart. Or I don't have to use this at all. So you tell me, Annie. What do you think I should do?"

"Liam, please don't hurt Andrew. I'll do anything you want."

Liam smiled. "I thought you'd say that, Annie."

He unzipped his pants, exposing his penis.

"Suck on it Annie. Make me really hot."

Annie shook her head no.

Liam placed his hands around her neck and squeezed lightly. "Do it or I'll inject Andrew with this needle."

Annie did as she was told. Liam became engorged, panting and moaning. Suddenly Liam pulled away from her, moving into the shadows.

The apartment was quiet.

Annie thought that Liam was done with her. She cautiously rolled over onto her stomach and slowly got up on her knees.

But just as she was about to stand up and run, Liam grabbed her from behind and ripped off her nightgown. Holding her hips, he slammed himself inside of her and pounded into her over and over again like a wild bull with a cow. Her knees and feet burned as Liam pushed and pulled her back and forth on the rough nylon carpet. Liam kept on ramming into her for what seemed like forever until he finally uttered a guttural moan and dropped Annie's limp body onto the floor.

Annie could hear Andrew crying out for her. Lying face down on her stomach, she frantically felt around the floor for the needle. She grabbed it and shoved it under her body to keep it out of sight.

From her vantage point on the floor, she could see Liam's shoes coming toward her in the dark. Suddenly, she felt a fierce pain, heard a terrible cracking sound, and then fell into total darkness.

When Annie woke, Karen and Fred were both kneeling over her.

"Where is Andrew?" she screamed.

"Be still, Annie." Fred said, concentrating on stitching her forehead.

Karen spoke softly, "Annie, Annie, be still. Andrew is fine. Let Fred finish stitching those cuts."

Annie cried out in pain when she tried to move, "My ribs."

Fred felt her right side. "That bastard must have kicked you. I think your rib is broken – maybe even two ribs."

"I'm calling the police," Karen said.

"No police!" Annie replied in a panic. "I have to get Andrew out of here. Where is he?"

Karen said, "Hush darlin', he's next door with my mother. The door is locked and he's fine."

Annie struggled to get up. "Help, me, please. I need to get dressed."

Fred stopped her. "We really should report this."

"Fred, he's my husband. They won't do anything about a husband raping his wife. You know that."

Fred nodded in agreement as he helped Annie stand up. "Karen is going to help you shower and put something on those rug burns."

Karen got Annie cleaned up, put petroleum jelly on the rug burns and helped Annie into some clean clothes.

Fred gave Annie several teaspoons of a pink liquid. "Here, swallow some of Eric's antibiotic. You'll need to take triple his dosage."

"That creep should get life in prison for doing this to you," Karen said bitterly.

"He should, but he won't. Domestic violence is not even considered a crime," Annie said.

"Until it becomes a murder. We'll get you to the airport and then I will have to put in a report." Fred spoke matter-of-factly. "Liam is bad news normally but he's been spinning out of control for weeks now. I hear that Taylor University put him on suspension and rightfully so. He doesn't belong in medicine."

"He doesn't belong anywhere. He doesn't deserve to live." Karen said.

Annie spoke in a weak voice, "We see women, who've been beaten up by their husbands all the time in the hospital emergency room, don't we Fred?"

"Yep, we do. I hate to see you travel in this condition but I'm more afraid for you if you stay."

Karen ordered Fred, "You help her down the stairs, Fred, while I get Andrew and her personal things. Mom already called a taxi."

Fred and Karen rode along in the taxi with Annie and Andrew to Hobby Airport. Annie took only the clothes on their backs, leaving everything else behind.

At Hobby, Fred helped Annie out onto the tarmac and carried Andrew up the metal stairs onto the Eastern Airlines plane. "Keep taking deep breaths Annie. I know it hurts with the broken ribs but, if you don't breathe deeply, you'll get pneumonia.

"Those rug burns will sting like crazy but they'll heal. Karen called Sarah. She and her mom know what to expect when they see you at LaGuardia."

Fred gently placed Andrew in the window seat and backed into the aisle so Annie could take her seat. "So long Andy. You and your mom are going to be with people who love you – just like me and Karen love you."

Andrew stared ahead, his eyes wide in fear.

"Thank you Fred. I love you and Karen," Annie whispered.

"Listen, Annie. This is very important. I wrapped that full needle in tin foil and put it in your purse. Get it to a lab and have it analysed. It's evidence that you may need one day. The police may not arrest him for raping his wife but they just might arrest him for stealing drugs."

"I'll do that. I promise."

Annie barely moved during the flight and Andrew slept soundly in the seat beside her.

PART V

NEW YORK CITY

Chapter 39

At LaGuardia Airport, a stewardess carried Andrew off the plane. Annie followed them, barely able to walk.

"Oh my God!" Sarah burst into tears when she saw Annie's face.

Catherine quickly masked her emotions, smiling at Andrew as she took him from the stewardess. "It's okay. Your mommy is going to be just fine.".

Sarah instructed the cab driver to take them to the Upper East Side of Manhattan. They pulled up at Esther Weinberg's elegant apartment building where the doorman helped them get from the cab to the elevator. At the seventeenth floor, the door opened into the foyer of Esther's magnificent apartment.

Esther yelled, "Ansha, darlink. No, no, I'm so sorry to see you like this. Just like during the War. These monsters destroy the innocent and face no consequence."

Annie wept when she saw Dr. Smith sitting quietly in Esther's spacious living room, waiting to examine and treat her.

Sarah made Annie comfortable in the guest bedroom. She folded back the purple velvet bedspread and placed soft white bath towels on top of the satin sheets.

When Annie was ready, Dr. Smith came into the sun-filled bedroom. Sitting on a chair beside the bed, he took Annie's swollen, rug-burned hand in his, delicate black fingers. "How's my favorite patient today? I spoke at length with your neighbour, Fred and we decided it would be best to treat you here in Esther's home to keep everything quiet. But if I run into any serious complications, I won't hesitate to hospitalize you. Okay?"

Annie nodded.

Dr. Smith examined Annie's injuries while Sarah watched, ready to help any way she could. "Your body will heal in time but it will be hard for you to get past the emotional part of all this."

He checked the stitches in black thread on Annie's forehead. "Fred did a fine stitching job but I'm afraid that there will be some small permanent scars. And I'll continue you on that same antibiotic that Fred gave you – only in pill form."

Sarah put an ointment on Annie's rug burns and laid her head back onto the plethora of satin covered pillows.

Dr. Smith spoke softly, "Now, tell me everything that happened last night. It's very important."

Annie recounted every horrible detail while Dr. Smith took copious notes.

She suddenly remembered something and struggled to sit up. "In my purse, over there, on the floor. Fred gave me the needle that Liam threatened me with and said to have it analysed."

"Wonderful - I'll take care of that." Dr. Smith retrieved the needle from Annie's purse and slipped it into his pocket.

"Now - I have two concerns - the possibility of Liam transmitting a disease to you and the possibility of pregnancy."

Annie answered, "This was the first time Liam did anything sexual. But I do know that he used condoms because I'd find them in his pockets when I did the laundry. I really don't know if he wore one last night."

"Well, the fact that he was in the habit of using condoms means that he, at least, protected himself from disease - so maybe we'll get lucky."

Annie nodded but there was still a look of terror on her swollen, bruised face.

Dr. Smith handed Annie a glass of water and a pill. "This is for the pain. I'll be back in a few days. But call me if you need me."

Sarah curled up next to Annie on the bed until Annie drifted off to sleep.

Catherine took Andrew for a walk over to Central Park using a stroller that Esther borrowed from her maid, Rosa Santos.

Then Esther wrote out a schedule to be sure that Annie would never be alone in the apartment. "Rosa, will be the main caretaker for Annie and Andrew but you are all welcome to visit or to relieve Rosa at any time."

Sarah offered to visit Annie and Andrew every night after work. "It's a short ride by bus for me from 46th Street. Mom can't come. She has to be careful. Desmond or Boss Garrigan's men may be watching her and we don't want Liam to know where Annie is. And she also needs to be close to home to keep up with what's going on with Keith."

"Don't worry, it is my joy to have Ansha here with me and, if need be, I'll hire extra help. Rosa has lots of friends and family who would love to help."

The next morning, Rosa Santos arrived early and took complete charge of the situation. She lived up on 114th Street in a two bedroom apartment with her mother, father, a brother, and a married sister with two small children – all recent arrivals from Puerto Rico. She adored the idea of working for the famous Esther Weinberg and she immediately fell in love with Annie and Andrew, fussing over Annie as if she were a broken doll.

Andrew became smitten with Rosa, imitating her lyrical Spanish accent by using *"si"* and *"gracias"* and *"por favor."*

Esther's work schedule consisted of performing every evening except Monday and doing matinees on Saturday and Wednesday. A sought-after guest, she usually attended some gala or party after the evening performances.

A few afternoons after Annie's arrival, Esther came back to the apartment, accompanied by the doorman who carried several shopping bags.

"Annie, darling, Rosa brought some clothes for Andrew that her nephew outgrew, but you, my dear, need some clothes.

"Esther, you are just too kind. But I can't accept this," Annie said.

"These are gifts. Please let me spoil you a bit, as if you were the daughter that I lost so many years ago. I think of you that way."

"I didn't even know you had a daughter. What happened?" Annie asked.

"In Vienna, before the war. It was a terrible time and she got lost."

"Is that why you were so sad when you first came to The Glen?"

"Yes, my darling, that is why. And you reminded me so much of her – with your blonde curls. But I love you because of you – your kindness, your intelligence," Esther said.

Annie smiled up at her old friend.

About a week later, Reggie Smith came to see Annie. "Wow this place is fantastic. I can't imagine living like this."

"Isn't it lovely," Annie said. It was her first day to really get dressed since her arrival. She wore red slacks, a black sweater and fuzzy white slippers – all gifts from Esther.

"So glad to see that you're up and getting around so well." Reggie kissed Annie on the forehead. He noticed the swelling and the rug burns on her face.

"So you've got your own law practice in the Bronx now," Annie said, tired of all the talk about her injuries.

"I do. You know how it is for me – it's difficult for a genius to work for anyone else so I'm on my own. And I've already begun your divorce process, Annie. But you need to sign all this stuff. Custody of Andrew is going to be a sticky issue so I'm not filing anything until we get you and Andrew out of harm's way. With Liam named as Andrew's 'father' on the birth certificate, we need to walk a fine line."

"Andrew can't be alone with Liam for even a minute – no visitation whatever – because Liam will hurt him. He told me that he would – and I believe him."

"Don't worry we'll get this straightened out for you. Liam really doesn't have any interest in Andrew."

"This is all my fault. I should have run away and not married Liam. It's my fault that Liam's name is on Andrew's birth certificate."

Reggie smiled. "If I had nickel for every father's name that is false on a birth certificate, I would be a very rich man. "We're getting you and Andrew out of the country."

Annie looked frightened.

Reggie said, "You can do this, Annie. Good thing you got that passport. You will stay with a friend of Esther's in Bamberg so you'll be right there when Keith is released."

"You're all so wonderful to me. I'll repay all of you. I promise."

"We're your friends Annie and we don't want to be repaid." Reggie leaned over and hugged her gently. "Just get stronger."

"I feel stronger just talking to you," Annie said as she smiled at Reggie.

Annie and Andrew fell into a happy routine at Esther's apartment. Rosa tapped into her endless familial source of toddler equipment and toys, securing a wooden playpen for Andrew to sleep in. And her cousin, Salvador, came to the apartment to reinforce the iron bars on all the windows to keep the curious little Andrew from toppling through the screen when he looked down at the street, seventeen stories below.

Esther usually got home well after midnight and slept until noon. The she'd wake and eat her breakfast while Annie and Andrew ate their lunch.

"I look forward to these meals together, Annie."

"Me too, Esther."

"You and Andrew chase away all my sadness. I adore having you here."

"I survived in Houston because of my wonderful friends. And I owe my friends here so much as well. I feel so alive here in New York City with you."

Esther pushed Annie's curls back from her face, to check out the stitches on her forehead. "I hate these scars. Nothing could make you look bad, Annie, but I hate to see a permanent reminder of Liam's cruelty."

"It's okay," Annie said.

"When I came to The Glen just before you were born, I vas a crazy woman." Esther's English was perfect now and quite elegant. But her accent tended to reappear if she became stressed.

Tears ran down Ether's cheeks as she talked. "It vas you and Sarah and dear sweet leetle Keith, you three innocent children, who made me whole again."

"Have you ever told anyone about what happened to you and your daughter?"

"No, even Catherine doesn't really know. I was very young when I left my parents' home in Czechoslovakia to perform in the Vienna Symphony."

Esther sighed, "I fell in love with a powerful musician, and, unfortunately, a married man. We had a daughter. It was a very dangerous time for Jews like me. He said that I should go to Switzerland with the baby – that he'd help me escape over the border. But as he drove me toward the border, he stopped the car and pushed me out onto the street."

Esther wept now. "He drove off and I never saw my daughter again. The underground found me, injured and miserable. It was they who got me to Switzerland. And so, you can see vy I vas truly out of my mind when I came to The Glen."

Annie nodded, "I'm so sorry." She took Esther's hand and kissed it. "Did you try to find your daughter when the war ended?"

"Yes, I went to Europe and I used every agency available and all my powerful friends to search for her, only to learn that she was killed in an air raid."

"Oh Esther, no."

"You know, vhen you vere a baby, I'd pretend that you were mine. You vere a motherless child and I, a childless mother. It was a only game of pretend but it helped me to get through a very bad time. And now, all these years later, we are truly close friends."

Annie threw her arms around Esther. "Yes, we have a very deep friendship now."

When Annie was strong enough, Reggie and Sarah took her to lunch at the Tavern on the Green. They sat in the garden room, with its walls of glass that looked out onto the park and its many chandeliers that resembled huge floral bouquets.

"This is so lovely. I've never seen anything like it." Annie said.

Reggie added, "Yes this is a most unique place. And we wanted to talk to you in peace and quiet. Not that I don't enjoy Andrew but he does limit conversation."

"Just a bit." Sarah agreed, rolling her eyes.

Annie nodded. "Yes – well it's really just been me and Andy but now he has so many people – a true audience for his antics. He adores Rosa and he was so excited to go to her nephew's birthday party. He's never done anything like that."

Reggie ordered the special of the day for everyone, quiche with endive salad. When they were almost done, he told Annie what he had in mind. "Listen, Annie, things are going to come to a head with Keith pretty soon. If you are in Germany, you will be there for him when he gets out. And I'd feel better with you and Andrew out of the country because I can't legally stop Liam from getting visitation. Don't get upset, but he has already filed a petition to the court for a week's visitation in Houston."

"Oh, no – he can't – he doesn't want to see Andy. He just wants to hurt me by hurting Andy."

"I agree. And that's why we are getting you out of the country."

Annie looked from Sarah to Reggie.

Sarah took the tickets from her purse. "We have tickets for you and Esther has a friend in Bamberg who can provide you and Andrew with a room."

"How can I ever thank you!"

Reggie took Annie's hand, "You're a brave girl, going off to a foreign country like this on your own."

"Keith will be with us soon. I can't wait for him to see Andrew." Annie looked at Sarah. "And I am not expecting anything from Keith – I know things may have changed – not for me – but maybe for him. Still, but he has to know his son."

"Annie, things will never change between you and Keith."

"I hope not." Annie looked pensive.

Reggie stood up, ready to go. "You'll be safe in Germany while you wait for Keith and he'll be thrilled that you are there for him. And I won't have to produce Andrew. No one will be able to serve you with a subpoena."

They walked out of the lovely restaurant into Central Park and strolled along a winding path that led them to 59th Street.

Annie noticed that Reggie and Sarah held hands.

Annie had spent two wonderful months recuperating at Esther's New York apartment. She knew now that Liam's attack had not left her with either a sexually transmitted disease or a pregnancy. She felt free of Liam finally.

And now she was strong enough to leave. She hugged Esther and then Rosa, both of whom cried openly.

Sarah hugged Annie so tight that they both squealed. To Annie, Sarah was everything - her sister, her "girlfriend," her confidante and mentor. But most of all, Sarah was a strong link to Keith.

Annie tearfully said goodbye to Catherine.

"I will fly over as soon as Keith is released. I'll see you in a few weeks – it can't be too soon," Catherine said, hugging Annie and then Andrew.

Too long a goodbye would only be painful - so Annie took Andrew's hand and followed Reggie into the elevator without looking back.

But Andy looked back, blowing kisses to everyone.

Reggie accompanied Annie and Andrew to Idlewild Airport in Jamaica, New York where they boarded a Pan Am flight to Munich, West Germany.

PART VI

BAMBERG,

WEST GERMANY

Chapter 40

Esther's friend, Helmut Rodiger, an American attorney working for the State Department in Munich, met Annie and Andrew at the airport. Recognizing them both from Esther's description, Helmut called out, "Hello, Annie, over here, yes, yes, I'm Helmut." He walked over to Annie, smiling. "It's my great pleasure to meet you."

Helmut guided Annie and the exhausted, very cranky, little Andrew through Customs. Speaking fluent German, he engaged the aid of a porter to carry their bags out to his car.

As they drove out of the airport, Helmut said, "So you will be living in Bamberg for a while." He maneuvered the car onto the highway and accelerated the vehicle to a very high rate of speed.

"Yes," Annie replied, holding tight to Andrew, not at all used to riding in a car, and certainly not used to such high speed.

Helmut calmly chatted, pulling his car out into the left lane from time to time to pass other cars and then back into the right lane in front of them.

"Moving here was quite a challenge for my wife and children. Munich is not Boston or New York and my wife is anxious to meet you and help you with the transition."

"What a kind offer. I can't wait to meet her," Annie replied, feeling extremely uncomfortable as the car sped its way down the new two lane highway.

"And our dear friend, Esther, made arrangements for you to have a room at the Riveredge Inn in Bamberg. Maria Vanderhorne, the owner, is another friend of hers."

"Esther knows so many people – all over the world," Annie commented.

"Yes, she is quite a woman. You and your son will be comfortable and safe at the Riveredge. The rooms are big and the café serves wonderful food."

Annie smiled, hiding her trepidation.

When Helmut introduced her to Maria Vanderhorne, all Annie's fears disappeared. Maria's loving eyes sparkled and her soft voice soothed both Annie and Andrew.

"Velcome, Ansha," Maria said, leading Annie down the hall to the very last room at the back of the Inn. It was large with a double window, lace curtains, a huge brass bed and a crib in an alcove at the far right side of the room.

"There ees bathroom across da hall dat is shared by only three rooms – and both are presently empty. You vill eat at the café any time you like."

"It's lovely," Annie said, holding Andrew's hand as she looked around. She walked over to the window that looked down over a path and then the river.

Maria said, "So, freshen up or vhatever, and ven you are ready, come to de café for some food, yah, dear?"

Annie nodded. "Thank you."

Alone in the bedroom, its walls covered with a faded, pre-war floral wallpaper, Annie peeked at herself in the big mirror above the oak dresser. The bruises and the swelling were gone but she could still feel the pain and the overwhelming fear. The stitches in her forehead had been removed but a cluster of small scars remained, covered most of the time by Annie's overabundance of unruly blonde curls. No one looking at her would ever guess what she had been through. But deep inside, in her heart, there were deep scars that refused to heal until she could be with Keith again.

Chapter 41

In the very early hours of June 25, 1960, a hand touched Annie's shoulder, waking her from a sound sleep. "Anika, eez telephone for you."

"Maria, you frightened me."

"Ze man on ze phone - he say ees urgent."

Annie instinctively checked to be sure that Andrew was asleep in his crib. "Okay, I'm coming. It better be important to wake us up in the middle of the night like this." She didn't bother with slippers or a robe but ran barefoot down the long hall to the lobby and picked up the black receiver lying on the reception desk. "Yes, this is Annie Lynch. Who is this?"

"It's Captain Lawrence. We have Keith. He's okay. Just sit tight and wait for more information." There was a sharp click and then nothing.

Annie clutched the receiver to her heart.

"Vhat es 'appen?" Maria asked.

"That was Keith's commanding officer. Keith is free. I don't know how or where."

"Such gud news." Maria hugged Annie. "You're shivering. Go to de bed now, yah? Ze morning vill bring more news."

"I'm sorry your sleep was disturbed, Maria."

"Eez okay as long as de news is gud. Und now you vill sleep, yah?"

"I'll try." Annie walked down the hall to the back of the small hotel. Closing the door to her room, she went to Andrew's crib in the alcove. Carefully, she slid the side of the crib down and picked her sleeping son up into her arms.

She gently placed him in her bed and snuggled up beside him, beneath the warm comforter. She kissed his head and whispered, "Your daddy will be with us soon."

But when Annie closed her eyes and tried to sleep, images of Keith and Andrew together played out in her head like a silent movie.

Listening to the steady rhythm of Andy's breathing and his occasional faint snore, Annie began to imagine Keith lying there with them, his arms tight around her. But, it wasn't until every possible thought about Keith and every conceivable prayer of thanksgiving passed through her mind that the merciful stupor of sleep finally overwhelmed her.

Andrew woke up early, happily surprised to find himself in his mother's bed.

"Momma, I sleep here," he said, hugging her.

"Good morning. I overslept a bit so we'll have to rush now."

Helmut Rodger had pulled a few strings and secured a part-time nursing job for Annie at the Bamberg Clinic. She loved the job and Andrew loved the day-care center nearby.

Annie slipped into a freshly ironed white uniform and put on her white stockings and white nurse's shoes.

But Andrew sensed something different about this particular morning. He refused to dress. Annie had to gently coax her son to put on his shoes.

And down the hall in the café, Andrew dawdled over breakfast.

When Annie finally kissed Andrew goodbye at the Kindergarten Day-care Center next door to the Bamberg Clinic, he pitched an uncharacteristic tantrum.

Annie felt frazzled. She got to work late. And by now, she had a wicked headache. So, of course, it turned out to be an unusually busy morning at the Clinic. The time flew by and, mercifully, her mind was just too occupied to think much about Andrew or Keith.

Near the end of her half-day shift, the floor nurse rushed up to her, "Annie, you need to report to Colonel Nolan's office on the main floor. Go now, dear, I'll finish up for you."

Annie knew that Colonel Nolan was the head of the Psychiatry Department. She'd seen him around the hospital but had never actually spoken to him.

When she got off the elevator, she saw Colonel Nolan pacing in the hall outside his office. He was a tall, grey-haired man in his early fifties. "Ah, you must be Annie?"

They shook hands.

"It's good to meet you, Colonel Nolan."

"Come in. I hope it's okay if I call you Annie?" He pointed to a big tan leather chair in front of his desk. "Sit down."

She sunk into the chair.

"Do you prefer Annie to Mrs. Fogerty?"

A hot blush inched up Annie's neck. "I use my maiden name, Lynch. But this must be about Keith. When can I see him?"

"But Fogerty is your legal, married name, isn't it?"

"Yes it is. Where is Keith now?"

"Sergeant Brandon is recovering from corrective surgery on his leg. And he's doing remarkably well."

"Surgery? Why? Take me to him! Please!"

"That's not possible right now. But rest assured that he is getting excellent medical care. You can see him in a few days when they transport him back to his unit here in Bamberg."

"Please, can I at least talk to him on the phone?"

"Not just yet. I have some concerns."

"Concerns?"

"Yes, concerns about you and Keith."

"I don't understand. Doesn't Keith want to see me?"

The colonel sat back, staring at her. "I didn't say that." He looked down, rifling through some papers on his desk. "Sergeant Brandon's life has been on hold for a long time. My job is to help him adjust. So you and I, as well as his mother and sister, need to work together."

"Of course."

"Then you'll answer my questions? I understand that you're close to Keith's family?"

"Keith's mother and grandmother raised me. He and Sarah are my best friends."

"Yet Keith does not know that he has a son?"

"I didn't know about the baby until after Keith went missing."

"Yet you married Liam Fogerty and it's his name that is on the boy's birth certificate."

Annie hesitated, not eager to share the story. "Andrew was born at a home for unwed mothers where babies were routinely put up for adoption. I only agreed to marry Liam so that I could keep my son, Keith's son, from being adopted."

"Let me get this straight: your son is biologically Sergeant Brandon's child but you are still legally married to this Liam Fogerty who, according to his birth certificate, is legally your son's father."

"You make it sound sordid."

"Those are the facts," Colonel Nolan retorted.

"I have filed for divorce. And I hope to get an annulment later on."

Colonel Nolan sighed. "Another problem – as Catholics you'll need an annulment. Surely, you understand what a mess this is for Sergeant Brandon."

"The mess, as you call it, exists because Keith was snatched away from his own life."

The colonel leaned forward. "If you want access to Sergeant Brandon while he's here in Bamberg, you'll have to go through me. Now, your son's name is Andrew Fogerty, right?"

"You obviously already know that Fogerty is the name on my son's birth certificate. But Andrew is Keith Brandon's son. All you have to do is look at him to know that."

"So, I've heard. Okay, that's all for now. You can go back to work."

"Please, let me see Keith," Annie pleaded.

"You'll see him in a day or two. And, when you do see him, keep things light, no histrionics. Don't press him for decisions and do not ask him about his time as a prisoner. Do you understand?"

"I understand." Annie bit her lip

"I'll be in touch." The Colonel dismissed her.

Annie stood, walked toward the door and then turned back looking at the Colonel.

"Dr. Nolan. I don't intend to make any demands on Keith. But he has a right to know his son."

She was at the door of the colonel's office when she heard him say, "Sergeant Brandon has been asking for you, Annie. Be patient for another day or two."

Annie smiled, knowing that whatever test the Colonel had just given her, she had evidently passed.

Chapter 42

July 7, 1960. - day four since Sergeant Keith Brandon walked across the no man's land at the Moldareith Border Crossing between East and West Germany with Soviet guns at his back. And, today, Keith was being transported back to Bamberg to rejoin his unit. The Bamberg Base Emergency Room overflowed with personnel eager to welcome back one of their own. The steady hum of animated conversation had an upbeat tone. And above the heads of the crowd, wide streaks of the late afternoon sun beamed through the ceiling high windows bestowing an almost spiritual quality on the usually dull, sterile atmosphere.

Catherine and Sarah Brandon waited with Annie Lynch, surrounded by a sea of uniforms. Annie was so excited that she could barely breathe. Yet, even here, half a world away, she still feared that Liam Fogerty might harm her young son, Keith's son.

Annie felt a kinship for the beautiful, orderly city of Bamberg. Like Annie, Bamberg kept the dark secrets of its past buried deep beneath a classic beauty and an outward calm. She checked her watch and nervously brushed her unruly blonde curls back off her face. "He should be here by now."

"It's not even three o'clock yet. Be patient." Sarah, calm, smiled at Annie.

"Sarah, it's so wonderful to see you. I've missed you so much."

"Mom and I have missed you and Andrew."

Just then, a harsh buzzer rang out and the huge emergency room doors opened outward, revealing a brown army ambulance, parked carelessly, back doors open and still swinging. Two attendants pushed a gurney toward the entrance ramp.

As the stretcher crossed the threshold into the Emergency Room, a roar of applause and raucous whistles erupted. The gurney made its way through the crowded room, being stopped every few feet by someone wanting to shake Keith's hand and wish him well.

At last the gurney reached Annie, Sarah and Catherine.

Keith looked up at them. He reached up to touch Annie's face just as she took his hand in both of hers and pressed her lips into his palm.

"You're really here, Annie. Every night I saw your face close to mine but, when I tried to touch you, it was just my mind playing tricks."

Keith's gaze moved from Annie to his mother, to his sister, and back to Annie again. Catherine wept and Sarah made the sign of the cross.

Words were inadequate.

A voice from behind called out, "Let's keep things moving. We need to get the Sergeant settled in."

Keith's hand slipped from Annie's grasp and the gurney moved on, disappearing into a maze of hospital corridors.

"Sarah, go on ahead. I'll catch up with you." Annie ran to get Andrew from the nurses who had been kind enough to watch him at the reception desk. She scooped her little son up into her arms and buried her face in his soft, wet neck, kissing him over and over until he squealed in delight.

"My momma!" he yelled.

"My Andy!" she answered. "Now we have to catch up with Grandma and Auntie Sarah."

Catherine and Sarah had joined a young corporal and were following him into the elevator. "Y'all come with me to Sergeant Brandon's room." he said.

Annie noticed the patch on the corporal's shoulder was the same patch that Keith wore. He led them to the fifth floor, then down the hall and stopped in front of a room marked PRIVATE.

"Y'all wait here. It'll just be a few more minutes."

But Andrew grew restless. "Dr. Nolan may be a great shrink for soldiers but he doesn't know a thing about toddlers," Annie confided. "This is just too much for him."

Catherine nodded in agreement. "Darling, come for a walk with Grandma, okay?"

Andrew ran to Catherine and they walked down the hall together. Catherine chatted with him as they waved to patients in the rooms where the doors stood ajar.

The door to Keith's room opened and a young nurse emerged. "Okay, ladies, Sergeant Brandon is all yours now."

Sarah put her hand on Annie's back. "You go in. Mom and I will let Andrew run off some of that energy. We'll be along in a few minutes."

"But, we're supposed to go in together."

"Go!" Sarah smiled, giving Annie a gentle push.

Annie entered the room and walked slowly over to the bed where Keith lay flat on his back, his right leg encased in a thick plaster cast, elevated in a sling. He smiled, watching her come closer. His striped cotton pajamas had the right leg cut out to accommodate his cast.

Annie knelt on the chair beside his bed, resting her head on his pillow, their faces almost touching. "You smell of soap and shaving cream," she said, feeling awkward.

Keith looked deep into her eyes and whispered, "Things went so wrong but the worst part was not being able to tell you what happened." He took Annie's face in both his hands.

"Your Mom and Sarah and I - we went insane with worry. There was something in the newspaper about a soldier who wandered across the border and, somehow, we knew they were talking about you. But we also knew that you would never, could never, get lost."

"It's going to be a while before I can tell you about it."

"I know. We've all been briefed and prepped."

Keith ran his thumb over her lips.

Annie leaned in close and kissed him.

She ran her finger over his mustache. "So this is new. How come?"

"I was a hairy, lice-ridden mess who had to be deloused and shaved but I figured I'd keep the moustache to impress you."

"Well, I am impressed."

"Impressed enough to marry me right here, right now, or tomorrow morning at the very latest? We've already lost so much time."

"I intend to marry you, Keith Brandon, so don't think for one minute that you'll be getting out of it. But you need to get stronger."

"Get up here on this bed and I'll show you how strong I am," Keith teased.

Annie laughed.

"I missed your laugh so much. The guards in that hellhole would taunt me. They said that my girl forgot all about me and married someone else."

"I could never forget you, Keith."

"I know. It was your sweet love that kept me alive."

Keith made a gesture of ownership, brushing Annie's hair back, away from her face and he saw the cluster of scars on her forehead. "What happened?"

"Oh, nothing, just a clumsy fall."

Keith was about to question Annie more when Sarah came into the room. Catherine followed behind her, holding Andrew in her arms.

Keith stared at Andrew and the intensity of his gaze frightened the boy. Andrew wiggled out of Catherine's arms and ran to Annie. Grabbing her tight around the legs, he peeked out at Keith from his vantage point of safety. "Dis my Momma."

Instant comprehension flashed on Keith's face.

Catherine stuttered, "Well, from the mouths of babes, eh? Here we all struggled to find the right way to introduce you to your son and Andrew did it all by himself."

Sarah teased, "Andrew is very much like you, Keith darling, only much sweeter."

Annie pulled herself free from Andrew's grip and lifted her little boy up into her arms.

Tears formed in Keith's eyes as he motioned for Annie to bring Andrew closer.

"Hi, Andrew, my name is Keith. I'm a soldier and I've been away for a while. That's why I couldn't meet you until now. But I want very much to be your friend. Hey, look at this plaster thing on my leg. Do you think you could draw a picture on it? It's kind of boring the way it is now."

Keith's suggestion interested Andrew.

Annie sat Andrew down on Keith's bed and gave him a crayon from her pocket.

The little boy scribbled his artwork on Keith's cast, smiling and looking to Keith for approval.

"That's so great. This big clumsy thing looks much better now," Keith assured Andrew.

But Andrew couldn't stay with one activity very long. He wiggled off the bed and lunged full speed at Sarah who picked him up while almost falling backwards.

"How about some ice cream?" Sarah asked..

"Yes, yes, yes!" Andrew yelled, looking to Annie for permission.

Annie smiled and nodded a yes.

"We'll see you later," Sarah called over her shoulder, carrying Andrew out of the room.

Catherine mumbled, "I need some coffee. Can I bring some back for you?"

Annie and Keith uttered perfunctory, disjointed replies, "Not for me," and, "thanks but no."

And then they were alone again.

Keith took Annie's hand and pulled her down onto the bed with him. Her head fell onto his chest as he wrapped her tight in his arms, burying his face in her curls, kissing her head over and over. "That shrink Nolan told me to be prepared for changes but I didn't expect a son! Our son!"

"Andrew is so like you, Keith. He's protective and affectionate and strong and good."

"I didn't protect you this time. I should never have let this happen. It must have been so hard for you and I can just imagine your father's reaction."

Annie shook her head, "Keith, listen. Andrew is not something that happened to me. We created him out of our love for each other."

Keith's dark blue eyes pierced her soul.

As Annie looked up at him, her body trembled with the raw, physical need for him.

Keith felt it and pulled her even closer.

"Keith I never let myself think of how much I needed you. I was afraid that I might slip over the edge into madness. So I put everything into keeping Andrew safe. But now you're here with us and . . ."

Keith kissed her nose, her chin, her eyes. "I'm just thankful that you had Mom and Sarah . . ." he whispered. And then his mouth covered hers in a long, penetrating kiss.

Annie shuddered, knowing that by this time tomorrow Keith would know that his tormentors were right. She had married another man.

Chapter 43

It sounded like a grenade exploding. Annie jumped. Keith's body tensed. "What the fuck!"

A dinner tray on wheels hit the door to his room so hard that it forced it to slam into the wall. And right behind the tray, a nurse walked into the room, her grey hair pulled back into a bun, her starched white uniform so stiff that it crackled when she moved.

"Sorry if I startled you. I could have knocked, but then this *is* a hospital, not a hotel."

Annie understood and eased herself off the bed. She recognized Captain Andrea Collins immediately. The woman was a living legend among Army nurses.

"Open wide, Sergeant," Captain Collins said to Keith as she retrieved a thermometer from her pocket and held it up.

Keith glared at her.

Coyly she said, "Sergeant, I outrank you."

Keith took the thermometer from her hand and placed it in his mouth.

Satisfied with his temperature, Captain Collins gave Keith a glass of milk from the tray. "Take these two pills." She glanced at Keith's chart and spoke at the same time. "Sergeant, your mother, sister, and that cute little boy, are dining in the cafeteria with Colonel Nolan so you two can dine here alone." She looked directly at Annie. "I hear that you're an excellent nurse so just be sure to maintain your professional demeanour while the Sergeant is a patient in this hospital."

Nurse Collins left the room, closing the door, gently and quietly, behind her.

"Who was that? The hospital bouncer? " Keith asked.

"Captain Collins. She's known for, um, well, handling difficult patients."

"Oh I'm going to be difficult for sure," Keith agreed, "because I'm goddamn sick of being a prisoner."

"Okay, Keith. But for right now, let's just eat something."

Annie lifted Keith's leg out of the sling and placed it on the bed. She went to the foot of the bed and cranked it up to a sitting position so that Keith could reach the food tray. And then she propped extra pillows from the chair behind his back.

"Captain Collins should have set you up to eat but I guess she wants to keep me busy nursing you and not kissing you."

"Well she and that shrink, Nolan, can go to hell. I want my life back and I want it now."

Despite his agitation, Keith ate well, devouring everything on his tray, even the ubiquitous green jello.

But Annie only picked at her dinner. "You'll be back at your normal weight in no time with that appetite."

"I've been hungry quite a lot and I've seen so many others go hungry every day. And what was that about you being an excellent nurse?"

"We have so much to catch up on. I took a practical nursing course and I work part time here at the clinic."

Keith looked uneasy as he began to realize how little he know about Annie's present life.

"Keith, we have a lot to talk about. But you're tired now."

"Can you bring Andrew to the hospital again tomorrow?"

"Darling, he's your son. I'll bring him to see you every day."

"No - just tomorrow! I don't intend to be here after that." Keith winced in pain as he pulled his body up on his arms, trying to reposition himself.

"Let me help you," Annie said. "I can be your very own private nurse." She moved the tray away and placed his leg back in the elevated sling while checking his toes for swelling.

Keith reached out and took her wrist in his hand, pulling her close to him. "Does being my private nurse include giving me a sponge bath?"

"You just had a bath. But that kind of teasing is a really good sign."

Keith yawned. "I think those pills are making me sleepy. Will you stay until I fall asleep?"

"Sure." And then, despite Captain Collins' dire warnings, Annie climbed onto Keith's bed and snuggled beside him. She clung to him like a kitten to the mother cat, savoring his scent, feeling his warmth, breathing in unison with him until he drifted off into a deep, drug-induced sleep.

Chapter 44

July 8, 1960 - day five since Keith crossed the border and his first morning to wake up in Bamberg since before he went missing. Groggy from the pain medication, Keith pressed the call button and asked for coffee. He struggled to get the heavy cast out of its sling and pushed himself up into a sitting position.

"Good morning, Sergeant Brandon." Captain Collins pushed an empty wheel chair into the room.

"You again? Don't tell me that thing is for me," Keith said rudely.

"Ah but it is. We're taking that heavy cast off your leg today and then you can take a hot shower. If your x-rays are good, then we'll fit you with a removable brace." Captain Collins said cheerfully.

"Great." Keith smiled at her for the first time. And he was still smiling when an orderly wheeled him back to his room, showered, shaved and fully dressed in his uniform.

Catherine and Sarah, who had arrived at the hospital early, waited patiently for him.

"Good morning," Keith happily greeted his mother and sister. "The heavy cast is off and I feel great." He looked around. "Where's Annie?"

Catherine kissed her son. "You look wonderful, dear."

"Yeah, the lighter leg brace is a lot more comfortable than the cast. When will Annie get here?"

Sarah replied, "This afternoon. She wanted to give us some time alone with you."

Keith nodded. "Oh I see. You're all manipulating me and taking turns to fill me in on things. Mom, Sarah, give me a break. I've been a prisoner for far too long. Please be honest with me."

"Okay, son." Catherine said.

"I can sense that you need to tell me some bad news. Annie alluded to the fact that there were things I 'should know.' So go ahead. Mom, you do the talking."

Catherine told Keith everything, from how they struggled to get information about him, to Annie's pregnancy, to the fury Desmond Lynch unleashed on her, right up to Annie's disappearance.

Sarah interrupted, "It was pure hell for us to have both you and Annie gone and not know where you were."

Finally, Catherine told Keith that Annie had been forced to marry Liam Fogerty. "There was no other way for her to keep Andrew from being adopted." Catherine's voice cracked, "Annie suffered the wrath of society and she was sold to a monster by her own father. Desmond called Andrew an 'illegitimate bastard.' It wasn't until after Andrew's birth that Annie was able to telephone us to tell us where she was and how she had made a deal with devil in order to keep Andrew from being adopted. She begged us to forgive her and she's worried now about whether you will forgive her."

Sarah cried, "Oh Keith, it was hell for Annie – and for you – and for us, too."

Keith looked down. "I'd like to kick Desmond's ass for treating Annie that way. And I'm sorry that I put you all through this."

"Son," Catherine whispered, "you're not responsible for any of it and neither is Annie. Garrigan's goons kidnapped her. They even came to the house and threatened me to make me stop going to the police to look for Annie. They said we owed back taxes and threatened to take the house."

There was a knock on the wall and Colonel Nolan leaned into the room, "May I join you?"

"Why not?" Keith replied sarcastically. "Let's all dig in and hash over the wreckage of my life."

"Keith, we're here to help you sort through all of this," Colonel Nolan said, sensing that this was a time just for family. "I just want to say that I'm here for you for whatever you need." He smiled at Catherine and Sarah, wished them a safe trip home and left, closing the door behind him.

Annie and Andrew ate breakfast in the café at the Riveredge Inn. Maria fussed over Andrew, telling everyone that he was her favorite guest.

Annie buttered a fresh roll for Andrew as she spoke, "We're going to the hospital later this afternoon to see Keith again. Would you like that, Andrew?"

Andrew looked unsure but he nodded yes. And he behaved very well all day, even taking an early nap.

It rained in the afternoon so Annie dressed Andrew in blue overalls and a navy blue sweatshirt with a hood. It was chilly enough for her to wear her brown corduroy slacks and a yellow sweater set. She hailed a taxi to take them across town to the Bamberg Clinic. Andrew stood up on the back seat and Annie held him tight as the taxi lurched and darted through the afternoon traffic. The occupation of Germany was obvious with more American Army vehicles on the streets than German cars.

At the Clinic, Andrew ran into Keith's room ahead of Annie. She watched from the doorway, as he threw his arms around Catherine and kissed Sarah. Then Andrew looked over at Keith, smiled and waved to him.

Keith was comfortable on the leather lounge chair with his leg stretched out over a matching ottoman.

"Hey Keith," Annie called out.

When Keith looked at her, she tossed him a small bag of potato chips, which he caught in mid-air, much to Andrew's delight.

Keith ripped the bag open, literally inhaling the chips. "These are great. The Commies don't have fun food. Hell, they don't believe in having fun." He turned to Sarah, "Hey, Sis, hand me the crutches, please?"

Sarah helped Keith stand up and gave him one crutch at a time until he could stand unaided.

Sarah and Catherine took Andrew to get some ice cream.

Keith walked over to Annie, dropped one crutch on the floor and pulled her close with his free arm. "I love you Annie. Can you ever forgive me for not being there for you?"

She threw her arms around him and buried her face in his chest.

"Keith, can you forgive me for not being stronger?"

"You kept Andrew safe. That's all that matters. It's hard for me to think of you living with Liam but I love you too much to care. And none of this would have happened if I had been there for you."

"I was never 'with Liam' – not the way you mean."

"Living together in the same apartment? You couldn't be like that and not . . ."

"In all that time, we never made love. Liam is not capable of loving."

"Those scars on your forehead - did he hurt you?"

"Liam is nothing. You're back now and it's over."

Keith whispered, "I'll kill him if he hurt you."

"Don't even think that way. You must never do anything that would take you away from us again." She couldn't hold back the tears. "I couldn't be apart from you again."

"Don't cry, Annie. Please don't cry. I'm getting out of here tomorrow. Mom and Sarah have to get home and so do we."

But Annie stiffened at the mention of "home."

"Andrew and I have a room near the Old Village. It's very spacious, with a great café and you can stay with us while we figure things out."

"As long as we're together, I don't care where it is," Keith said, relieved to have a plan in place.

Annie said, "Please don't hate me for marrying Liam."

"I could never hate you, Annie."

"I used to see all those shotgun weddings and those couples having babies much too soon after the wedding with everyone counting the months backwards. And I foolishly thought that was the worst that could happen to us."

"Are you still married to Liam?"

Annie nodded. "But it was never a marriage. Andrew and I were show dogs for Liam."

"Don't worry. We can handle anything now that we're together," Keith assured her.

"Reggie helped me file for divorce. But things are so complicated. Liam's name is on Andrew's birth certificate. Andrew's surname is Fogerty."

"It doesn't matter. He's my son." Keith kissed her. "So do I know everything now?"

But Annie didn't seem to hear the question and did not answer.

The next morning an army jeep dropped Keith off in front of the Riveredge Inn. Annie and Andrew were waiting out front for him and they walked Keith, who was maneuvering quite well on his new crutches, through the lobby and down the long hall to Annie's room.

Keith looked around. "It's nice."

"Maria brought the ottoman to the room this morning so that you can sit with your leg stretched out."

"I think I'll do just that."

Annie stuffed a bed pillow behind his back.

She hung up his jacket in the wooden wardrobe and started to unpack his duffle bag.

It was a bit cool for July with a crisp breeze that smelled of fresh cut grass and forced the long lace curtains to blow into the room.

"It's really nice, Annie. We can hear the sounds of the river."

"Yes, I love that sound."

Andrew showed Keith his newest toy truck.

"We'll be comfortable here until we go back home. Right Andrew?" Keith looked over at the crib in the alcove.

Andrew brought all of his trucks over to show Keith.

"I always played with cars and trucks as a kid. And these are great. Where'd you get this one?"

"Granna gave it to me." Andrew smiled.

Keith smiled back. "I used to call my grandmother, Granna, too."

After lunch, Andrew and Keith napped while Annie helped Maria set up a table in the café. Catherine and Sarah, out shopping in the Old Village, had plans to join them at the café for an early dinner.

Annie got back to the room just as Andrew woke up. She took him to the bathroom across the hall, bathed him and dressed him in a new outfit – a gift from Sarah. She carried a basin of warm water back to the room for Keith to shave.

"You've got your hands full with two babies," Keith said.

"I love taking care of my two men. Oh look at the time. They're probably at the café waiting for us. You and Andrew go on down to the lobby and I'll change. Can you make it okay on the crutches?"

"With Andrew's help, I can." Keith smiled down at his son.

When Annie got to the café, she peeked through the French doors at everyone sitting at the big table, laughing and talking. A great peace descended on her. It was a kind of happiness that she had not felt for a very long time. She felt sorry that Catherine and Sarah had an early morning flight back to New York the next day.

Keith struggled to get up when Annie joined them, but Annie put her hands on his shoulders. "Darling, don't get up, please."

"Annie, this café is wonderful. Now don't get too spoiled with all this service because it won't be that way when you're home in The Glen," Catherine teased.

"I can't wait to get home, Mom," Keith said.

Annie looked down and Sarah reached for her hand under the table. Even with all their time apart, Sarah always knew exactly what Annie was thinking.

They enjoyed the roast pork, buttered noodles and fresh string beans, topped off with apple strudel for dessert. But soon Andrew got restless. Sarah and Annie took him for a walk, allowing Catherine and Keith to finish their coffee and have some time alone to talk.

Sarah looked at Annie and asked, "You're afraid to come back, aren't you Annie?"

"Yes. I'm afraid that Liam will get visitation rights with Andrew. Even a few minutes alone with Liam could be deadly for Andrew."

"You've got to tell Keith everything. He needs to know."

"He's been through enough. And he feels so guilty as it is."

"Tell him. If he feels that he can protect you and Andrew, that may help fix that guilt he is feeling now."

"I'll try, Sarah."

"Take a week or two just to be together – the three of you. You need it."

"Sarah, things seem to be really good between us. I was so worried about how we'd be with each other but I know now that Keith still loves me."

"Of course things are good. You've loved each other forever. And I love you as well." Sarah hugged Annie and tears filled her eyes. "Come home to us soon."

Later on, Catherine and Sarah said their goodbyes in the lobby, "So long, for a little while, Keith. And just for the record, you are the best brother in the world and I love you."

"I love you, Sarah. We'll be home soon. I promise."

Keith, got clearance to travel almost immediately but Annie found excuses not to go home,

"Keith, let's stay at least until you finish physical therapy on your leg."

"Annie, we have got to get back home to America where there are private bathrooms and showers. This is quaint but . . . we need to go home."

Annie mocked anger. "Are you telling me that you don't want my sponge baths anymore?"

Keith laughed. "You can only bathe me for the next twenty years or so. Then, they just have to stop." He grabbed Annie and pulled her down on the bed beside him, kissing her neck and tickling her.

Andrew jumped on the bed with them. "Me too, Daddy, tickle me too," Andrew shrieked with laughter as Keith tickled him. And Annie uttered prayers of thanksgiving for the wonderful gift of hearing Andrew call Keith, "Daddy." But then she thought of how Liam tried to force Andrew to call him "Daddy" and how Andrew would put his head down and cry.

That night Andrew fell asleep on the middle of the double bed between Annie and Keith. When he was in a deep enough sleep, Annie carried him to his crib and tucked him in. She pulled the drape across the alcove opening and walked back to the double bed.

Keith reached for her and pulled her close. Even with his limited mobility, Keith made love to Annie with such intensity that he seemed to enter her very soul.

"We have this room for two more weeks and then I have a surprise for you. I booked us passage on the brand new liner, the S. S. United States. It will be like a five day honeymoon."

"Keith that sounds wonderful."

"And when we get back to The Glen, we'll stay with Mom and Sarah until we find a place of our own."

"I'm a little nervous about going back, Keith."

"But Annie, we can't just hang out. I'm not re-enlisting so I've got to get a job. I have a lot of back pay but still we need to start really living again– at least I do."

Annie smiled. "Okay, in two weeks, we'll go home. But for right now, let's just enjoy being here." She held him close. "All I dreamed about for the last few years was being next to you, listening to your heart beat."

"Annie, we got into such a mess. Me in prison and you forced to marry that miserable piece of crap. Your father hated me so much that I was always afraid he'd take you away from me forever. And he sure tried."

"My father hates everyone. I'll never forgive him for handing me and Andrew over to Liam. Still, I would live it all again, except for you being in a prison, just to get to where we are right now, the three of us, here, together."

"We're going to build a good life together," Keith whispered.

Satiated as well as exhausted, they fell asleep wrapped in each other's arms, not moving a muscle until Andrew woke up at five the next morning.

"Hush dear, let Daddy sleep." Annie slipped on jeans and a cotton tee shirt and took Andrew down the hall to the café. It was already crowded with early hikers and local residents buying fresh bread and rolls.

Andrew carried a white paper bag with fresh buttered rolls back to the room while Annie managed a tray with two coffees and a hot chocolate.

"Surprise! Breakfast in bed," Annie said, entering their room.

Andrew, never one to be still long, ate his roll while playing with his trucks all lined up along the window sill.

Keith said, "Our little Andy is by far the handsomest little boy I've ever seen."

"Oh, he is, he definitely is." Annie smiled, hugging Keith. "And he looks just like his father."

"I don't know," Keith teased. "He's much better looking than his old man."

Annie interjected, "The only difference is that his old man has a mustache and Andrew does not."

As they watched, little Andrew rubbed the skin just above his upper lip, not looking up, and then went on playing with his trucks.

Keith said, "I didn't even think he heard us."

"He hears and remembers everything. He's smart like his father," Annie replied, wondering if Andrew actually could recall anything about their life in Houston and that terrible last night.

Chapter 45

"Why are you so afraid of Liam knowing where you and Andrew are?" Keith asked Annie.

"Liam may demand that Andrew visit him in Texas. He is legally Liam's father and I don't know if I can face that."

"Annie, you don't have to face Liam alone anymore. I'll protect our son. You have to trust me."

"I trust you. But I put Andrew in this danger. I'm responsible for this mess. I should have just run away from that convent in Maine."

"I never saw you like this Annie. Stop the regrets. You did what you had to do. Who knows what your father and Boss Garrigan, might have done if you had not married Liam. And by the way, do you know why Garrigan is so involved with Liam?"

"No. I only knew that if Andrew had been adopted, we'd never be able to find him. Those records are sealed forever."

"Let's go outside for a walk. You always feel better when you're out in the fresh air."

They walked together along a worn path through the pines next to the river. Andrew stopped every few feet to pick up stones. Then, he'd look up at Keith and ask, "I keep?"

Keith would nod and say, "Sure, you can keep."

When Andrew discovered a red ball under a pile of leaves, he asked Keith to play catch. But it was Annie who had to chase all their missed balls and wild throws. "Hey guys, you're wearing me out." Annie collapsed, sitting down on a flat rock.

Andrew climbed onto her lap. "Momma's kisses tickle." He laughed, as Annie kissed his neck, making loud smacking noises.

Keith watched them smiling, "You were right, Annie. We needed this time here together before going home."

"You hear that Andy? Mommy was right. Now don't you forget that."

When they got back to their room, Annie found a telegram on the dresser. She tore it open. "Keith, it's from Reggie. I'm divorced. I'm free of Liam."

"Let me read it," Keith asked, "What's a 'quickie divorce' through Nevada?"

Annie shrugged her shoulders. "Who knows? I've never even been to Nevada. But if Reggie says it's legal, then it's legal."

"Reggie wants us back home to deal with the paternity issue." Keith took Annie in his arms. "How about we get married, here, right away?"

Andrew grabbed Keith around the legs. "Me too, me get married too?"

"Of course, you, me and Mommy - all three of us will get married."

There were no hitches with the paperwork because everyone at the Bamberg Base bent over backwards for Keith.

They opted for a simple ceremony at the Interfaith Chapel on Base. Maria Vanderhorne and Keith's C.O., Captain Lawrence acted as witnesses. Outside the Chapel, Annie fussed over and complimented her two men, kissing them tenderly as she gave her final approval of their appearance. "Keith, you look like a movie star and, Andrew, you are magnificent."

"What's mificent?" Andrew asked.

"It means handsome ten times over." Keith smiled, answering his son.

"Mommy, you're mificent."

Annie wore a street length aqua silk dress and matching pumps with the traditional Bavarian ivy and edelweiss crown. Keith placed it carefully on Annie's head and intertwined the white ribbon through her blonde curls. "My beautiful bride."

"This is a perfect wedding day," Annie said softly, pushing back tears as she thought back to that dreadful wedding ceremony at the home for unwed mothers. At the altar, Andrew stood next to Keith holding his favorite toy truck – one Keith purchased for him at the PX.

The ceremony was short. "And now you may kiss the bride," the Minister instructed Keith. It was a long kiss that ended only when Andrew impatiently pulled them apart.

Keith hoisted Andrew onto his shoulders as Captain Lawrence snapped pictures. Maria hosted a small reception at her Riveredge Café. Annie and Keith were amazed at how many people came to wish them well. Most of Keith's unit managed to drop by for a while and nurses from The Bamberg Clinic came. Helmut and Mrs. Rodiger and their three children were there. Even Colonel Nolan and Captain Collins managed to stop by.

Captain Lawrence made the toast. "Here's to Mr. and Mrs. Keith Brandon, and Andrew. I wish them a long life of happiness together. They have a very special and strong love."

"Here, here!"

"Prost!"

"Shlante!"

Andrew laughed. "Me too."

Annie and Keith Brandon left Bamberg for Le Havre, France later that evening by train. Two days later, they boarded The S. S. United States, the newest, fastest and most luxurious passenger ship on the ocean.

The ultra-modern ship even had a special kindergarten where Andrew could meet and play with children close to his own age and give his parents some time alone.

Keith wore his leg brace only a few hours a day now and slept without it. He even managed to slow dance with Annie at least once every night after dinner.

But when the fast songs played, Annie took Andrew in her arms and spun around the dance floor with him.

"Keith, I love this voyage. I feel so isolated at sea - so safe."

"I love you, Mrs. Brandon and I'm going to see to it that I make you and Andy just as happy every day as you are today."

Andrew smiled. "Me happy."

Keith relaxed but he was never out of touch, receiving daily telegrams from Captain Lawrence – and one very important wire from Reggie Smith finalizing plans for them to meet at Reggie's Law Office in the Bronx the day after their arrival in New York.

PART VII

BACK IN THE GLEN

Chapter 46

The S. S. United States Liner docked at its berth on the Upper West Side of Manhattan and the passengers lined up to go through customs. Then they walked through the huge area on the covered platform above a two story parking garage to pick up their luggage.

A porter carried their bags, as Keith carried Andrew, and Annie followed, outside to a waiting hired car. The driver sat on the fender holding a sign that read, "Brandon." The long, sleek black car sped up West Side Highway over the high bridge into the Bronx and then into the City of Yonkers.

The big car maneuvered through the narrow streets of The Glen, bouncing on the old trolley tracks that were still embedded in the center of the main streets. Andrew stood on the back seat while Keith held him tight, pointing out landmarks along the way.

Annie was unusually quiet. Her apprehension increased as they got closer to The Glen Center and her hands began to tremble.

"What is it?" Keith asked.

Andrew felt her tension and began to cry.

When the car pulled up in front of Catherine's corner row house, Keith jumped out and called to his mother who stood on the front steps. "Mom, Annie is sick. Take Andy inside, will you?"

Sarah, waiting on the porch, understood. She ran to Annie and helped her into the house, up the stairs into Keith's bedroom where the two women sat on Keith's bed together. Sarah held Annie's hand and stroked her hair.

Annie cried quietly, "Every happy memory of my childhood is here in this house with you and Keith. But everything outside these walls terrifies me. I'm so afraid for Andrew. And it's really strange to see my father's house next door."

"Your dad's been gone from the row house for so long, Annie. And he's in a bad way - at St. Teresa's Nursing home. Boss Garrigan lives full-time in Albany now and has no interest in The Glen. We have a black mayor."

Annie smiled at Sarah. "Really? Oh Sarah, you look wonderful – too wonderful. Are you in love?"

"Maybe," Sarah teased.

Annie noticed the newspaper on the night table with a thick bold typed lead-in that read, *"Local Hero Returns to The Glen."*

She grabbed the paper and read it.

Local hero, Army Sergeant Keith Brandon arrived home today after years in captivity behind the Iron Curtain. Nothing is known about why he was held so long or where but a statement issued by his commanding officer, Captain Wayne Lawrence, described Sergeant Brandon's actions as being "far beyond the call of duty and a fine example for all Americans."

The Sergeant's homecoming also has elements of a storybook, romantic ending. Last week in Germany, the Sergeant married his childhood sweetheart, Angela Marie Lynch, who also grew up right here in The Glen.

Annie flung open the bedroom door and ran down the stairs to confront Keith. "Look at this! Andrew is in terrible danger. You don't know what Liam is capable of doing if he reads this."

Keith tried to take Annie in his arms. "Take it easy, Annie. Liam is in Houston. I've checked everything out - where he is and what he's doing. I've got it covered."

Annie pulled away from him. "Boss Garrigan and his men aren't that far away. And my father is bound to hear about this from someone who reads it in the local newspaper."

"Exactly! Garrigan is a politician. He won't let anything happen to a hero's son – not while the world is watching. I wired this story to the newspaper. And I did it for Andrew. Right now, you and Andrew are safer out in the open than you would be hiding in the shadows."

"You sent this to the newspapers? And you never even mentioned it to me. How could you?" Annie's face was deep red.

"Annie, I've never seen you like this before."

"Yeah, well I never had a son to protect before." She stormed up the stairs, into Sarah's room and slammed the door.

Keith looked at his mother, shrugging his shoulders. "She was ecstatic on the ship. I have an appointment with Reggie tomorrow, so would you please stay with Annie and Andrew. Let her hide in the closet and keep the curtains drawn if that's what she wants to do."

"I'll take care of Annie and Andrew. Don't you worry," Catherine reassured Keith.

The next morning, Keith and Sarah caught an early commuter train into the city together. Keith got off the train at 125th Street, leaving Sarah to go on to her job in mid-town. He walked three blocks east to Reggie's office building, passing store owners just as they were beginning to pull aside the metal gates that protected their glass store fronts during the night.

People of every size, age, nationality and color, rushed through the streets going to work or to school; young men carried portable radios blaring loud rhythmic songs; and senior citizens dragged empty metal carts to carry their purchases back to their apartments in the government project buildings. Cart vendors hawked everything from fake designer handbags to hot pretzels. "Buy a pretzel, nice and hot – only ten cents."

Life on the streets in the Bronx played out in stark contrast to the orderly, bland silence behind the Iron Curtain. When Keith got to the address Reggie had given him, he looked up at the four story brick building. He chuckled to himself as he read the huge cardboard sign with a big black arrow pointing to the office in the cellar. "Authentic Gypsy Fortune Teller. No Appointment Necessary."

Running up the six steps to the first floor entrance, Keith opened the door marked "Legal Office." Reggie spotted him through the half glass door of his private office and ran out to greet him, "Welcome back, Keith!"

The two men shook hands and hugged briefly.

"Hey, you don't look bad for an ex-con. There's an article in Life Magazine about you Special Forces guys – no names, no faces, of course – just says they only take the best of the best and that's sure what they got in you, Keith."

"Thanks Reg. But look at this place – and it's all yours."

"Yeah, well, you know me. I have to go it alone - can't work for anyone else. Most of my clients can't even pay but I still love it."

"Say, what goes on in the basement with the gypsy fortune teller? Remember that family in The Glen."

"I remember and this is the same family – they're quite successful these days."

"You mean the same family that lived in the store front in the Glen - the ones that Annie went to for her reading. You mean they operate their business downstairs?"

"Yeah – they do. And they do a lot of work for me."

"Doing what?"

"They keep me knowledgeable about what's going on in the neighbourhood – for a fee, of course. They're okay – really – they don't do any harm – and they provide me with more information than any private detective could."

"Reggie, you are a sly old dog."

"I am."

"And thank you, my friend, for Annie's divorce. I don't know what you pulled off with that Nevada 'quickee thing' but it worked because she is now Mrs. Keith Brandon."

"Good! Congratulations on your marriage. But didn't Annie tell you that I'm a legal genius?"

"She did mention that – several times." Keith laughed.

Reggie closed the door to his private office.

"Listen, Keith, things with Liam Fogerty are far from settled. He may sue for full custody of Andrew or, at the very least, he will sue for visitation rights."

"That's just what Annie fears so much. I contacted the newspapers like you said and they ran the story. But the whole notoriety thing got Annie really upset."

Reggie nodded. "She's terrified - and with good reason. Liam can legally force visitation rights and Andrew is not safe with him. As I see it, that leaves us with one option. We have to force Liam to sign away his paternity rights."

Reggie grabbed a folder from the top of his desk and gave it to Keith. "This is our ammunition. Read it all. But I warn you, it's nasty stuff. It details Annie and Andrew's last night in Houston with details about the beating and the rape."

"What? Annie said Liam got angry that last night but . . ."

"Yeah, well, Annie wouldn't tell you about it."

Keith read Dr. Smith's report. "That creep injured Annie so bad that she can't have more children. He's a fucking dead man."

"Take it easy. We'll talk when you're done." Reggie put his hand on Keith's shoulder. "Annie signed waivers because she knew we might have to use this stuff. If Liam refuses to terminate his paternity rights, then all this will go public. Andrew's life is at stake. And Annie will do anything to keep him safe."

"This won't need to be published because I'm going to kill Liam first."

Reggie spoke sternly, "Wouldn't you rather have Andrew safe than get revenge?"

"I want both."

"I know that killing Liam would be satisfying, but it won't help Andrew. And Annie cannot endure anymore. She just can't."

Keith's blue eyes turned cold. "I'll tell you, Reggie, killing is not all that satisfying. I've done it. But it is final."

Reggie gave Keith the rest of the depositions. "These are from Karen and Fred, Annie's neighbors in Houston. I sent a private detective to meet with them."

"Annie talks so much about Karen, I feel as if I know her," Keith commented, reading a part of Karen's deposition out loud.

"When I heard Annie screaming, I ran to her front door and started banging on it and ringing the bell. Liam finally opened the door. He walked out of the apartment, right past me without even seeing me. "

"The apartment was dark. I found Annie on the living room floor, half naked and bleeding.

Andrew was in his crib calling for his mother. All Annie cared about was finding that hypodermic needle to be sure that it was still full and hadn't been used on Andrew. She would do anything to protect that child. I always knew in my heart that Andrew wasn't Liam's son. "

Keith mumbled, "No wonder, Annie's having anxiety attacks. And, me, like a jerk, I've been telling her to calm down."

Reggie and Keith went over the depositions from the Eastern Airline employees and from the taxi driver who took Annie and Andrew to the airport in Houston. Esther Weinberg and her maid, Rosa Santos, gave statements testifying to Annie's physical condition when she arrived in New York. Everything backed up Dr. Smith's medical report.

Reggie's secretary brought them mugs of hot coffee on a tray.

"Cassie, you must be psychic. This is Sergeant Keith Brandon. Keith, meet Cassie Flack, my right arm, guardian angel and secretary."

Cassie smiled. "I've heard so much about you, Sergeant Brandon, and I know your sister, Sarah, from the Katherine Gibbs Secretarial Program. You two look very much alike."

Keith stood up and shook her hand. "Cassie, it's nice to meet you. There's a family resemblance but Sarah is the good looking one."

As Keith put the file on Reggie's desk, two photographs fell to the floor and he went down on one knee to pick them up. "Oh my God, is this Annie?"

"Yeah, pretty gruesome, huh? My dad took those Polaroid shots. But there's even more and it's very interesting."

"Interesting?" Keith repeated, sarcastically.

"Yeah! Interesting!" Reggie reiterated. "Boss Garrigan pissed me off when he sent the cops to question my dad after Annie disappeared from the hospital. I wondered why Garrigan was so deep into Desmond and Annie's business. So I had the best private detective on the East Coast do some digging."

"You know you'd make a great Special Forces guy, Reggie."

"Damn right, I would!" Reggie nodded. "Garrigan and Fiona Fogerty, Liam's mother, had an affair that lasted for years. Garrigan has got to be Liam's biological father. Everyone says that Old Doc Fogerty used to sleep in his office and hardly ever went home to Fiona. Oh – I got so much on that family. Look here - a newspaper reporter at The Glen Dispatch said that Garrigan paid a large sum of money to the editor to kill a story about Liam being arrested for beating up a high school girl."

"So, that's the connection between Liam and Garrigan," Keith said.

"Garrigan couldn't chance his constituents finding out that he had an illegitimate son with a married woman. Fiona and Garrigan both wanted to hide the fact that their son is a 'sicko.' That's why Garrigan got Desmond and Annie involved. And old Desmond always did Garrigan's bidding."

"My grandfather, Frank O'Connor, loved Desmond like a brother but even he acknowledged that Desmond had a huge blind side."

"Garrigan paid big bucks to have Liam Fogerty's arrest record expunged. He covered everything up."

"So Garrigan used my Annie and my infant son to cover up for a monster and make him look like a good family man. And he probably sent Liam to med school in Houston to get him away from the trouble."

"You got it, Keith! I talked to the principal at St. Simon's, myself, and to Liam's roommate at Georgetown. They both said that bad things just seem to happen to women when Liam Fogerty is around."

"Despicable." Keith shook his head,

"With Annie pregnant, Desmond only cared about getting her out of public view. He didn't care what he did to Annie as long as he didn't look bad. And that's when Garrigan put all of this into play."

"Annie and Andrew were in danger everyday living with that sadistic monster."

Reggie nodded. "I'll give old Desmond this – he would have forced you to marry Annie when he found out she was pregnant with your child - not that he would have had to. But with no alternative plan, he went to Garrigan for advice and Garrigan played him by getting Annie out of sight and into that home."

Keith mumbled, "Once a long time ago, at St. Simon's, Liam said something sleazy about Sarah. We fought and I knocked him out cold."

"Well, yeah, Liam is no match for you, Keith. He only beats up girls and little children. And he hated you for that knockout so I bet he took it out on Annie."

"You know, there was this really nice girl from St. Gabriel's who went to the prom with Liam. Gracie Burns - I heard stories that she tried suicide."

"I'll check her out. Gracie Burns you say? Liam is not the kind of dude most fathers want their daughters to marry."

"Desmond was such an idiot!" Keith said, his body stiff with anger.

"Listen, Keith, this is what we need to do."

Reggie laid out the details of his plan to force Liam into signing away his paternal rights to Andrew.

"Brilliant, Reggie - almost as good as killing him."

"Ah but my plan doesn't turn you into a fugitive – something Annie could never deal with."

Reggie called a friend at the Houston Daily News while Keith finished reading the file.

"Everything's in place, Keith. Go home now and get things going there."

"You've done a ton of work here. I need to pay you for all this."

Reggie shook Keith's hand. "You can pay the private detective. But my work is done out of friendship. Friends for life, remember?"

"Friends for life!" Keith repeated, "And now, we have to make a deal with the devil himself."

Chapter 47

When Keith got home that afternoon, Annie was preparing dinner. Catherine and Andrew sat at the kitchen table playing "Go Fish."

Annie's eyes met Keith's.

"You know?" she asked.

Keith nodded. "Reggie has a plan."

Annie whispered, "Okay."

"I have to make some calls." Keith went to the phone in the front hall,

"Long distance operator, please. Connect me to St. Gerard's Convent in Ellsville, Maine."

Sister Rita answered, "Sergeant Brandon, a friend in Washington told me that you were home. We prayed for your safe return every day here at St. Gerard's."

"Annie and I are together - with our son. I want to thank you for the care you gave my wife and child."

"You're kind, Sergeant Brandon, but I made a terrible mistake allowing that sham of a marriage to take place. I've learned since then that some rules are meant to be broken and I'll carry that particular burden of guilt to my grave."

"I share in that guilt about what happened to Annie and my son – they were the unwitting victims of evil men with ulterior motives. But right now, Sister Rita, I need a favor."

"What can I do?"

"I'd like my mother and my son to stay at the convent for a day or two. It's only a precaution, to insure their safety. But no one can know they are there."

"Being discreet is what we do best here at St. Gerard's. Your mother and son are most welcome."

"Thank you. They'll be driven to St. Gerard's by a private detective, Joe Kline. They'll probably arrive late tomorrow afternoon. The detective will drop them off and wait somewhere in town to take them home."

"Perhaps your detective could dress a bit like a gardener and stay here on the convent grounds. Ellsville is a very small town and I fear that a stranger hanging around at the hotel might attract undue attention."

"That's even better. Thank you."

When Sarah got home from work, the Brandons gathered around the dining room table for the evening meal.

"Can I bathe Andrew and tuck him into bed tonight?" Sarah asked. "I don't get to see him as much as I'd like."

"Yes, yes, yes." Andrew smiled.

Annie and Keith said "yes" together.

Keith made a somber announcement. "After Andrew is asleep, we all need to talk."

It was after nine when the family returned to the dining room table.

"I'm sorry to inconvenience everyone but . . ." Keith outlined Reggie's plan and detailed the part each of them would play.

Catherine, Sarah and Annie went upstairs to pack while Keith telephoned Reggie to go over the details one more time.

It was almost eleven when Keith slid into bed next to Annie. He pulled her close and whispered, "I'm an ass for telling you to calm down."

"I hoped you'd never have to know what Liam did, but," Annie sighed, "I wish I'd been smarter and stronger."

"You're the bravest, smartest person I know. And I'd give anything to spare you seeing Liam again. But we have to do this."

She kissed Keith on the neck and the chest. "Be quiet now," she said, wrapping her body around his, "and make love to me."

At five thirty the next morning Joe Kline pulled his Chevy Kingswood station wagon up to the curb in front of the Brandon's row house.

Keith, carrying a small overnight bag, walked little Andrew and Catherine out to the car

"I'll take good care of them," Joe assured Keith.

A half hour later, another hired car picked up Sarah, Annie and Keith, taking them into Manhattan to Sarah's office building on Madison Avenue at 46th Street.

"Go with God and be safe," Sarah said, kissing first Keith and then Annie.

Keith warned his sister, "Go straight to Esther's apartment after work. Rosa is expecting you. And no matter what happens or what anyone tells you, don't go home until either Reggie or I give you the okay. I don't want you near the house in The Glen until I know it's safe."

"Okay Keith," Sarah replied. She turned and waved just before entering the huge marble and glass lobby.

"La Guardia Airport, the Eastern Airlines Building," Keith said, slipping his arm around Annie. "Hey, I like riding in the back seat like this. We can make out like teenagers all the way to the airport."

"Keith, be serious," Annie scolded him.

"I don't want to be serious. I want to be silly and carefree and I want all this crap behind us so we can have the life we've missed out on."

"We will, Keith. We will."

The flight departed LaGuardia on time, arriving at Hobby Airport in Houston early in the afternoon.

Annie stared at the familiar flatness of the Houston topography. "It's so different from landing in Munich; so flat with open fields; but lovely in a different way."

"I never got to see the landings in Germany – no windows on the plane."

"Let's switch seats," Annie said.

"No way! I want to watch the wonder on your face."

Keith picked up the rented car that Cassie arranged to have waiting for them. As he slid behind the wheel, he realized that this was the first time he would be actually driving a car since that day when he was ambushed in East Germany and taken prisoner.

Annie read Cassie's directions as they drove south along the Gulf Freeway to the Alameda Mall. They ate at a new Hamburger Hut at the end of the mall, enjoying fries and milk shakes along with a huge Texas-size burger.

"Hey this is delicious," Keith said as he wolfed down his food.

"It is. Andy would love this."

They strolled through Foley's Department Store before checking into the Alameda Motel, the only motel on the Gulf Freeway between Houston and Clear Lake.

"We'll just have to come back and bring Andrew," Keith said.

"Yes and we can visit with Fred and Karen. I feel guilty being here and not calling them."

"Next time!"

They settled into their room where Keith drilled Annie on every possible scenario, the same way he would drill an operative in his unit. When he felt that they were done, Keith fell back on the bed exhausted.

Annie snuggled next to him.

"Remember, no matter what Liam says, don't react. He'll try to provoke us both by saying terrible things. Seeing you will catch him off guard for a short time but he'll recover and then he'll be more angry and even meaner."

"I get it. I really do. And I can do this. It's like I'm saying to Liam, 'you hurt me but you didn't cripple me'."

Keith brushed Annie's hair back and kissed the cluster of small scars that Liam's brutal attack had left behind. "He should be going to jail but this is going to have to be our day in court. And, when it's over, we'll never say his name again. Deal?"

"Deal!"

The next morning they showered, dressed, had coffee and toast in the hotel lobby and checked out. Keith drove south on the Gulf Freeway toward Galveston.

"Annie, you're a great navigator."

"These directions make it easy."

Keith exited the freeway at Landry, Texas, and followed the two lane country highway three miles to the newly constructed Landry Hospital, a satellite of the prestigious Taylor University Hospital in downtown Houston.

Keith said, "Garrigan must have saved Liam's hide again. Reggie says that he's on probation here but that creep shouldn't be practicing medicine at all."

"You're right. Liam should not be allowed anywhere near patients."

Keith parked in the first row just a short walk from the ultra- modern building. "This building looks so out of place next to flat grassy fields where cattle are grazing."

Annie sighed. "This is the real Texas. I never got outside of Houston in all the time I lived here. We have to come back with Andy and see the whole state."

"That's a plan for sure."

They entered the massive lobby and approached a pretty young receptionist sitting at a marble podium.

"Good morning." Keith gave her his most charming smile. "Well, now I see what they say about Texas is true."

"Excuse me, sir?" The young girl blushed as her eyes met Keith's dark blue eyes.

"Well I've been told that they grow pretty girls in Texas and, looking at you, well, obviously that's very true." Keith, always irresistible, distracted the young girl as he placed Joe Kline's expired private detective license on the podium, keeping his finger strategically placed over the photograph and date. "We have urgent business with a Dr. Liam Fogerty. Do you know him?"

"Yes sir, I know who he is." She picked up the phone. "Please send Dr. Fogerty to the lobby." Pointing to a door behind her, she said, "Go on into the conference room and wait. He'll be down in just a few minutes. Would y'all like some coffee?"

"Thanks but no. We won't be here all that long,"

Keith took Annie's hand, leading her into the huge marble room decorated in teak and steel, totally windowless but well lighted. They stood beside the long chrome and glass conference table.

Suddenly, the door opened and they were face-to-face with Liam Fogerty. He peered at them through the thick lenses of his dark rimmed glasses, his cold, grey eyes magnified and menacing. His face showed momentary surprise but he masked it instantly. "Well, well, what do you two idiots want from me now?"

Keith, taller than Liam, stood straight, protecting Annie. He held the folder out to Liam. "We came to give you something."

Liam ignored the folder and focused on Annie. "Cut the theatrics and get on with it. I signed the divorce papers. Now what?"

Annie stared back at Liam.

Liam smirked and then looked at Keith. "I came to Annie's rescue after you knocked her up and abandoned her. I even gave that bastard kid of hers my name but all Annie ever wanted to do was humiliate me. She's a total bitch, Keith, so watch your back. But she sure does know how to give a guy a great 'blow job'."

Keith calmly responded, "We came to let you look at this folder before we take it to the press. There are sworn depositions from credible witnesses, and even a lab report that proves you stole hospital drugs and threatened to inject Annie and Andrew with them."

Liam took the folder from Keith's hand and flipped through it.

"Blackmail eh? Well since you didn't just go ahead and publish this, I'm thinking there's a deal to be made."

Keith smiled. "Sign this dissolution of paternity form regarding my Andrew and there will be no publication."

"I'm right again. You two dummies are so predictable!" Liam shook his head making his deprecating remark even more insulting.

Keith dropped the form and a pen on the glass conference table.

Liam read the form over and looked up at Keith. "I'll sign gladly. I want nothing to do with the little bastard."

Liam rolled the folder into a tube shape and shoved it into the pocket of his hospital jacket.

Staring at Annie, Liam said, "So I guess this is the end for us, Annie. I sure hope you're happy with the man who abandoned you when you needed him most. But, don't worry little Blondie, we'll always have the memory of that last, very special night together."

Annie's expression never changed. She was calm, enigmatic.

Keith picked up the signed form and took Annie's hand.

They walked out of the conference room.

Just before closing the door behind them, Keith looked back. "Maybe I'll just publish this stuff anyway or maybe mail it to Dr. DeBann."

They walked fast, almost running, out of the lobby and across the parking lot, jumping into the rented car. Keith gunned the engine and drove the speed limit back to Hobby Airport. Neither of them said a word.

Parked in the airport lot, Keith put his hand under Annie's chin and kissed her on the lips. "Well done."

Annie shivered. "Liam is a devil."

"He is. But it's over," Keith whispered.

"Not completely. You still have to adopt your own son." Annie reminded him.

"I'll do whatever it takes."

Annie put her arms around Keith and wept silently.

Inside Hobby's spacious airport lobby, Annie freshened up while Keith used the pay phone to call Reggie. "That creep taunted us but we kept our cool and we got what we came for."

"Good. He's probably so frustrated now that he's looking to buy drugs even as we speak. Is Annie okay?"

"Yeah, she did great. I think it actually helped her to face him and see him for the coward that he is."

"Come on home and get that signed paternity form to me as soon as possible because I've already filed for you to adopt Andrew."

"You did?" Keith said, surprised.

"I knew you'd do it. And I'll bring Sarah home tonight. Don't want her to be traveling alone right now. We can't be too careful," Reggie said.

"Thanks. I don't want her to be alone either."

Keith called Sister Rita at St. Gerard's Convent in Maine. "You can send my mother and my son home with Joe Kline now. And thank you for helping us."

Sarah answered the phone on her desk and heard Reggie's excited voice. "It's over. They got what they needed with no violence and they're on the flight home now."

"Thank God. You do great work, Reggie."

"I know, I really do. Listen, Sarah, I'll pick you up at work and go back up to The Glen with you. I don't want you at the house alone just in case Annie and Keith get delayed. Humor me and let's play it extra safe, okay?"

"Sure. See you around five in front of my building."

Reggie called his father. "They did it, Dad. And Annie is okay. I'm coming home to The Glen tonight. I'm taking Sarah to dinner and then bringing her home."

Reggie and Sarah ate at the Algonquin Hotel dining room on 44th Street before taking the train up to Yonkers. They arrived at the row house in The Glen at nine o'clock, right after Annie and Keith. Sarah made tea for everyone while Reggie announced that he had even more news. "I got some additional information about Liam today. Dad has a psychiatrist friend at NYU who claims that they categorize men like Liam Fogerty as 'sexual sadists.' Evidently these types only experience sexual pleasure when it hurts women."

"In the old days, we just called guys like Liam 'scum bags' but now there's a medical term for it?" Keith's tone was angry.

"Yeah," Reggie answered. "It doesn't qualify as insanity so he could still be charged criminally. That is what should happen. And that's my goal, to get him charged as a criminal and have him locked up where he can't hurt anyone else."

"It took every bit of strength I had not to strangle him," Keith muttered.

Reggie put his hand on Keith's arm. "But today wasn't about Liam. It was about Andrew. And there's more. My secretary found Grace Burns. She talked to her for over an hour and Gracie said that Liam raped and beat her up the night of the senior prom. But she was too ashamed and frightened to go to the police. Her parents moved the family to Boston to get Gracie away and let her start over."

"Poor Gracie - she was a real nice girl," Keith said.

"But Gracie was right. The police would not have done anything because the police in The Glen were all in Garrigan's pocket," Annie said. "And violence against women is actually blamed on the women themselves. It is so sick. I saw much too much of it when I worked at the hospital in Houston."

Keith was furious. "So Boss Garrigan knew that he was handing Annie and my son over to a monster. Do you think Desmond knew about Liam?"

Reggie thought for a moment. "I don't think so. Garrigan never shared personal information or anything else for that matter. But here is the biggest news of all. I am really close to proving that Boss Garrigan is Liam's biological father. He had an affair with Fiona Fogerty for years and that's why Garrigan went to such lengths to protect Liam no matter who else got hurt. People also say that Garrigan had something on Desmond that he used to force Desmond to make Annie marry Liam."

Keith asked, "What would Desmond ever have done that Garrigan didn't order him to do or wasn't a part of?"

"It would have to be something big, something no one else would know about," Reggie said.

Keith realized that Annie was getting uncomfortable with all the talk about her father. He put his arm around her. "This can wait until later."

Annie spoke softly, "My father was always so complex, as if he lived somewhere deep inside of himself. No one ever knew what he was thinking. All I ever wanted was for him to love me, but he just couldn't seem to."

Sarah spoke softly, "I think Desmond did love you Annie – in his own strange way. Maybe that's why he arranged for Mom and Granna to take care of you. He didn't want some housekeeper raising you. Give him that much. He sent you to us and we had a really happy childhood together. Just forget all the rest."

Reggie stood up. "Well, tomorrow is a work day and I've got to get some sleep."

"Speaking of work, I have a job interview at the U. N. next week," Keith said.

"You'll need a new suit for an interview, Keith," Sarah piped up. "You've been wearing uniforms for so long that your civilian clothes are outdated, fifties looking."

Annie agreed with Sarah. "You do need some new clothes, Keith. You have nothing recent."

Just then Annie heard Joe Kline's car pull up outside. "They're back," she said and ran out to the curb.

Andrew was wide awake and tumbled out of the car. He ran to Annie, saying, "Mommy, we saw nuns and I played with a giant."

"I know that gentle giant. He was there the night you were born."

Catherine thanked Joe. "I want you and your family to come to dinner. I'll be calling your wife."

Keith shook Joe's hand. "Come in and stretch your legs. Have some tea."

"No thanks, Keith. It's late and I'm anxious to get back home. I like driving this time of night because the traffic is less."

"You did something really important for us, Joe, and we are all very grateful. Annie needed to know that Andrew was safe while we confronted Liam. And you gave her that security. Thank you."

"I'm glad you got what you needed in Houston. Personally, I had a blast." Joe laughed. "I never slept at a convent before."

Reggie shook Joe's hand. "Good night everybody. Sleep well," he called out, walking past Desmond's old row house to his parents' place.

Sarah and Catherine went up to bed. But Keith and Annie stayed up with Andrew, playing games and reading to him, until he finally dozed off in Keith's arms.

Chapter 48

It was a new world for Annie – finally free of Liam Fogerty's threats against little Andrew.

Catherine related some funny stories about Andrew at the convent. "St. Gerard's may never be the same. Andrew had everyone playing hide and seek with him, in and out of every dusty corner in the main building. But those beds are so hard. Annie, darling, I don't know how you got any sleep at all. But the breads and the soup. Oh my, but the food was superb."

Annie smiled. "Didn't I tell you the food would be the only good part?"

"Mom, you were great to take on that trip with Andy." Keith hugged her.

"But, Catherine, you really should rest today," Annie said, looking very concerned about her mother-in-law.

"Nonsense, I had a solid night's sleep and I'm ready to enjoy my grandson again."

Keith smiled. "Good, because I need you to watch Andrew on Saturday, probably all day, because Annie and I have to wrap up a few things."

"Things? What things?" Annie asked, smiling up at Keith.

"You'll see," he answered. "I have to get to the city now."

Catherine added, "Minding Andrew is a snap when he's not restricted to the back seat of a car."

"Hey Sarah," Keith yelled from the foot of the stairs. "Hurry up. I'll be late for that resume guy."

"Don't forget, Keith, we need to do some clothes shopping for your interview next week." Annie shook her finger at him.

Sarah ran down the stairs, past everyone. "Okay, let's go, Keith, what are you waiting for?"

Keith followed, running after her, slamming the door behind them.

Catherine shook her head, "Honestly, it's like they're still ten years old, squabbling and carrying on."

Annie picked up Andrew's trucks from the floor. "Darling, you can't leave these all around like this - you'll trip Granna."

Catherine hugged Annie. "I just hate the thought of you leaving this house. Although I do realize that you and Keith need to have your own place."

"Well, we won't be far. If Keith gets that job translating at the U. N. – and who would not want to hire him – we will take that little apartment on the east side. And he's already enrolled at Hunter College for evening classes."

"And you, dear, what will you do to continue your nursing studies?"

"I'm looking into a Registered Nurse program at Hunter. But I've enough to think about today. You need a little quiet time and we could use some fresh vegetables. So I'll take Andrew shopping in his new stroller."

Annie and Andrew headed toward the stores on Broadway. It was very hot for so early in the day. The baker's wife gave Andy a sugar cookie, fresh from the oven and still warm. "Such a handsome boy. He'll break many hearts one day."

Passing Mario's restaurant, Annie noticed that no one sat by the front window anymore. And three small shops filled the space that used to be O'Brien's Pub - a record shop selling the latest 45's, a bodega stocked with Spanish-style foods, and a television store displaying the new Philco "portable" TV in the front window.

The only thing in The Glen that had not changed was the uniformed policeman directing traffic at the main intersection.

"Hey, Annie," a young cop called out as he walked over to her, "Remember me? Pat Madden, from St. Joe's. I used to sit behind you in school and play with your curls."

"Pat, of course. How are you?"

"I'm fine. And you're looking great, Annie, like always! Your son, right?"

"Yes, this is Andrew."

"He's looks just like Keith Brandon. My brother was in Keith's class at St. Simon's. Keith was a hero even back then. Remember that time when he stood up for that black girl, you know, the doctor's kid, the one who died?"

"How could I forget?"

"Yeah, you're right. No one will forget that. Keith was really something that day."

"I'll tell Keith that we met." Annie tried to walk on.

But Pat did not move out of her way. "Hey Annie, where were you all that time when Keith was missing? I never believed that story about you and Liam Fogerty running off to get married."

Little Andrew tried to climb out of the stroller, almost tipping it on its side.

"It's a long story, Pat, I'd love to talk but my son gets so restless."

"Oh, sure, go ahead. And I'm sure sorry that your dad is so sick. Desmond was a tough guy back in the day but he treated me and my family real good."

Annie smiled. "It was great seeing you, Pat."

"Tell Desmond that I send my best."

"Thanks, I'll do that."

Anne couldn't get over how everything had changed so much. It was as if the lives they all once lived never even existed.

A sudden sense of urgency overwhelmed her. She collapsed the light weight stroller, hung it over her shoulder, picked Andrew up in her arms and boarded the sleek new bus that displayed The Village of Fleetwood as its destination.

She sat behind the driver with Andrew on her lap. The bus swayed, bouncing roughly over the old trolley tracks. As the bus' engine strained, it climbed the first steep hill and then speeded up to a swooping glide as it passed the prestigious homes on Park Place. Annie held on tight to Andrew and to the back of the driver's seat when the bus barrelled down the other side of the hill like a run-away roller coaster.

Annie and Andrew got off the bus in front of St. Teresa's Nursing Home. Unfolding the light-weight stroller, Annie settled Andrew comfortably into it and headed toward the grey brick building whose elegant exterior looked exactly the same, its windows sparkling, hedges neatly trimmed and the front door, as always, a newly painted deep red. Entering the lobby, Annie felt the same sad emptiness that she felt all those years ago when she visited her mother there.

"Is Desmond Lynch well enough for visitors today?" Annie asked. The nun at the reception desk looked up at Annie, squinting, her pale, wrinkled face a harsh contrast to the tight black veil wrapped around her head.

"You may visit Mr. Lynch but he probably won't even know that you're in the room. Sign the visitors' log, please."

"Is that at a big witch, Momma?"

"No, silly, she's a nun, just like at St. Gerard's." Annie kissed Andrew's forehead.

She left the stroller at the reception desk, carrying Andy down the hall and entered her father's private room. Annie stood beside his bed, looking down at the man whose love she once so desperately needed, the father who so cruelly allowed her to be used by Liam Fogerty.

Desmond snored, his mouth hanging open, saliva dripping down his chin. The odor of stale urine and harsh disinfectants made her nauseous, almost dizzy.

Andrew whispered, "Momma, monster, monster," and he buried his face in her neck.

"Don't be afraid darling. He's only a sick old man."

Suddenly Desmond's eyes popped open and he looked up at Annie. "Am I dead? Are you here to punish me?"

"You're not dead, Daddy. It's me, Annie, and this is your grandson, Andrew."

"You're not Annie. She ran off to Europe after that Brandon boy, left a fine husband, a rich doctor – all for that no-good Brandon boy."

Desmond looked away, mumbling, "Just like his father he is, taking his pleasure with my Annie and then leavin' her alone and disgraced. I'll fix him like I fixed his father. They think the money came from the veteran's pension but the Army would never have a drunk like him."

"And just how did you fix Michael Brandon?" Annie asked.

But Desmond drifted off to sleep again.

"Mommy, go home," Andrew whimpered.

Annie returned to the reception desk. "Please make arrangements for Mr. Lynch to see a priest. I'm his daughter and here's my telephone number. Please call me if he gets any worse."

They boarded the next bus back to The Glen and Andy fell asleep as soon as the bus began to move. Annie wondered just what her father meant when he said that he would "fix" Michael Brandon.

Back home, Catherine came running to the door, "Annie, dear, we were so worried. Keith is back from the city and he's frantic."

Andrew ran to Keith. "Daddy, Daddy, we saw two monsters today." The little boy held his right hand up, extending two fingers."

"What's this about monsters? Where were you?" Keith bent down to take Andrew in his arms.

Annie stammered, "I ran into Pat Madden. He's a traffic cop now and he went on and on about you and what a great guy you are and about my father and how sick he is. And, well, before I knew it, I was on the bus going to St. Teresa's Nursing Home."

"Is your father one of the monsters that Andrew's talking about?"

"Yes, Andy got frightened by the nun at the front desk and by my father's appearance. Granted, he does look terrible. "

The kettle whistled and Catherine interrupted, "Come have some tea and tell me what happened. I heard that Desmond had a stroke."

"He's dying," Annie said. "I made arrangements for the Last Rites."

Catherine took her hand. "You've always been such a kind, forgiving soul."

"I realize now, of course, that I shouldn't have taken Andrew to the nursing home, especially without telling you, Keith. I'm so sorry."

Keith's expression softened, "If you'd said something about wanting to see your father, I'd have taken you there."

Annie was suddenly very tired. "I know. But for some reason, I just had to go there today."

Keith put his hand under her chin, lifted her face to his and kissed her lips. "Please don't shut me out, Annie. You're not alone anymore."

Andrew ran off into the living room to play with his trucks.

Chapter 49

Keith's "special surprise" would take place on a Saturday that dawned as one of those "once-in-a-summer" kind of days that always follow the hot, humid "dog days" of August.

A cool, dry breeze with just a hint of autumn made the atmosphere so clear that you could see for miles.

Annie, awake early, went down to the kitchen to make coffee. She pushed the screen door open and went out onto the back porch to breathe in the fresh air.

Although she was looking forward to this adventure with Keith, she just couldn't get the image of her father's frail body and his utter helplessness out of her mind. If Keith had not rented a car for the day and made such a fuss about "his big surprise," she might have asked him to change plans. But Annie couldn't disappoint him now.

Andrew thundered out onto the porch and began badgering her with questions about the sun and how high the clouds were and where the sky ended.

"Andrew, darling, please go back upstairs and wake Daddy. He must get up now and he knows the answers to all your questions."

Andy pouted, stomping back up the stairs, making enough noise to wake Keith as well as Catherine and Sarah, and possibly the entire neighbourhood, too.

A few minutes later, Sarah, dressed in jeans and a gorgeous orange sweater, beautifully made up, joined Annie on the porch.

"You look lovely, like you're on a mission," Annie commented.

"I am indeed on a mission. It's a gorgeous day and Mom and I are going to take Andy to the Bronx Zoo. Say, Annie are you okay? You're awfully pale and Mom said you had a rough time of it yesterday."

"I'm fine, really. Just a bit tired. I'd better bring some coffee up to Keith. He wants to leave early - to go wherever it is we're going. You know, Sarah, you look like a New York model."

"I'm getting pretty skillful at this makeup and eye shadow stuff. My next project is to make you up."

"Great, maybe tonight."

"No, this morning - right now." She followed Annie back up the stairs. "You can go off with Keith on this mystery tour looking like a movie star."

An hour later, Annie was kissing Andy goodbye. "Be good, sweetheart. We'll be back later this afternoon."

Sarah answered for him, "He'll be fine. And, oh what fun we'll have on this beautiful day."

Annie followed Keith out the front door to the little red car parked at the curb.

"It's a Corvair, something new from Chevy. It's like the Volkswagen with the engine in the back, kind of like a sports car but a heck of a lot cheaper." Keith held the door open for Annie.

As she slid in, she said, "I don't know if I like these bucket seats."

"Why?" Keith asked.

"Because I can't slide over and snuggle up beside you."

Keith smiled, handing Annie a sheet of paper. "Be my beautiful navigator again?"

"Sure."

She guided Keith through city streets all the way to the Hutchison River Parkway and onto the beautiful Whitestone Bridge, suspended high above the shimmering waters of Flushing Bay.

"Keith, look at how clearly you can see the Manhattan skyline from here. Oh, it really is a spectacular morning!"

"I'm glad you feel better today. You look absolutely gorgeous."

"It's this makeup job Sarah gave me."

"It's not the makeup – it's you."

"Keith, I need to go see Desmond tomorrow."

"Sure. Can I come with you?"

"I'd rather go alone. You need to stay with Andy."

"Okay, if that's what you want."

They arrived in Flushing, Queens. "Slow down. We get off the parkway here and we have to find a street called Bayside Boulevard."

They drove a few blocks. "There it is, up ahead." Keith pointed. "And that's the apartment house over there, the one with the long green awning out front. And there's a parking space right out front. You always bring me good luck, Annie!"

Keith skilfully executed a parallel parking maneuver and turned off the engine. "Let's go."

Annie got out of the car. "And just when are you going to tell me what's going on?"

Keith took her hand. "We're here to visit a woman named Olga Krupchik and her father-in-law, Stefan Krupchik. One of my assignments in Europe was to smuggle Olga and her husband, Milos, out of East Germany. I couldn't tell you about any of this until now because there were others still being held – until a few days ago."

Inside the small lobby, Keith scanned the columns of buttons and pressed one. When the answering buzzer sounded, he pushed open the door and they entered a white marble lobby with floor to ceiling mirrors.

Keith led the way onto the elevator. When the doors opened on the third floor, Olga Krupchik stood there, waiting to greet them. She threw her arms around Keith's neck and kissed him, European style, on both cheeks.

"Moya Keiz, darlink, all prayers ver answered ven zey let you go free." Olga rattled on and on in what Annie recognized as Czechoslovakian.

And all the while Annie experienced the very unpleasant sensation of jealousy as she observed Olga's and Keith's familiarity with one another.

Then Olga turned her full attention to Annie, kissing her on both cheeks as well and taking in every detail of Annie's appearance with her gorgeous brown eyes.

"So at last I get to meet ze love of Keith's life. Anishka, you are more beautiful even zan Keith tell me. Come, follow me."

They followed Olga to the open door of her apartment.

"Zis is great day that you are here," Olga said in English and then rattled on in Czech once again.

Annie grudgingly noticed how tall and slim Olga was and the fact that her exquisite features were set in a perfect complexion. Her straight, brown hair, cut blunt just above her shoulders, was the very latest style.

Annie self-consciously pushed the unruly blonde curls off her face and followed Keith and Olga into the living room where an old man in a wheel chair struggled to stand up.

Annie moved toward him, quickly. "Please don't get up."

He stopped struggling and took Annie's hand in his. "Annie Brandon, your beauty brings joy to these old eyes of mine." He kissed her hand like a gallant knight pledging loyalty to a queen and his sparkling blue eyes shimmered like a young boy's – a stark contrast to his gnarled body.

Keith shook the old man's hand. "You must be Stefan Krupchik."

"Sergeant Brandon, it eez my pleasure to shake your hand. You save my Olga from prison. Sit please, both of you!" He pointed to the salmon colored velvet sofa.

"This room is beautiful." Annie couldn't help but comment on it. Lovely oil painted landscapes in gold frames hung on the wall. An elegant end table with a cut glass lamp and beige silk shade stood beside the couch. Two dark green velvet chairs flanked Stefan's wheelchair in front of a big window accented on each side with salmon velvet drapes..

"Olga, she sew and do everything," Stefan said proudly. "You should see vat mess before she come here to live vith me."

"Olga is very talented," Annie commented, hoping to ward off her demons of envy with kind words.

Olga darted back and forth between the kitchen and living room, bringing platters of delicate finger sandwiches, cookies, and pastries along with cups of steaming hot coffee.

"Can I help you Olga?" Annie asked.

"No, no, please sit. I vanted to cook big European meal but Keith, he say no. So, next visit, you vill bring son and Keiz's mozer and sister and I vill cook for all."

"Everything is wonderful, Olga, thank you." Feeling queasy after the long car ride, Annie popped a thin sandwich into her mouth.

Stefan cleared his throat, "I'm citizen here in United States since 1938. My wife, she die in childbirth. I left my son with my parents in Prague. I vork very hard here and ze vorld seem to go crazy. Germans take my country. My son ees married now to Olga. Then Russians take my country from Germans. No freedom. Ze communist order my Miloslav and Olga to move to East Germany."

Stefan wiped the tears from his eyes. "My Milos is smart scientist so they force him do research." He sipped his coffee. "But ze communist government don't trust Milos but they use him. Then they say - he is a spy. He is in big trouble if he do it or even if he don't do it." Stefan started to cough.

Olga continued for him. "Some Americans, Keiz and others, ze came to take me and my Milos over border to ze west. Keith speaks languages vith good accent and he ees wonderful actor. You know, he blends in."

Keith interjected, "I was sent over the border to get Olga and Milos out of East Germany, but Milos was arrested just hours before I got to them. Olga would have been arrested next so I took her with me. For days we hid out and we were constantly just a few steps ahead of the secret police. We slept in the sewers and ate from garbage cans. Once we even pretended to be the parents of a school girl so that we could get inside the school and steal some lunches from outside a classroom. We ran in circles to confuse the secret police until I finally got Olga across the border. Stefan arranged for her to come here to live with him."

Olga smiled. "Later, Milos escaped jail and I don't know it but Keith and another American go back to East Germany to get him."

Keith spoke again because Olga began to cry. "We were betrayed and everything went terribly wrong. We kept missing Milos because someone was messing things up. My partner, Joe McDermott and Miloslav were both arrested. I was on the run, alone, for maybe two months. I hurt my leg jumping from a second story window and the underground got me to a doctor. The secret police followed me and arrested me right at the border. I was with Miloslav and Joe in prison in Bratislava – and there were other American and British prisoners there as well. "

"They held the westerners for as long as they could and then deported us. But Miloslav is a Czech citizen and there were no deals to be made for his release. Keeping him from being executed has been our only success so far."

Olga nodded. "We lie and say that Stefan has citizenship here, and how you say it, make smokey screen zat ees keeping Milos alive because Stefan swears that Milos is an American citizen too. My Milos don't get killed yet so we pray and we write letters."

Olga looked directly at Annie. "That prison so cruel. They put Milos and Keith in front of firing squad day after day but shoot someone else. Then take them back to cell. Try to make them crazy."

"Oh no!" Hearing that, Annie felt shock waves run through her body.

"Anishka. I'm sorry, I thought you knew."

Annie shook her head.

Olga continued, "My Milos life is in more and more danger every day."

Keith put his arm around Annie as he spoke to Stefan and Olga in Czech. Finally he said, in English, "We will never give up, I promise. Miloslav is alive and that is the most important thing right now."

Annie spoke hesitantly to Olga, "Yes, knowing that Miloslav is alive means everything. When I knew for sure that Keith was alive then I was able to do things that I never thought I could do."

"Anishka, your Keith is such a good man, like my Milos. Keith save my life and he even make me laugh when I am so desperate and so sick. That is good thing, no?"

Annie smiled. "Yes, that is a good thing. Keith can always make people laugh, even at the worst times."

Olga moved to the couch and took Annie's hands in hers. "Keith talk all the time about his Anishka but he never tell me he has a son."

"He didn't know about Andrew."

Annie told Olga and Stefan what she endured while Keith was in prison.

Stefan cried out, "Why, why these people must always hurt and control ze other people. It ees the same in all countries, and in all the vorld. And always ze innocent must suffer."

The conversation became intense as Olga and Annie reached a level of intimacy, on this, their first meeting, that only close friends of many years are able to achieve.

"Annie, I envy you your son. Keith help me, he steal food and water, and blankets for me but still I lost my child." She wept. "And I have nothing of my Milos now."

Annie put her arms around Olga.

It was time to leave. Annie and Keith promised to write letters to Senators and Congressmen on behalf of Milos to beg for government intervention and get Milos released from prison.

"I am so happy to meet you both and we will stay in touch and see each other often," Annie vowed as they left the lovely little apartment.

In the car on the way back to The Glen, Annie said, "They are good people caught up in a situation that is not of their making - like us, like so many."

Keith nodded. "Milos and Olga deserve better."

"When I first saw Olga, I was jealous. She's so beautiful."

Keith looked at Annie, surprised. "Olga is a good woman. But you never need to be jealous, Annie. Don't you know that?"

Annie smiled. "Keith, what were you thinking when Olga spoke about losing Milos' baby? I noticed how intently you looked at her."

"I noticed how she said, 'Milos' child' - over and over – connecting everything about her love for Milos to her baby. That's when it finally dawned on me that Olga wanted that part of Milos no matter how hard it might be for her. And I knew then that was how you felt and I was finally able to let go of my guilt about not being there for you. That guilt of mine was getting in the way. It must be something primal that women understand long before men do."

"Some men never get it. Keith, I never resented you, not for a second. I never regretted making love to you. Without Andrew, I don't know what I would have done."

They drove the rest of the way home in that special silence that only two people who really understand each other can share.

Chapter 50

When Annie and Keith got back to The Glen, they found Monsignor Murdock at the row house sitting in the living room with Catherine.

Annie knew instantly that her father was dead.

The monsignor stood up to greet her. "Annie, I'm so sorry. Desmond passed away early this afternoon. But he was at peace. He accepted the last sacraments. And his final words were about you and the many regrets he had about his relationship with you."

Annie felt a loss, not the kind of loss one feels when someone is really part of your life, but a loss nonetheless. Desmond had never really been a part of her life. But she had shed so many tears already over the fact that her father just could not love her that she had no more tears left.

"My father was such a complicated man," she murmured sadly.

Monsignor Murdock took Annie's hand. "Aye, that's true. But he did a lot of good things along with the bad. And he'll be judged, like all of us, by his Maker, and not by you and me. Just know that at the very end, he begged for forgiveness and he requested to be buried next to your mother. He left the plot to you. As for anything else, well most of your father's money went for his nursing and medical care."

Keith came up behind Annie. "I'll take care of Desmond's funeral and whatever else is owed to St. Teresa's."

"Desmond gave generously to Saint Teresa's over the years so nothing is owed. And Desmond gave to St. Joseph's as well, so I'll be glad to help you arrange a proper funeral for him - something dignified - him being a fixture in The Glen for so many years."

Saint Joseph's Church was filled to overflowing on the morning of Desmond Lynch's Funeral Mass. Old cronies and former residents came back to The Glen, their cars lining the curbs on both sides of Broadway as far as the eye could see.

Boss Garrigan drove down from Albany. Retired police and firemen filled row after row of the church. And a few unsavory looking characters filled the pews in the back.

As Annie entered St. Joseph's, a large older woman grabbed her hand. "Your father was a loyal friend to me over the years. I tell you he put food on my table and got me through some tough times."

"It's kind of you to tell me that and thank you for coming." Annie inquired, "and what is your name?"

"Just call me Henrietta and these here are friends of mine who also knew your father." She introduced her two female companions, both adorned with thick makeup and too much jewelry, as Peggy and her sister, Maggie. Peggy hugged Annie and Maggie shook her hand.

Dr. and Mrs. Smith, Reggie Smith, Esther Weinberg, and Olga and Stefan Krupchik took up the second and third pews on the right side of the church directly behind Catherine, Sarah, Keith, Annie and Andrew who filled the first row.

Annie gave the eulogy.

"My father came to The Glen from a cruel place during a very troubled time. He never spoke of his childhood nor did he ever try to go back to Ireland. I know nothing about his family there - my family - nor do I know what his life there was like. Many of you are here out of respect for my father and you've said some very kind things about him. For that, I am truly grateful. Some of you think of Desmond Lynch as a man who broke the rules, while others think of him as a savior and a benefactor.

"I guess my father was all of these things. He could be a loyal friend to those he respected and a fierce adversary to those he did not. And I've heard tell that my father never ran from a fight. When I was born, he knew that he couldn't care for me. But he did make it possible for me to grow up in a happy home where I was truly loved. He gave me what he never had, a safe, happy childhood, one quite different from his own.

"I loved my father and I know that I'm strong like him. And I also know that I let him down. But I believe in my heart that he did love me and he forgave me. And I'm trying very hard to forgive him. So thank you all for coming. Please say a prayer today for the soul of Desmond Lynch. Try to remember the good things about him. And join me in praying the he will find the peace in the next world that he never enjoyed here on earth."

Almost everyone received Communion. But Annie and Keith could not. In the eyes of the Church, Annie's divorce from Liam did not exist and she lived with Keith in sin every day of her life. Keith whispered to Annie, "We'll get busy on that annulment so you can receive the sacraments with Andrew."

Annie replied, "Maybe one day we'll do that for Andrew. But I don't need that annulment. I know the difference between love and sin and I know the power of forgiveness."

Keith kissed the curls on top of his wife's head and held her hand through the rest of the funeral mass. Later, he invited everyone at the Gates of Paradise Cemetery to stop by the Wild Geese Inn down the road for refreshments.

Once at the restaurant, Catherine kept a close eye on Annie to be sure that she was alright. "That eulogy was lovely, Annie. And I'm so glad that you got to see your father before he died. I believe that just trying to forgive has freed your soul, and your father's soul as well."

"I hope so, Catherine. Sometimes I feel so wicked, like I am really just the way people talk about me – a wild young girl who got pregnant, ran off with a bad man, leaving him to chase Keith Brandon all the way to Europe. They think two marriages and having Andrew out of wedlock are terrible sins. Oh, I've heard it all and I'd like to shout at the world to tell them how stupid and unfair all this talk is."

"I know that feeling very well too." Catherine hugged her daughter-in-law. "But I know how good you really are!"

Sarah and Reggie sat together, completely absorbed in a serious conversation. Little Andrew ran around the tables talking to everyone. He didn't understand the happenings of the day but he knew that he belonged there with his family.

Monsignor Murdock grabbed Keith. "I hear that your mother is selling the row house. She'll be the last of the old timers to leave."

"Yes, we already have a buyer. She and Sarah took an apartment in the same building with me and Annie. I think the city will be a welcome change for Mom. She wants to be close to Andrew and she can enjoy the plays and the concerts and everything the city has to offer with Esther."

"Well, I wish you all the best."

"Thanks," Keith said. "But we'll be back to visit you and the Smiths and some others."

"Good, don't be a stranger at St. Joseph's when you do visit."

Keith shook the old priest's hand.

As he turned around, he almost fell over Boss Garrigan. Keith's face registered surprise but his natural reflexes made him react with a polite, "Excuse me, sir."

Garrigan, shrunken with age, appeared small and vulnerable.

"Keith, my boy, I haven't seen you in years. Welcome back, son."

"Thank you," Keith answered politely as he tried to walk away.

But Garrigan grabbed Keith's hand. "I'm speaking at the Veterans of Foreign Wars' meeting here in The Glen next Saturday night and I'd like to officially invite you to our annual dinner. The Vets would love it if you'd say a few kind words to them about what's going on in Europe. It would be my privilege to share the podium with you."

"And it wouldn't hurt you with the voters either, right?" Keith quipped.

"Well, that's true." Garrigan grinned. "But it's also true that, you, my boy, are an inspiration to all of us."

"Perhaps one day I will speak at the VFW Hall but I have no intention of sharing a podium or anything else with you. I know the part you played in what happened to my wife and son. If you'd like to read the ugly details of what Liam did to them, well, I can arrange it for you."

"My part? All I did was help Annie. It was I who got her into Saint Gerard's after you used her and left her to face everything alone. Desmond believed that you went AWOL to get out of your responsibility for Annie and the baby. He cursed you to hell and back and vowed to kill you."

Keith scowled. "You arranged to kidnap Annie and take her to St. Gerard's against her will. You manipulated Desmond, using his shame to further you own agenda which was all about Liam. Annie would have been well taken care of by my mother and sister. Even Esther Weinberg would have taken Annie into her apartment in New York. Annie didn't need St. Gerard's nor did she need to marry Liam."

"You wanted Annie for Liam and you used her and my son, threatening an adoption and scaring Annie into believing that she would never see our child again – all that just to force her to marry Liam."

Garrigan laughed, appearing taller now, and more threatening. "You're a father yourself now. You should understand how Desmond felt. No one wants their child to be the center of vicious gossip. Where is Annie? I'll talk to her. That young woman was wild. She was always a handful, impudent and willful. And she used Liam to get out of a jam and then humiliated him in front of the faculty at Taylor University. It's her fault that he's not a doctor today."

"Liam is scum and you know it. Nothing is Annie's fault. All she wanted was to keep her son - my son. She saved Andrew and she even forgave Desmond for much of his part in all of it. But me, I'm not ready to forgive anyone – not you and not Liam."

Keith glared at the shrunken Garrigan, "I know all about your affair with Liam's mother, Fiona, and I know that Liam is your biological son – your only child, in fact. That's why you took such an interest in setting up Liam's education and making sure he had a family to show off. You stole my wife and child – putting them both in grave danger - so that Liam could pass himself off as something other than a sick pervert. You knew all about Liam's violent past and the women he hurt. The secrets of The Glen are out in the open now."

Everyone heard Keith's voice as they stood shocked, staring at him and at Boss Garrigan.

Garrigan pointed his nicotine-stained finger at Keith. "I helped Annie after you used her and ran out on her."

"Come on Garrigan, you knew that those fine folks at Taylor University would never have allowed Liam to stay in their medical program unless you presented him as a family man and a father, not as the criminal he is."

"You give me far too much credit, Keith. I'm a simple man. It was Desmond who used Liam to place Annie in a higher social position. He had access to my office. He read all those accusations against Liam and used that information to blackmail me into making Liam marry Annie."

Furious, Keith said, "Desmond did none of that - he never even knew about Liam's criminal record or about you being Liam's father. Desmond never even learned how to read."

Garrigan pushed his shoulders back, trying to appear stronger. "That's ridiculous. Desmond Lynch was my right hand man. I'd know it if he couldn't read."

"You never saw anyone as they really were. You only saw how you could use them. Desmond never learned to read but he was a fine actor and he covered it well."

Garrigan's chest swelled up like a poisonous puffer fish. "Mine aren't the only secrets in The Glen. Why don't you look into what really happened to your own father, Keith?"

When Annie heard that, the color drained from her face and Reggie stared at her in desperation.

Garrigan shouted, speaking to the entire room now, "Desmond Lynch killed Michael Brandon. He murdered your own father, Keith." Pausing only long enough to be sure he had everyone's attention, he went on. "Oh, Desmond loved your grandfather, Frank O'Connor, but he hated Michael Brandon and he blamed Brandon for Frank's untimely death. "

Gasping now, Garrigan took a deep breath and continued his diatribe.

"Now how's that for one of the secrets of The Glen? And how's that for a family skeleton for your son over there to live with? He'll always know that one of his grandfathers killed the other. Nice family history for the boy to grow up with. But he wouldn't have that stigma if Annie had stayed with Liam."

Boss Garrigan stormed out of The Wild Geese Inn with his two flunkies running to keep up with him.

Reggie grabbed Keith by the shoulder. "Fine job, Keith. You got some satisfaction and you didn't kick the old man's ass. I'd say this worked out well."

Keith looked at Annie. "I made a scene. I'm sorry."

Reggie commented, "That two-faced pig deserved all that, and more. That stuff, Keith, about your father, well, just forget it. I dug through all sorts of papers and I found out that Michael Brandon died in 1943 at Bellevue Hospital in New York City. He was struck by a taxi as he staggered out of a bar.

"Are you sure, Reggie?" Annie asked.

"Yes, Annie, I'm sure," Reggie replied, "and I also found out that Desmond faked that veteran's pension that he gave to Catherine. That money came from his own pocket because he felt an obligation to take care of Frank's family after he died."

"It's hard to believe that Desmond would give my mother money," Keith said, "since he blamed my mother for bringing Michael Brandon into their lives and causing my grandfather's death. And he hated me for being Brandon's son. I really don't understand."

"Desmond did it out of love for his only friend, Frank O'Connor. He believed that it was his duty to take care of Frank's family."

Annie asked, "Are you sure it was Keith's father who died at Bellevue in 1943?"

"Well I can't bring him back to life and prove that it was the same Michael Brandon, but he was the same age, the same physical height and weight – it had to be Keith's father. His parents had already drunk themselves to death, so no one claimed the body. He was buried in that potters field on that island off the Bronx. He was half way to drinking himself to death just like they did."

Annie put her hand on Reggie's shoulder. "Thank goodness! My father was out of his head when I saw him at the nursing home and he ranted on and on about paying a pension to Catherine and taking care of Michael Brandon. Knowing my father's violent nature, I guess I just jumped to conclusions. I let my imagination run wild and I was afraid that my father was confessing to killing Michael Brandon."

Sarah overhead, asking, "Afraid Annie? Afraid that Desmond killed my father? You had nothing to do with any of that."

Reggie interrupted, "Sarah. Desmond blamed Michael Brandon for Frank's death and I am sure that he beat him to a bloody pulp but he didn't have anything to do with killing him. The nasty drunk had one foot in the grave anyway. Desmond knew that. He'd just as soon have let him die slow - suffering as only drunks suffer. He would never have made it easy for Brandon. Sorry, but that's the truth of it."

"And those things Garrigan said?" Sarah asked.

"Boss Garrigan would not know the difference between a fact and a lie. He hasn't dealt with the truth in years. But I deal only in facts. You know that, Annie and Sarah, and you as well Keith. Who do you trust, me or Garrigan?"

"Oh, Reggie I trust you with Andrew's life. I believe you over Garrigan, of course." Annie assured him.

Sarah said, "We all believe you, Reggie."

By now, only close friends and family were left in the dining room of the Wild Geese Inn.

Keith folded Annie into his arms and looked around the room at Doctor and Elaina Smith, Reggie and Sarah, his mother and Esther.

"I apologize for this upset and the harsh words. Annie and I thank you all for coming. And, dear friends, the next time we get together will be at our new apartment in New York City,"

Annie pulled Keith's face down to hers, whispering directly into his ear, "We'll have to invite everyone to join us in welcoming the new baby next spring."

Keith wasn't sure that he heard Annie correctly. "What did you say?"

Annie smiled up at him, nodding yes. "Shh, don't say anything out loud but you heard right."

"I, I, didn't think we could."

Anne shrugged. "Well, it appears that we can, and, we are."

Keith hugged her. "This time I'm not missing out on anything. I'm going to be with you every minute, taking care of you and rubbing your chubby tummy."

Annie grinned. "If it's a girl, we'll call her "Keira" after you."

Keith pushed the curls away from Annie's forehead. "Keira Brandon. I like that name a lot. And I'd love to have a beautiful little girl who looks like you - but another boy would be just fine as well. Everything's falling into place. Even those little scars on your forehead are fading."

"Being with you is forcing all the bad memories and the scars to go away."

Keith looked over at Andrew, now sitting with Olga and Stefan Krupchik, intently showing off his newest truck. "We have to tell Andrew first. He'll be so excited to be a big brother."

"We'll take him for a walk later and make an announcement to him alone. And then we'll let him tell your mom and Sarah and they can tell everyone else."

Keith and Annie walked hand-in-hand over to Reggie and Sarah.

Reggie took Sarah's hand. "I'm sorry I had to blurt out all that stuff about your dad's death but I didn't want any false rumors to surface that might hurt you and Keith – or little Andrew."

"It's okay, Reggie, really it is." Sarah replied, kissing his cheek. "Don't forget that I know all too well what and who my father was – a mean, abusive drunk. Anything could have happened to him."

Reggie sighed in relief. "I'm guessing that Desmond probably made damn sure that your father would never return to The Glen and I'm certain that the Michael Brandon who died in New York City in 1943 was your father."

Sarah said, "My father brought tragedy to everyone around him. But no more – let's just forget Michael Brandon, please."

"You're right, Sarah, we all need to look to the present and to the future. Forget the past. It didn't belong to us. But "right now" belongs to all of you - and to me," Reggie said emphatically, sounding like a wise old sage, "let's just be happy because it's a good time to be alive – it's a time of hope."

And, indeed, it was a time of hope - and a time of peace, however brief; a time when Americans felt entitled to own a home, a car or maybe two cars. They were confident that hard work had rewards and that it was their right to raise a family in peace. And Americans were very aware of their place as the undisputed leaders of the free world.

Times were changing. A descendant of Irish immigrants just might be the next President of the United States. Civil Rights were discussed openly and many Americans envisioned equality as their future, despite the bloody, past.

A few brave dreamers even believed that the future might just include mankind escaping the very boundaries of the earth itself.

"To the future!" Dr. Smith toasted, holding up his half-full glass of Pepsi.

"To the future!" Everyone responded.

Keith kissed Annie and whispered, "This seems to be our very own happy ending."

Annie smiled up at him. "Oh, no, Keith, my love, this is just the beginning."

About The Author

Dorothy Ann Searing published an award-winning essay at age twelve and has been writing ever since – everything from technical product descriptions, advertisements, corporate training courses and safety newsletters. But. only recently, has she indulged in writing fiction – her first love.

And right out of the gate she won Honorable Mention in a Writers Digest short story contest for, "Remember Me" which published in several periodicals. She also recently published "My Florida Valentine," as part of an anthology, *Florida On My Mind*, with ten other Florida writers.

Although *Secrets Of The Glen* is her first novel, the story and the characters have been a part of her soul for a very long time. And the sequel promises to be even better.

Originally from New York and Connecticut, Dorothy and her husband, Richard, now reside in Tarpon Springs, Florida.

You may contact the author by emailing cawdorburn@gmail.com

Made in the USA
Charleston, SC
07 November 2013